THE CAMELOT CRIER

ABOUT TOWN: Richmond, Virginia

A proposition to remember!

It seems that the prim-and-proper princess of Camelot, Ashley Kendrick, has been snagged by rugged contractor Matt Calloway. But it's not what you think! Ashley, who was running a gala dinner to benefit the East Coast Shelter Project, was well and truly mystified when Matt unexpectedly put another item on the docket: Miss Ashley Kendrick herself! Sources who attended the event state that Matt offered up one hundred thousand dollars for Ashley to actually help build a Shelter Project house. And Ashley has risen to the challenge. She is scheduled to work in Gray Lakes, Florida, in August. It's also been confirmed that the handsome bachelor Matt will be joining her there. Clearly, their days will be spent on the construction site, but just how will these two be spending those hot August nights?

Dear Reader,

Well, June may be the traditional month for weddings, but we here at Silhouette find June is busting out all over—with babies! We begin with Christine Rimmer's *Fifty Ways To Say I'm Pregnant*. When bound-for-the-big-city Starr Bravo shares a night of passion with the rancher she's always loved, she finds herself in the family way. But how to tell him? *Fifty Ways* is a continuation of Christine's Bravo Family saga, so look for the BRAVO FAMILY TIES flash. And for those of you who remember Christine's JONES GANG series, you'll be delighted with the cameo appearance of an old friend....

Next, Joan Elliott Pickart continues her miniseries THE BABY BET: MACALLISTER'S GIFTS with *Accidental Family*, the story of a day-care center worker and a single dad with amnesia who find themselves falling for each other as she cares for their children together. And there's another CAVANAUGH JUSTICE offering in Special Edition from Marie Ferrarella: in *Cavanaugh's Woman*, an actress researching a film role needs a top cop— and Shaw Cavanaugh fits the bill nicely. *Hot August Nights* by Christine Flynn continues THE KENDRICKS OF CAMELOT miniseries, in which the reserved, poised Kendrick daughter finds her one-night stand with the town playboy coming back to haunt her in a big way. Janis Reams Hudson begins MEN OF CHEROKEE ROSE with *The Daddy Survey*, in which two little girls go all out to get their mother a new husband. And don't miss *One Perfect Man*, in which almost-new author Lynda Sandoval tells the story of a career-minded events planner who has never had time for romance until she gets roped into planning a party for the daughter of a devastatingly handsome single father. So enjoy the rising temperatures, all six of these wonderful romances…and don't forget to come back next month for six more, in Silhouette Special Edition.

Happy Reading!

Gail Chasan
Senior Editor

Please address questions and book requests to:
Silhouette Reader Service
U.S.: 3010 Walden Ave., P.O. Box 1325, Buffalo, NY 14269
Canadian: P.O. Box 609, Fort Erie, Ont. L2A 5X3

Hot August Nights

CHRISTINE FLYNN

Silhouette®

SPECIAL EDITION®

Published by Silhouette Books

America's Publisher of Contemporary Romance

To Pam Wede, a wonderful friend whose strength and easy charm I admire so very much.

 SILHOUETTE BOOKS

ISBN 0-373-24618-8

HOT AUGUST NIGHTS

Visit Silhouette Books at www.eHarlequin.com

Printed in U.S.A.

Books by Christine Flynn

*The Whitaker Brides
†The Kendricks of Camelot

CHRISTINE FLYNN

admits to being interested in just about everything, which is why she considers herself fortunate to have turned her interest in writing into a career. She feels that a writer gets to explore it all and, to her, exploring relationships—especially the intense, bittersweet or even lighthearted relationships between men and women—is fascinating.

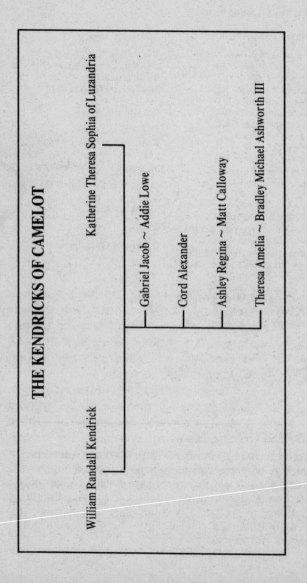

THE KENDRICKS OF CAMELOT

William Randall Kendrick ~ Katherine Theresa Sophia of Luzandria

Gabriel Jacob ~ Addie Lowe

Cord Alexander

Ashley Regina ~ Matt Calloway

Theresa Amelia ~ Bradley Michael Ashworth III

Chapter One

Ashley Kendrick's day had started out badly and gone downhill from there. She'd thought the worst was the snag she'd hit at noon when a paparazzo had followed her into a deli and drawn so much attention to her that she'd left without her lunch. She figured it had actually hit rock bottom about twenty minutes ago.

She had learned to live with people who unsettled her. Strangers on the street routinely pointed or stared. Paparazzi and reporters emerged from nowhere, startling her with the flash of their cameras, assaulting her with questions inevitably designed to expose something—anything—personal or sensational about any member of the Kendrick family.

She was accustomed to the attention. She wasn't always comfortable with it, but she had come to accept the near constant publicity that came with being a Kendrick. Her baby pictures had appeared in the national press, as had those of her siblings each time her wealthy, now-retired senator father and her mother, a princess who had given up an entire kingdom to marry him, had produced more progeny. America had watched her grow up, and over those years she had learned to handle the disconcerting situations that occurred with astounding regularity.

She pretended she could handle them, anyway, which was the best she could hope for considering how unsure of herself she often tended to be. But when Matt Callaway had answered her knock on her brother's door, she had been forced to admit that no one had ever unsettled her more than her brother Cord's best friend.

She hadn't seen Matt in ten years, but he still disturbed her. Not the way strangers did when they encroached upon her privacy. But in a far more fundamental and primitive way. The man was six feet, two inches of sandy-haired, carved and sculpted muscle, tension and testosterone. His steel-gray eyes had a way of looking at her that made her feel totally exposed, totally vulnerable. And she had never once been in his presence without feeling she would be totally susceptible to him if she didn't keep her guard in place.

He had also just become the only man who'd ever driven her to drink.

Granted, the drink was a rather excellent California chardonnay that she'd found in her brother's wine cellar. And having a glass gave her something to do while she waited on Cord's deck for him to get home. But discovering that Matt Callaway could still make her uneasy enough to seek the first available excuse to avoid his company had her frowning at the nearly empty crystal goblet. That, and the fact that she didn't want to be where she was to begin with.

She had planned to work tonight. As far behind as she was, she desperately needed those uninterrupted hours. But her father had insisted her work could wait. He considered it far more important that she used her time to track down her brother and have Cord sign a trust amendment he had forgotten to sign when he'd been in Richmond last week. Her dad, who ruled the Kendricks' multimillion-dollar empire from a suite of offices ten stories above her decidedly more modest one, had informed her she could work late tomorrow night.

Having to make a two-hour drive from Richmond to Newport News frustrated her enough. In the time she spent on that round-trip alone, she could have done serious damage to the piles on her desk. But her mother had started exerting her considerable influence on her time, too. Just that morning, her mom had informed Ashley that she would have to give up her position as director of the scholarship program she helped administer if she intended to assist with fund-raisers like the gala charity auction she was currently working on twelve hours a day to have ready for next week.

It hadn't mattered that the auction was for the East Coast Shelter Project, her mom's new favorite charity. Or that Ashley had insisted that she truly could handle both. Her mother had said there was absolutely no need for her to work that hard.

What Ashley did had nothing to do with need as her mother had meant it. It had to do with feeling that she was earning her own way.

Smoothing the hem of her short red jacket over her white slacks, she settled back in the deck chair. Not liking her mood, hoping to change it, she told herself she might as well enjoy the break.

The effort lasted long enough for her to cross one knee over the other. One low-heeled sandal dangling from her French-manicured toes, she restively swayed her foot and glanced past the wide, tiered deck and her brother's sailboat moored fifty feet beyond the cedar railing.

She knew that working for her family must be like working for any other employer. Suspected it was, anyway, as she watched the sun set on the sailboats in the long inlet on Chesapeake Bay. She'd never worked for anyone else to know for certain. She loved her family. She truly did. But she was twenty-eight years old, had never in her life done anything that wasn't by the book, and she was getting really tired of being told what to do and when she could do it.

Ten feet away, the glass deck door rumbled open in its track.

"Do me a favor, will you?"

The sound of Matt's deep voice had her foot going still an instant before she carefully uncrossed her legs. Knees together, she automatically crossed her ankles, abandoned her mental mutiny and set her wine on the glass-topped table beside her. As she did, she glanced toward the blond jock filling the doorway.

Matt was still dressed as he had been when he'd answered the front door. His loose gray tank top exposed enough of his beautifully cut arms, shoulders and pectorals to leave no doubt about what had to be an impressive six-pack of abdominal muscle. Below the baggy hem of his navy gym shorts, his powerful thighs glistened with sweat.

The front of his shirt was stained with it, too.

He'd obviously finished the workout she'd interrupted when she'd arrived.

"If I can," she said, hurriedly dragging her eyes from his chest.

"I just need you to listen for the phone." His glance slid over her, bold and assessing, much as it had when he'd opened the front door. He'd seemed as surprised to find her there as she'd been to find herself faced with his decidedly large and impressive body. Within seconds of her unconsciously stepping back, he'd also seemed just as edgy with her as he'd always been. "I'm getting in the shower and won't be able to hear it. Cord said he'd call if he got held up.''

Without looking up, swearing she could feel that edginess radiating toward her, she nodded. "Sure."

"If he does call, tell him he doesn't need to stop by the construction site. I have the reports he left there."

The construction site. That would be the major mall Matt's company was building outside Newport News for Kendrick Investments. Apparently, he'd come down from Baltimore to check on its progress and was staying with Cord while he was here.

She might not have seen Matt in years, but that didn't mean she didn't occasionally hear about him through the somewhat tangled family grapevine.

"I'll do that," she quietly assured him.

Restively pushing his fingers through his hair, he turned away. A heartbeat later, he turned back. "And tell him that if he wants me to help him with his boat, he's going to have to pick up some graphite. His ignition switch is jammed."

"You're working on his boat?"

"I'm helping him get the winter kinks out of it as long as I'm here. He just had it brought from dry dock yesterday."

She gave him another nod, tried not to stare at his thighs. At least now she knew why he was here.

"I'll pass that on, too."

She thought he would leave then, go inside and leave her to stew in the lovely late-June evening. She hoped he would, anyway, since she couldn't think of anything else to say with him watching her so closely. She could practically feel his quiet scrutiny move from her low ponytail to where her bare toes were now tucked, ladylike, beneath her chair.

He was about to say something else. She felt certain of it.

Or, so she was thinking when she saw him slowly shake his head and the door finally rumbled closed.

Her breath escaped in a long, low rush.

All Matt had said when she'd asked if Cord was home was that he expected her brother in about an hour. He'd then stepped back, more to allow her her space than to get out of her way, told her she might as well come on in and disappeared in the direction of the weight room.

With him going one way, she had immediately decided to wait for her brother in the other—which had put her out on the deck.

She picked up her wine again, took a healthy sip.

In the space of seconds, he'd thrown her back ten years. She hated that he still made her nervous, but she'd at least grown up enough to carry on a relatively normal conversation with him. When she'd first met him at the tender age of fourteen—a full year before her parents had banned him from the house because he'd turned out to be such a bad influence on her brother—he'd intimidated the daylights out of her.

He'd been big even back then. Tall, broad-shouldered and filled out more like a man than a prep-school senior. The years had carved an appealing maturity into his beachboy good looks, and his effect on her now was actually rather intriguing considering how much time had passed. Yet every time she'd seen him back then, her teenage heart had done a pirouette in her chest. The way he would narrow his beautiful steel-gray eyes and tell her she could at least say hello had tied her tongue, literally stolen any clever thing she might have said right from her head.

Then, she had begun to overhear the concerns her parents had expressed about him. About how Matt had been suspended from school for fighting. About how he'd stolen liquor from another friend's home. About how they could no longer trust their son in his company because Cord had picked up his unruly behavior and Cord had already been difficult enough as it was.

Had she been the rebellious type herself, she supposed she would have found Matt's defiance of authority terribly attractive. And she had—in a safe, James Dean teenage-fantasy sort of way. But her parents pampered and protected their children. Their girls, especially. She had been sheltered all her life from people who lacked manners and breeding and, being a good and dutiful daughter, she had avoided him like the proverbial plague long before he had been declared persona non grata at the Kendrick estate. Even after Matt and Cord had hooked up again in college, she had found herself avoiding him.

Not that their paths had crossed often. Until she had arrived at her brother's that evening, she hadn't seen Matt since his and Cord's college graduation. And then, only at a distance. The most exposure she'd had to him was to hear his name in connection with the astonishing growth of his company and, occasionally, to hear her mother complain that Cord had taken off with him yet again to risk his neck in pursuit of an adrenaline high.

She crossed her legs once more, her foot slowly swaying as she nursed her chardonnay. She had the distinct feeling that Matt's and her brother's mutual love of adventure was why they had remained such good friends despite the temporary ban from each other in their youth. Cord climbed mountains simply because they were there. He sailed, scuba dived and flew his own plane. If there was a force to be conquered, he met the challenge head-on. More often than not, according to her mom, Matt was the one who introduced the challenge in the first place.

Still stewing about her day, she rather wished she had that sort of nerve herself. Make that guts, she thought, unladylike as the word sounded. She rather wished she had such *guts* herself.

She would never admit such a thing aloud, of course. It wouldn't be dignified and heaven knew she needed to be that. At that moment, though, feeling constrained by her parents, her life and her own inability to buck the tide, she couldn't help thinking that she would love to abandon the conventions she lived with and lose herself in something that made her feel truly…free.

She finished the last of her wine. Vaguely aware of its effects draining the tension from her muscles, she also decided it was time she stopped letting Matt Callaway get to her. Years had passed. People changed. As she had already reminded herself, she was twenty-eight, not an impressionable eighteen. More importantly, not letting him intimidate her would at least return some control to her day.

By the time she decided she wouldn't be able to work on her little self-improvement project without seeking Matt out, something she hadn't quite worked up the nerve to do, she had retrieved the bottle of wine from the refrigerator. Twilight had settled deeply over the tranquil view and she had polished off a second glass. Feeling quite relaxed, and certain she would soon feel brave enough to venture inside, she poured another splash simply because sitting there sipping it was the most pleasant thing she'd done all day.

She sank back in her chair.

Across the wide inlet, the trees had turned black against the last light of day. An occasional pinpoint of white indicated a house as isolated as the one her brother had chosen for his escape. Water lapped against the dock. Her brother's sailboat, its sails furled and masts bare, rocked gently with the incoming tide.

It was peaceful here. Something that surprised her. She wouldn't have thought Cord could stand all this lovely quiet.

Ten minutes and another splash of wine later, the rumble of the door put an end to tranquility.

Her strappy red sandal slipped from her toes. It hit the deck as she glanced up hoping to see her brother standing there.

Matt leaned against the doorjamb.

He didn't bother to turn on the porch light, but even in the low glow of the lamps coming from farther inside, she could easily see that he had showered and changed. He'd combed his damp hair straight back from the angular lines of his face. A loose V-neck sweater hung casually over comfortably worn jeans. She couldn't tell the sweater's color. She could tell only that it was pale and that it clung rather impressively to his broad shoulders.

The clothing covered him commendably. It didn't do a thing, however, to disguise the power in his big body. Or, maybe, she thought as he crossed his arms, that power was just the latent tension that surrounded him like a force field.

"Cord just called."

Reminding herself that she wasn't going to react to him any differently than she would any other guy, she toed at her shoe. She succeeded only in pushing it farther away. "I didn't hear the phone."

"You probably couldn't hear it through the door," he replied, his face shadowed in the deep dusk. "He won't be back until tomorrow."

Ashley glanced up. "What time is it now?"

"About seven-thirty."

She'd been there since six-fifteen.

"He knew I was coming. I left a message on his cell phone."

"I don't know anything about that."

"Did he say why he wouldn't be here?"

"I think her name is Sheryl."

Give Cord a choice between a good time and responsibility and responsibility lost nearly every time.

"Great," she muttered, and set her goblet down with a clink beside her purse and the manila envelope beneath it.

She didn't feel relaxed anymore. The drive had been a total waste.

"Tell me," she said, leaning forward again to see if she could see her sandal, "is he really playing tonight, or is he just doing what he tends to do when it comes to his family and avoiding me?"

"He didn't say what he was doing."

Liar, she thought. He and Cord were as thick as thieves.

"Tell me where he is and I'll take the papers to him. All I need is two minutes."

"He didn't say where he'd be."

Exasperation threatened to surface. Years of biting back anything that might sound less than agreeable kept it from her tone. "You don't have to protect him from me," she assured him, drawn by his loyalty as much as she was annoyed by it. As a Kendrick, it wasn't easy knowing who to trust. Cord could obviously trust Matt, though. "I'm not asking him to donate an organ. I just want his signature."

"He'd probably give you the organ."

"Then, tell him I need a lung and that I'm on my way."

The corner of his mouth crooked, the expression dangerously close to a smile. "For some reason, I think he might not believe that." With lazy masculine grace, he pushed himself away from the door. "Leave me the papers. I'll see that he gets them."

"I can't leave them with you." Still probing for her shoe, she barely noticed the way Matt came to a halt at her flat refusal. "I know my brother. He'll let them sit around until I have to come back for them. Or he'll lose them," she decided, hearing boards creak as Matt resumed his stride.

"Then the lawyers will have to redraw them and I'll have to waste hours chasing him down again. He could have signed these two days ago, but he was in such a hurry to get out of his meeting and up to New York for some concert that he totally spaced it."

"Maybe he spaced it on purpose."

"I can't imagine why. It's not as if he's getting cut out of anything. It's just an administrative formality that Dad wants taken care of this week."

She nudged her chair back farther, pine legs scraping against cedar.

"Would you turn on the light, please? I can't see."

There were times she would like to take a hike from responsibility, too, she thought. At the very least, she would love, for once, to know what it felt like to do what she wanted to do, the way her brother did, instead of what was expected of her. There were times she felt so stifled she could scream.

But that wouldn't be dignified, either.

A while ago, she'd only felt frustrated by her parents and her life in general. Now, she felt frustrated by a brother who obviously had never learned the value of other people's time. It didn't help that she couldn't find her shoe.

The clean scent of soap and something hinting of citrus, musk and warm male filled her lungs an instant before she glanced up. Matt crouched in front of her. With one hand braced on the arm of her chair, he reached under the table. His arm brushed her leg as he did, the feel of it as solid as granite against her calf.

He picked up what was little more than a dainty heel and a few intersecting ribbons of leather. In the dark, the crimson leather was practically invisible.

"Is this what you're looking for?"

Ashley's glance slid from the breadth of his shoulders to

the dainty shoe he held in his big hand. With it extended toward her, he openly studied her face and waited for her to take what he offered.

From the unblinking way he watched her, it was almost as if he were daring her not to.

She had no idea where the odd thought had come from. "Thank you," she murmured, taking the shoe from his hand.

Without a word, he rose, dwarfing her, and stepped back so she could slip the little straps over her foot.

Dismayed by how quickly her heart was beating, she glanced up to see him hold out his hand.

Refusing to let him rattle her was her goal for the day. Utterly determined to have at least that much go her way, she curved her palm over his, willed herself to ignore the heat seeping into her skin and rose from the chair before she could spend any time thinking about the flutter the contact put in her stomach.

She stood too fast. Suddenly light-headed, wanting to ignore that, too, she turned to pick up her purse, keys and the envelope beneath them.

The quick lack of equilibrium wouldn't be overlooked. Swaying just enough for her to consider that the last splash of wine might not have been the best idea, she steadied herself against the first thing she could reach—which happened to be Matt's chest and a forearm that felt like hammered steel.

The man wasn't just solid. His body felt as hard as concrete. Even his fingers felt as if they had no give at all when they automatically locked around her upper arms to keep her upright.

Beneath her hand, she felt the steady beat of his heart.

"Are you okay?"

"I'm...fine." She was aware of the scowl in his voice,

more aware of the heat wherever her body touched his. Each little point of contact seemed to physically burn—her palm where it had flattened against his chest, her arm where it lay against his. "I just got up too quickly."

She shifted, getting her footing, trying to ease back.

Still holding her by one arm, he picked up the bottle of wine and tipped it. The scowl deepened. "Was this full?"

"It was when I opened it."

"You sat out here and drank half a bottle by yourself?"

She was tempted to point out that he could have joined her. He just didn't give her a chance. His frown had settled hard on her mouth. The displeasure carved in his face seemed to be slowly fading, though. It turned to something that looked far more like curiosity. And heat.

The air in her lungs went thin. She wasn't sure she was even breathing when his eyes finally locked on hers once more.

"Give me your keys."

"Excuse me?"

"Your keys," he repeated, finally deliberately letting her go. "You're not driving anywhere."

She had already realized that she'd had more wine than could be considered wise. She'd realized, too, that his power to rattle her went a tad beyond anything she might be able to physically control. Yet, all she truly cared about at the moment was that he was the third person that day to tell her what she couldn't do.

Curling her fingers around her key ring, she tipped her chin, reminded herself not to be intimidated and politely said, "No."

The sound he made leaned heavily toward exasperation. "Don't do this."

"I'm not doing anything," she replied ever so reasonably. "You asked for my keys. I said no. End of discussion."

"It might be the end of the discussion, but it's not the end of the issue." The determination in his eyes met the uncharacteristic stubbornness in hers. "Don't make me have to take them."

"Well, I'm afraid you're going to have to," she informed him.

Her tone mild, her expression faintly mutinous, she slipped her hand under her jacket, beneath her blouse and tucked them into her bra. She was perfectly capable of keeping her keys in her possession while she figured out how to get home without driving there herself. She wasn't drunk, but she doubted she could walk a perfectly straight line, either. The last thing she wanted was to be stopped for driving under the influence. Worse, harm someone in an accident she caused. The press would have a field day with that one.

Remembering that the press was always out there, lying in wait for some mistake in judgement or unguarded comment to exploit, did nothing but add another layer to the sense of frustration she was beginning to feel with her life. Or, so she was thinking when Matt's glance slipped to the V of flesh between the lapels of her jacket.

Seconds ago, he had sounded considerably less than pleased with the position he found himself in. Now, with her keys nestled between her breast and her bra, he simply seemed intrigued by it.

"Now, that's a move I never would have expected of you."

"Maybe I'm tired of doing what's expected," she murmured, a little surprised by it herself. "Chalk it up to a bad day."

"All the more reason for you to not get behind a wheel. And by the way," he said, his voice surprisingly patient, "I wasn't implying that you had to stay here. If you give me your keys, I'll drive you.''

There was a deep cleft in his upper lip. Realizing she was staring at it, hoping he didn't, she jerked her glance up. ''All the way to Richmond?''

''I was thinking more along the lines of a hotel. There's a Hyatt right down the road.''

''It wouldn't look right to check into a hotel without luggage.''

Especially if someone recognized me, she thought.

Having encountered yet another thing she couldn't do, she picked up the goblet. Since she wasn't driving, there was no reason not to finish what was in it. It was far too good a vintage to let it go to waste.

Watching her, looking unwillingly intrigued, Matt narrowed his eyes. ''Why was it such a bad day?''

''It wasn't really that bad. Not in the overall scheme of things,'' she qualified. It really hadn't been any worse than any other. Except for running into him, it hadn't even been *unlike* any other.

She glanced toward the sky, wondering if she'd find a full moon. That might help explain the odd sense of dissatisfaction that had sunk its claws into her.

She didn't see the moon at all.

''It was just…frustrating.''

''Because your brother didn't show?''

That sounded so petty. And it was. But it wasn't any one thing getting to her. It was the accumulation.

''Among other things,'' she murmured.

There was a time when Matt would have told himself to let it go. To pack her into a cab and get her out of there. This was the woman who had backed away from him every time he'd come within ten feet of her, who had barely said a word to him even when he'd gone out of his way to get her to speak. From the time he'd first laid eyes on her, when she'd been all legs and long hair and all of fourteen, she'd done everything but twitch her nose to disappear in order to avoid him.

He could have sworn she had intended to continue to treat him like one of the great unwashed when she'd first arrived. Yet, it seemed that he had misread her. She didn't seem at all intent on avoiding him now.

He watched her swirl the pale liquid. Her expression pensive, her thoughts clearly troubled, she seemed far different from the untouchable little princess he'd last seen nearly ten years ago. There was no mistaking her polish or refinement. There was a grace about her that went beyond the impeccable clothes and flawless skin. Yet, even looking as privileged as she truly was, she seemed softer to him, more... touchable.

In the muted light spilling through the windows, her hair looked like pale silk. The way she had it caught at the back of her head fairly taunted a man to undo the intricate clasp restraining it, free it to tumble over her shoulders. And her skin. In the shadows it looked as smooth and perfect as marble. Her eyes were what drew him, though, the gentleness he saw there.

Curious, taunted by a vulnerability he never would have expected, he heard himself ask, "Like what?"

"Well for one thing," she said, looking as if she might be struggling to admit it, "I've discovered that I lack... guts."

"Guts?"

"You know. Nerve."

Fascinated by the admission, he watched her frown.

"Anything in particular you want this nerve for?"

"To do something freeing."

"Freeing?"

The pinch of her delicate forehead deepened, her pensive expression making him wonder if the wine might be making her a little more thoughtful, or more candid, than she might have otherwise been.

"Make that something...outrageous."

"For instance?"

"Oh, I don't know." Looking very much as if she were only now considering it, she moved to the railing and lifted the goblet toward the dark water. "Maybe taking that boat and heading off where no one could find me."

"You sail?"

She shook her head, turned her glance back to the water. A faint breeze tugged at her hair, loosening a few of the shorter strands around her face. "Not without a crew. And that would defeat the whole purpose."

"That's not outrageous. That's just escape." He recognized that need easily enough. He'd just never expected that she would feel it. "Next choice?"

"How about throwing my dinner at the next waiter who interrupts eight times to ask if everything is prepared to my liking?"

"A food fight at Four Seasons. Yeah," he muttered, nodding as he considered. "That might be a little shocking." He smiled. "What else?"

She pondered for a moment, clearly searching for what, for her, would be scandalous behavior. "Skinny-dipping."

His glance cut to where she stood at the rail. He didn't know how tall she was. Five-five maybe, without the heels that brought her to his chin. But he had no trouble estimating the size and proportion of the rest of her slender, supple-looking body.

He'd been conscious of her since the moment he'd opened the front door. He had not, however, been prepared for the jolt of pure physical awareness he'd felt when he'd caught her by the arms moments ago. He'd barely had his hands on her, barely breathed in her subtle, faintly erotic scent and every nerve in his body had gone on alert. Then, she'd looked up at him and his glance had settled on the gentle part of her lips. Her lush mouth had looked soft, moist and as ripe as a peach. And the prospect of tasting her had turned certain parts of his anatomy as hard as stone.

"You think you'd do that?" he asked casually.

"No." She sounded disappointed. "But it sounds like something that would take nerve."

"For some people."

"Have you done it?"

He lifted one shoulder in an offhanded shrug. "The water's warm in Tahiti."

Ashley's glance moved from his broad shoulders to his narrows hips, then jerked back to where the low security lights made shadows on the boat in the distance. She had a profound appreciation for art in all its forms and his body, magnificently, gloriously naked would definitely be a work of art. As for experiencing the freedom of being naked in the water herself, she couldn't imagine the sheer lack of inhibition doing something like that would take.

At the moment, growing more relaxed by the wine, protected by the darkness, she realized she truly hated being inhibited.

"What does it feel like? Being that…free."

She felt rather than saw the faint lift of his shoulder above hers. "Good, I guess."

"I mean really." She waved her glass toward the vast darkness beyond them. "How does it feel to not care about convention and just go where the moment leads you?"

"What makes you think I know?"

She knew he did. Actually, she was dead sure of it. Her memory about why that was just seemed a little fuzzy at the moment. And, as relaxed as she was and, surprisingly, not feeling nervous at all, it didn't seem to matter anyway. "You don't?"

Matt reached over, slipped the glass from her fingers. "Maybe," he conceded. "But we're not talking about me. We're talking about you." He took a swallow of wine. Rather than handing the goblet back, he kept it for himself. "In your mind, is going for a swim without a suit the most outrageous thing you could do?"

He spoke quietly, thoughtfully, as if he really wanted to know her secrets. As if learning them might tell him something he had always wanted to know.

The thought that he might have always wanted to know more about her drew her eyes to the shadowed angles of his face. The years had carved character into his compelling features and made him far more dangerous than he had ever been in his reckless youth. Dangerous because he was far easier to talk to than she ever would have imagined. Dangerous because he drew her in ways she didn't totally understand, didn't trust and at the moment really didn't care to consider.

Looking from the sensual line of his mouth, wondering if it would feel as hard as it looked, she could easily think of something far more shocking than diving naked into a pool. For her, anyway.

"No," she heard herself quietly admit. "It's not."

"So, what is?"

She shook her head. The thought of curving her arms around his neck, stretching herself up against his chest and thighs and unabashedly kissing him felt bold enough. No way would she say it aloud. Especially no way could she tell him that, at that moment, what she would really like to do was tug off his sweater and let her hands roam over all those beautiful muscles. She'd never fantasized about seducing a man before, but if she were to do it, he would definitely be her fantasy.

Realizing she *was* fantasizing, her eyes widened. Dragging her glance from his mouth, she heard Matt chuckle. The deep delicious sound washed over her like the caress of warm velvet.

"Come on," he gently coaxed. *"In vino veritas."*

"In wine there is truth," she translated, smiling. "That does seem to be true." She'd already exposed far more of herself to him than she had anyone else. "But some things are definitely better admitted only to oneself."

"But I already know you have a deep-seated wish to throw food and swim naked."

"That's just between you and me." She quickly glanced up, her eyes suddenly serious. "Okay?"

"I won't tell a soul."

"Promise?"

"Promise," he replied, and reached over to tuck back the strands of hair that curved by her mouth.

His touch was light, oddly reassuring and, at that moment, felt like the most natural thing in the world. It seemed strange that she should feel such certainty about him, but she didn't doubt that she could trust him with everything she said. Not once in all the years he'd known her brother had he ever said a word about a Kendrick that had shown up in print.

Even in the lovely fog relaxing her body and mind, she knew that alone was worth its weight in platinum.

His hand slowly fell. Over the tranquil lap of water, she heard the faint clink of the goblet touching wood as he set it on the railing ledge.

"So." His eyes glittered on her face, down the line of her throat.

"So," she murmured back, feeling strangely warm everywhere his glance touched.

"Are you going to give me those keys or not?"

She swallowed, drawn by that delicious heat, drawn by him.

"I hadn't planned on it."

Humor glinted in his eyes, tugged the corner of his mouth. "Do I have to go after them?"

Her heart bumped her breastbone. The thought of his big hand slipping inside her jacket and inside her bra pooled that heat low in her belly.

"You wouldn't." She swallowed, thinking she should feel far more alarmed than she did by the thought. Or, at least, alarmed by the jolt of anticipation it brought. "Would you?"

He edged closer, making her tip her head back farther to look up at him. His grin was as seductive as the deliciously dark tones of his voice when he slipped his fingers along her jaw. "There's something you need to know about me, Ashley."

His head descended, making her pulse leap, her breath go shallow.

"What's that?"

His mouth hovered inches from hers. "I've always found it hard to resist a challenge. Right now," he said in response to her claim, "yes, I would. And not because I'm in any hurry to get you out of here."

The heat of his body seemed to radiate toward hers, surrounding her, drawing her closer. She wasn't in any hurry to leave, either. "Oh," she whispered.

"Yeah." His breath caressed her cheek. His lips brushed hers, the touch light, incredibly tender and far too brief. "Oh."

Lifting his head far enough to see her eyes, he waited to see what she would do.

When all she did was draw a shivery breath, his head dipped again and he covered her mouth with his.

Ashley's first thought was that his lips weren't anywhere near as hard as they looked. They were soft, warm and, when his tongue touched hers, the shock of that small invasion turned her insides liquid and threatened to turn her legs to mush.

He kissed her slowly, deeply, his unimaginable gentleness melting her bones by slow degrees. He eased her closer, his touch feeling far more like promise than demand. It occurred to her vaguely that she had never been kissed the way he was kissing her. It was almost as if he could be perfectly content to simply savor the shape of her mouth, her taste, and let her decide just how much more she wanted.

She sagged toward him, opened to him a little more, wanting more of the promise. Or, maybe, it was the feel of his hand and its gentle pressure at the small of her back that had her flattening herself against him as she had imagined only moments ago. She wasn't entirely sure. Lost in the sensations, in the haze, she wasn't even sure it mattered.

All she knew for certain was that she hadn't wanted his mouth to leave hers when he trailed a path of moist heat along her jaw to the sensitive shell of her ear.

"Are you going to tell me what you were thinking?" He whispered the words, his warm breath causing a delicious shiver to race along her sensitized nerves.

She let her head fall to the side, giving him better access. "I don't think that would be a very good idea."

He chuckled, the sound vibrating against her skin.

"Then just tell me if I'm getting hot or cold." His voice darkened, grew more intimate. "Did it have anything to do with this?"

His lips trailed down her neck, touched the pulse pounding between her collarbones.

"Warm," she murmured.

"And this?" He lifted his head, brushed his lips over hers, the sensation deliciously teasing.

"Warmer."

His mouth still hovered over hers when he lifted her hand, pressed it to his chest and murmured, "This?"

Her heart jerked. "Maybe."

"Hot or cold?"

As close as he was, every breath she drew brought his breath into her lungs. "Hot," she whispered.

"Do you still want to do something no one would ever expect of you?"

Slipping her hand over hard muscle, the feel of it drawing her closer still, she smiled. "I'm not going skinny-dipping."

"I wasn't even going to suggest it. The water's too cold."

"What, then?"

"Ever make love in a sailboat?"

She didn't know what she said. She didn't know if she said anything at all. As she raised up on tiptoe and lifted her lips to his, she just knew that while she didn't have the nerve to seduce him, she had no problem at all with him seducing her.

Chapter Two

Ashley should have known something would go wrong. When it came to something she needed to have go well, it almost always did. That was why she drove herself nuts trying to imagine every possible disaster and come up with a plan to cope with it. Especially when there were cameras around.

She stared across the ballroom of the Richmond Bay Yacht Club, her heart beating in her throat and her grip tight on the podium. Even with her totally obsessive attention to detail, she hadn't considered this particular possibility. Since she'd slipped from her brother's house last Wednesday morning, not an hour had gone by that she hadn't felt shocked to the core by what she had allowed to happen with Matt Callaway—or prayed that it would be at least another ten years before their paths crossed again.

She'd made it three days. He'd just risen from one of the tables at the back of the room.

She had just auctioned off the last item of the night—a weekend in Aspen that had gone for eight thousand dollars. It had been the highest bid of the evening, the frosting on the proverbial cake for the gala dinner and auction to benefit the East Coast Shelter Project. Enthusiastic applause rang through the crowded and glittering room of beautifully gowned and tuxedoed guests.

She barely heard it.

Looking totally at ease in black tie and cummerbund, Matt moved toward the middle of the tables. He drew the eye of every female he passed. The men noticed him, too. The aura of quiet power surrounding him had them all sitting taller, straightening their shoulders as males who competed for money or power often did when faced with a prime example of their own.

With an easy smile, he motioned to the assistant handling the portable microphone.

Ashley had long ago learned to cover nerves with grace, disappointment with a smile, challenge with composure. Now was definitely not the time to forget what she'd been taught. Not with the society editor of the *Richmond Times-Dispatch* and five hundred of the wealthiest and most influential citizens in Virginia as witnesses.

Applause was still ringing when other guests began to turn in the direction of her frozen stare.

"Before you conclude the auction, Miss Kendrick. I'd like to bid on one last item."

Matt's rich, deep voice filled the ballroom. Applause quieted. Conversations died.

Ashley made herself smile as her own microphone carried her voice back to him. "I'm afraid those were all the donations we had. There isn't anything left."

"Sure there is." His tone was deceptively, good-natured. Almost dangerously so. "There's you."

She could swear her heart stopped. Sheer will kept her tone unremarkable. "I beg your pardon?"

"You," he repeated easily. "I'll bid fifty thousand dollars for you to actually help build a Shelter Project house yourself."

Murmurs rolled through the crowd as the cream of Virginia society looked from the undeniably attractive man casually holding the mike to where she stood on the dais in her strapless pink gown.

Over the years, Ashley had learned to pretend an ease that was never truly present in public. She madly pretended that ease now as the low rumble of speculation and approval faded to expectant silence.

With a thousand eyes on her, aware mostly of the steel-gray pair locked hard on hers, two thoughts collided in her mind. Under no circumstances did she want to do anything to embarrass herself or her family. And she would give half of her sizable trust fund to have never behaved so irresponsibly with a man who obviously still behaved irresponsibly himself.

"Mr. Callaway," she said, feeling frantic, feigning calm. "Your bid is most generous." Pride and duty nudged hard. So did a rather desperate need to get him away from that microphone. "I would be more than happy to work on a Shelter Project house."

"Start to finish," he qualified. "You have to stick around to see it through. You can't just show up, then disappear."

He was too far away for her to see the challenge she felt certain must be glinting in his compelling eyes. But she didn't doubt it was there. She could practically feel it radiating toward her. She could hear it, too. An edge had slipped into his tone that indicated far more meaning in his last words than what anyone else was likely to hear.

You can't just show up, then disappear.

He was angry. At the very least, it seemed he'd been offended by what she had done. Or, more likely, what she hadn't. She hadn't wakened him before she'd left. She hadn't left a note. She hadn't done anything but hurry away before he could wake up and see that she was not at all like the woman who had eventually pulled off his sweater, unzipped his jeans and played out her little fantasy of feeling totally unrestrained.

Embarrassed to death by what had happened, she hadn't returned the call he'd made to her office the next day, either.

"Tell you what," he said, "you see it through and I'll make it a hundred thousand."

Low gasps went up around the room. Regatta Week in Richmond drew the movers and shakers, old money and new, and anyone who was anybody spent with abandon. Yet, even that rather exclusive crowd seemed impressed by the sum. Or, maybe, what impressed them was Matt's nerve.

Determined not to lose hers, she glanced around the room. Her expression as good-natured as her tone, her stomach in knots, she asked, "Are there any other bids?"

A smattering of laughter drifted through the room as guests craned their necks to see who might want to top him.

It seemed no one wanted to steal his thunder. Either that, or they'd maxed out on their charitable spending for the night.

With all the other items, she had rapped her small gavel against its block when the item had been won. It was a fair sign of how rattled Matt had her that she forgot the gavel now. "Then, one hundred thousand it is."

Matt's golden head dipped in a deferential nod.

The flash of a camera caught her as the crowd burst into enthusiastic applause for the unprecedented bid. The goal of raising a quarter of a million dollars to build adequate housing for the working poor had not only been met. It had just been quite handsomely exceeded.

Ashley barely heard the ovation that was for her as much as the man someone had just handed a glass of champagne. She was far more aware of Matt as he lifted the glass to her in a subtle but clearly triumphant toast.

Conscious of the press, her peers and her parents, she nodded back, smiling when smiling was the last thing she felt like doing. She didn't trust what Matt had just done.

She wasn't even sure why he was there. His name hadn't appeared on the guest list.

She knew Cord hadn't brought him. Her second brother never did "the charity bit," as he called it. She doubted Cord even knew about the event, involved in his own world as he was. She wouldn't have thought Matt interested in mingling with the local glitterati, either.

The thought that he had shown up just to get back at her somehow added more color to the subtle blush accenting her cheekbones. The fact that he'd chosen to do so in front of her friends, her parents' friends and several hundred total strangers only increased the discomfort she was desperately trying to hide.

Hoping that anyone who noticed would only think her excited by the size of his donation, she stepped aside so the gray-haired and bespectacled president of the Shelter Project could take the podium. As the distinguished-looking gentleman thanked Matt, thanked her and thanked them all for their generosity, she quietly slipped off the stage.

Hiding was not an option. Since it was also doubtful that a hole would conveniently open up and swallow her, or that a comet would strike and end the world as she knew it, it seemed she had no other option but to face Matt and be as gracious as possible with so many others around. She did not, however, have to do it until it was absolutely necessary.

Buying herself time, she headed toward her table and tried not to look anxious while she accepted congratulations for a job well done from guests who stopped her on the way. At any moment, she expected the society reporter from the newspaper to pounce, photographer in tow. Her acceptance of the check from the man everyone was now talking about would be a photo op no self-respecting journalist would pass up.

Ashley had to concede that the passing of the check would also be excellent publicity for the charity—and raising funds for the Shelter Project had been the entire evening's goal.

Her goal now was to prepare herself for the moment she would turn and find Matt behind her. The effort, however, was wasted.

The reporter appeared as predicted to obtain a quote about how delighted Ashley was for the opportunity to actively participate in the building of a Shelter home. Ashley also told the woman that she did, indeed, know the gentleman who had put her up for bid. His name was Matt Callaway, and he was a friend of her brother Cord.

Looking as if that association alone was enough to explain the man's clearly unpredicted—and unprecedented—actions, the reporter then directed her photographer to get a shot of Ashley and her committee and went off in search of Matt.

Matt, however, had disappeared.

She was one hundred thousand dollars short.

Ashley sat in her modest office with its art prints on the walls, blinds tilted to mask the less than impressive view of a rooftop from the tenth floor of the Kendrick Building, and frowned at the neat columns of figures on the sheet in front of her. Every single item that had been donated for the auction had been purchased and paid for. Season tickets to the opera, to the symphony, to Washington Redskins games. An original oil painting. Baskets of gourmet foods. Cooking lessons. Dinners at some of the areas finest restaurants. Massages. A facial peel. Golf clubs. A spa membership.

The list went on.

The totals added up.

Everything was accounted for. Everything other than the last item of the evening, which one of her committee members had written on the recap sheet as *Ashley K.-$100,000!*

Ashley would have smiled at the exclamation point had the bid come from anyone but Matt. And had she not dreaded having to go after him to collect it.

She reached for the coffee cooling by her neatly aligned in-box, stapler and mouse pad of Monet's water lilies. She would send a letter first. If that didn't work, she would send her no-nonsense, very married assistant Elisa Jenkins to ask for it, since Elisa could sweet-talk her way into or out of just about anything. She just didn't want to have to talk to him herself. She was too embarrassed, too confused by what she had done, and somewhere between baffled and furious about what he had done in return. Being painfully honest with herself, however, she had to admit she was far more upset with herself than she was with him.

She had spent years going out of her way to avoid any situation that could embarrass herself or her family. For most of her life, she had lived in fear of proving that she would never be as refined as her mother, as capable as her younger sister, or that she would make a mistake that will wind up all over the press the way it so often had with Cord. Like her oldest brother Gabe, a senator now running for governor, she understood her duty to her family and its reputation, and had learned long ago to suppress every rebellious instinct she'd ever had.

Or so she'd thought before last Tuesday night.

She set the blue mug with its bright sunflowers back down, rubbing her forehead as if the motion could somehow erase the memory. It seemed to be one of those annoying paradoxes that the more a person tried to forget something, the more she thought about it. And thinking about her behavior with Matt piled guilt on top of regret and a whole host of other emotions she knew she didn't deserve to escape. She'd never in her life had a one-night stand. Never even considered it.

Until Matt.

She'd always been afraid she was susceptible to him. She'd just had no idea how susceptible she truly was. It seemed he'd barely touched her and she'd not only thrown caution to the wind, she'd flat-out forgotten caution existed.

A movement across the room rudely interrupted her self-flagellation.

Dropping her hand, she felt her heart jerk against her ribs.

It seemed she wouldn't have to go after Matt after all. He filled her doorway, a six-foot, two-inch wall of raw male tension civilized by a beautifully tailored navy-blue suit.

His steel-gray eyes skimmed from the neat twist of her hair, down the buttons of her tailored black jacket and moved back up to settle with an invasive jolt of heat on her mouth.

The inhibitions he'd stripped away right along with her clothes returned in spades.

Taking a step into the functional but feminine room, he lifted his bold glance to her eyes. "You didn't return my call."

There was a reason for that. "I...didn't know what to say."

"How about, 'I made it home fine.' Or, 'I had a good

time. Yes, I'd like to go to dinner sometime. Maybe take in a play.''"

He didn't understand. The woman he'd been with, the one it seemed he'd wanted to see again, hadn't really been…her. "Please." She rose, glancing past him, uneasy with fear that her assistant might arrive any moment and overhear. "Would you close the door."

"No need." His chiseled features seemed as tight as the deep tones of his voice as he crossed the industrial-gray carpet. "I'm not here about anything but the auction, Ashley. I got your message loud and clear." He stopped in front of her desk, the overhead lights catching hints of silver in his sun-bleached blond hair. "I just came to bring you this."

Reaching inside his jacket, he removed a check from its inner pocket and held it out to her. "You don't need to work on the project. I'll donate the money, anyway."

She looked down at the bold writing on his personal check. He'd written it out to the foundation in exactly the amount he'd bid. But it was his hand that held her attention. He clearly didn't run his business from behind a desk. His hands were a working man's. Broad, blunt fingered, capable. There were calluses at the base of his fingers. She knew. She'd felt them when he'd cupped her face, skimmed them down her naked back.

The thought brought other memories she'd desperately tried to erase. Taking what he offered, she forced herself not to snatch it in her haste to mentally change the subject.

Her glance barely grazed his chin.

"I appreciate the donation," she murmured, relieved that he seemed as anxious as she did to forget what had happened. "And I appreciate that you want to let me off the hook. But I do have to do the work.

"The story about you bidding for me was in the society section of yesterday's paper," she informed him, politely, because manners were the shield she used to get through just about everything. "*Entertainment Tonight* and *People* magazine have already picked it up, and a network called this morning to send a crew to film my progress for a documentary. The money they offered to the foundation for the rights will build a hundred houses. I'm not in a position to back out now."

That had not been at all what Matt had been prepared to hear. He'd thought he'd walk in, hand over the check, tell her he expected nothing in return and let it go at that. But then, he had to admit that he hadn't been prepared for anything that had happened with her lately.

He could feel the acid in his stomach churning as his glance moved from her impeccable clothing to the painfully neat and organized space surrounding her. Not so much as a paper clip was out of place in the cool blues and grays of the surprisingly unassuming office. The prints on the walls—a Monet, a Renoir, a Degas—were nicely framed but inexpensive. Her oak desk and blue chair were very much like the one her absent secretary or assistant used in the outer office. He'd been under the impression that Kendricks did everything on a grand scale. The ones he associated with now certainly did, anyway.

The modern thirty-story building was populated mostly by law and accounting firms that rented space from Kendrick Management Company. The upper four floors belonged exclusively to The Kendrick Group, Inc. Located there was an enormous boardroom, her father's suite of offices, an office Cord saw maybe once a quarter, and the offices of the sizable staff it took to oversee a conglomerate involved in everything from computers and commodities to wineries and world-class sports teams.

Everything upstairs spoke of wealth and power.

By comparison, the offices of the Kendrick Foundation

were downright austere. What he saw here was pleasant enough, almost serene, he supposed, but it spoke of an almost obsessive bent toward order.

The rigid control she seemed to surround herself with probably explained a lot about her, he thought. But with her studiously avoiding his eyes, he was far more interested in how her air of untouchable refinement could still provoke defenses in him.

There had been a time when she had made him feel as if he were nowhere near good enough to deserve her attention, wasn't worthy enough for even a few moments of her time, much less her interest. The way she would turn away when she saw him coming, or hurry past without speaking had only added to the quiet rage of inequity that had simmered inside him for so long he hadn't even known it was there.

He could have sworn he had grown beyond the buried anger and resentments of his youth. After the other night with her, he'd thought she'd grown up, too, or at least grown beyond the snobbish, pampered-princess stage that had made it nearly impossible for her to go anywhere near him.

It seemed little about her had changed, though. Apparently, her mood and a half a bottle of one of California's better vintages had only masked her feelings about him. She hadn't even had the decency to return his call when he'd phoned to make sure she'd made it home all right.

She was clearly back to avoiding him again. Which was fine with him. The less he had to do with her himself, the better off he would be. It felt demoralizing enough to think that she'd had to nearly get drunk to let him touch her. It only added insult to injury that he couldn't get the feel of her out of his mind.

He was working on it, though. He just wished he hadn't totally forgotten about the media attention she would attract.

Jamming his hands into his slacks' pockets to keep from

jamming them through his hair, he mentally kicked himself for what he'd done. Watching her the other night, seeing her so cool and poised, he had simply wanted her to acknowledge that he existed. He had no idea now why that had mattered. He wasn't feeling particularly proud of his actions, either.

Picturing her on a construction site was impossible.

"I suppose you don't have a lot of choice now," he conceded, figuring he should probably be grateful all that polished poise was there. Considering what he'd gotten her into, it probably kept her from going for his throat. "When do you plan to go?"

"I haven't planned anything yet."

"There are a couple of projects scheduled here in Richmond for the first of September. Those will be the easiest in terms of proximity."

She shook her head, strands of champagne gleaming among shades of pale wheat. "September is when our scholarship recipients start school." There would be child care to help the ladies arrange. Paperwork with the various colleges to complete. Part-time jobs to find. "It's far too busy a time for me to be gone then. The only time I'm free is the first of August."

"The only projects then are in Florida. August is a miserable month there."

"It's the only time I can go."

"Go earlier. Get someone to cover for you." His voice tightened as he looked up from her smooth, perfectly manicured hands. He was trying to help her out here. He was trying to help both of them, actually. "You really don't want to go to Gray Lake, Florida, that time of year."

"I don't want to ask anyone to cover for me." Her delicate brow pinched. "And how do you know so much about Shelter's schedule?"

He knew the schedule because he'd helped draw it up. He'd donated a project supervisor and manpower to each Shelter project from the construction company he'd started ten years ago. He didn't care to explain that, though. He especially didn't care to explain how he'd become involved with the charity in the first place. Not to her. "The schedule was in the publicity material."

"In the newspapers?"

"At the dinner. It was on the tables."

"Why were you even there?"

It seemed she couldn't imagine any reason for his presence at such an event—except, possibly, to make her life miserable.

His defenses already up, Matt ignored the anxiety in her tone. All he heard was the phrasing that seemed to suggest he hadn't belonged in the socially and politically prominent circle she ran with.

Two seconds ago, he'd struggled with guilt and a fair amount of self-reproach for letting her get the better of him. Now, any guilt he felt about what his actions had committed her to disappeared like water drops on a hot griddle. Any desire for further discussion evaporated right along with it. Although he might have pointed out that she hadn't seemed to mind his lack of pedigree the other night had his basic sense of decency—and his friend—not stopped him.

"Hey, there you are. Dad's secretary said I'd find you here."

Ashley's glance jerked to her brother Cord as he stopped in the doorway. She couldn't remember the last time she'd seen him in a tie. His nod to family convention today had been to throw a sports jacket on over his collarless shirt and slacks. It didn't matter that the black shirt was imported silk, the slack's cashmere and the jacket a beautiful hand-tailored Italian cut that were hardly the uniform of a rebel. She suspected he refused to wear a tie simply because their father and their older brother did.

His rakish smile died as his glance bounced from her to the side of Matt's head. "What's going on?"

A muscle in Matt's jaw bunched as he pulled his hands from his pockets. "I needed to hand over a check. I thought I'd do it before our meeting."

"Dad's on his way to the conference room now. If we get ourselves up there, we can be out of here in an hour."

"Hey, Sis," he said to her, oblivious to the strain snaking through the room. "I'm sorry I missed you with those papers. Edna just cornered me with them."

Edna was their dad's personal secretary, had been for nearly thirty years. Knowing the amazingly efficient, no-nonsense woman as she did, Ashley could almost picture the sixty-something matron taking Cord by the ear, sitting him down in his office and insisting that he wasn't leaving until the document was read and signed.

As much as Ashley had hated being pulled off her own job to chase down her brother, she'd hated even more that she hadn't been able to accomplish what her father had sent her to do.

It had been a day of system failures all the way around.

"Come on, Callaway." Cord's voice cut through the strain. "As soon as we get through this proposal, I'm heading home. Sheryl has a friend in town. Want to go for a sail?"

It sounded as if the two of them had put together another project for the real-estate development arm of the Kendrick companies. Despite his penchant for play, Cord had proven himself a bit of a genius at spotting potential business properties and buying them for a song—which was undoubtedly why their father hadn't disinherited him over some of the messes he'd gotten himself into. Flings with models, female

rock stars and incidents with race cars and gambling estab-
lishments raised their socially and politically conservative
father's blood pressure enough. But a paternity suit last year
had nearly put him over the edge.

"I'll pass," she heard Matt mutter. "I need to get back
to Atlanta."

"You just came from Atlanta."

"That's because I've got another project going there."

"You need a break," Cord grumbled.

"Call it my own form of risk management. Work keeps
me out of trouble."

Standing the same impressive height as Matt and with his
blue eyes and sun-streaked hair, Cord could have more easily passed for the brother of the big man radiating tension
beside him than the one he actually had. Gabe was dark like
their father. So was their little sister, Tess. Ashley and Cord
had both inherited their mother's fair coloring.

Any other similarities between her and her next oldest
sibling, however, ended there. As much as Cord tended to
distance himself from family, other than for business, she
felt she barely knew him at all. There were only three years
separating them, but with their difference in interests and
attitude, those years could be measured at the speed of light.
From the time he'd been a teenager, it seemed he'd gone
out of his way to break the rules.

Matt's influence back then hadn't helped at all.

If she remembered correctly, it had been Matt who'd
shown him how to hot-wire a car.

"You're turning into a bad example," Cord informed his
friend. "If I hang around with you much longer, I might
almost turn respectable myself. Are you through here?"

She could practically feel Matt's finely honed tension
when he glanced toward her.

"Your sister and I have nothing else to discuss," he said, speaking to Cord, looking at her.

"Then, let's get out of here." Cord slapped him on the back. Without another word to her, they both turned to the door.

"What was the check for?"

"That auction."

"Oh, yeah," she heard her brother muse. "I can't believe you got her to agree to that. Are you really going to let her do it?"

Matt was already out the door. Cord was right behind.

She had no idea why her brother thought Matt had any say in whether or not she worked on a house. They gave her no clue, either. With their voices fading with their footsteps, she couldn't hear another thing they said.

She could, however, still feel the tension Matt had left in his wake. It rubbed her nerves like sandpaper, making it impossible to stay still.

Crossing her office, she closed the door before Elisa could arrive and walk in as she always did, eager to share whatever it was her precious six-month-old daughter had accomplished the night before and launch into her usual lecture about what Ashley really needed was a husband and babies. She would adore having a family of her own. Now just wasn't the time to think about how useful it would be to first meet the right guy.

With her hand still on the knob, she rested her forehead against the smooth wood. All she could think about now was what had happened with the wrong one.

It seemed that the Fates weren't satisfied with letting her stew in her own disappointment in herself. To make up for her lapse in judgement with Matt, she must now suffer a situation she truly did not want to be in.

She knew nothing about building a building. Her interests

were in her family and in her charities, in the scholarship program for single moms and in the impoverished women and children she tried to help by finding out where their needs were and raising funds to meet them. Her talents lay in organization and an eye for detail. That was why her mother had entrusted her with the Shelter Project fundraiser. But just because she could raise the money to buy bricks or boards, didn't mean she knew how to put them together.

Worse than that, the press would be around whether she wanted them there or not.

She lifted her head, slowly turned back to the papers on her desk. Only months ago, the press had had a field day with Gabe before he'd married their head housekeeper's daughter. Cord's name hadn't shown up in at least six weeks, so he was due to fall off the good-behavior wagon any day now. Their little sister, Tess, had settled into domesticity with her husband of barely a year in Boston and rumors were rumbling that her marriage was already in trouble. Tess staunchly denied it. But her smile had seemed awfully strained to Ashley when they'd met a few weeks ago for lunch.

Staying out of the limelight seemed impossible for Ashley, too. Just trying to avoid it had caused her problems enough. She'd tried lying low a few years ago and speculation had ranged from her being ill to her being a recluse. She'd had no problem overlooking the tabloid's claims that she'd been abducted by aliens, but her mother had finally made her face the fact that their family would never have the privacy others had. Unless she wanted to live her life in total seclusion, her only defense would be to hold her head high and give the world as little as possible to criticize.

She would do her best to do just that. But she couldn't help feeling a disaster coming on with the building thing. It seemed to her that the only positive in the situation was that what she would do would be for a very good cause. That, and now that she had his check, there was no imaginable reason for her to have to deal with Matt again.

Or so she thought until she came across his name two weeks later in a volunteer packet Shelter's home office had mailed her. The sponsor material she had seen for the fundraiser hadn't listed Callaway Construction among its benefactors. She was almost certain of it. But right on the back of the single-page brochure that listed the basics for each volunteer, listed under project management was Callaway Construction, Matthew J. Callaway, President.

The connection certainly explained his presence at the auction. It did nothing, however, to ease the trepidation she felt about what she had to do.

Preferring to be optimistic, she told herself the disquieting little discovery had no effect one way or the other on her. Her own father had his name on dozens of companies. Some of which he rarely set foot in. He made the decisions, but other people did the actual work. When she arrived in Florida, Matt would be off building major real-estate developments in Newport News, Atlanta or somewhere equally distant.

That logic stayed with her until the second week of August when she stepped off a chartered plane at the landing strip outside the little backwater town of Gray Lake, Florida. She'd barely glanced through the heat waves rising from the tarmac when she saw him standing, arms crossed, beside a big, bull-nosed silver pickup truck.

Converging ahead of him were three reporters and a camera crew.

Chapter Three

"Ms. Kendrick. Paula Littleton. WFAZ out of Sarasota." A tall brunette in a pale blue blouse and navy skirt stuck out her hand as Ashley reached the bottom rung of the commuter plane's short flight of retractable steps. The woman had amazingly white teeth and a grip that could rival any man's. "Will you be staying with the rest of the crew while you're working here?"

Ashley made herself smile as she glanced at the foam-tipped microphone the woman thrust in front of her face.

"I imagine I am. I'm not being treated differently from any of the other volunteers."

Pulling her hand from the Amazon's grip, she tried not to glance toward the man watching her from fifty feet away and popped up the handle on her black travel bag. Her smaller bag hung from her shoulder.

"What is it exactly that you'll be doing?" the reporter asked as Ashley started forward with her luggage.

"I don't know yet. I understand that I'll get my assignment at the site."

"Are you really going to work on this project until it's completed?"

Ashley kept her smile in place. "That's my intention."

"Miss Kendrick." Another microphone appeared beside the first, this one in the hand of an attractive gentleman with thick dark hair wearing an open-collared dress shirt. He apparently used the same toothpaste as his female counterpart.

"Tony Shultz. *Sun Daily News,*" he said, not bothering with a handshake. "It seems Senator Kendrick's constituents have welcomed his new wife with open arms. They're calling her marriage to him a triumph for the working girl. How do you feel about having one of your servants as an in-law?"

"I'm perfectly fine with it," she replied, deciding he wasn't so attractive after all. He was after dirt.

"But doesn't her background as your parents' gardener and the daughter of their housekeeper make it awkward for some of you?"

"Addie Lowe Kendrick is family," she replied, politely. "And I don't discuss my family with the press." She flashed him a smile. "I'd be happy to talk to you about the Shelter Project, though."

Slanting her male counterpart a look that clearly said he should have known better than to ask a Kendrick about a Kendrick, the brunette edged herself closer—only to be aced out by another reporter half hidden by Tony.

"Susie Ortega. *Evening Entertainment.* Miss Kendrick," came the voice attached to a white sleeve and a microphone, how do you feel about Jason Roberts's engagement to Sarah Bradford-Hill?"

"They're engaged? I'd heard he was seeing someone, but

I didn't know they'd made it official.'' Her smile turned pleased. ''I'm delighted for them both.''

Jason was Ashley's ex-almost-fiancé, a charming, brilliant, socially prominent attorney whose rising success had ultimately made her realize how totally ill suited they were for each other. Over the two years they'd been together, the more well-known he had become, the more he'd craved the publicity and attention she had always sought to avoid. With him, parties and a constant stream of strangers would have been a major part of her life. She might have forced herself to cope with such a lifestyle had he been able to understand her need for occasional downtime. But he hadn't, and they both eventually admitted that they simply weren't being fair to each other.

They had broken up over a year ago, quite amicably—much to the disappointment of the tabloids.

''Are you still seeing Eric Parks?'' asked the *Entertainment* reporter.

Eric? ''I've only been out with him once.'' And that had been over three months ago, if she remembered correctly. She'd met the young senator at a political dinner with her brother Gabe, and been totally impressed by his seemingly selfless interest in his causes. On a date, all he'd been interested in was himself and getting her influence with her brother.

''Will you see him again?''

Not in this lifetime, she thought. ''I'm sure I'll run into him somewhere.'' And others just like him, which was pretty much why her social life was limited to a few highly trusted friends.

Paula closed the gap. Ahead of them two cameramen and three photographers walked backward, cameras rolling. ''Why the Shelter Project, Miss Kendrick?'' she asked, edging out little Susie and blocking the male reporter as Ashley continued across the apron of the runway. Heat radiated up from the black tarmac, adding twenty degrees to the already sultry air. Matt had been right. It was hot there in August. The humidity was also thick enough to cut with a stick. "There are a hundred different charities you could lend your name to," the woman continued. "Why this one?"

"Because of what it does." She did her level best to avoid the pull of Matt's eyes. He was still watching her. She could feel it as she tried to focus on the question and the woman who'd posed it. When a microphone was in a person's face, she'd always found it wise to avoid distractions.

"It's actually one of my mother's favorite causes," she explained, terribly distracted anyway. "I've become interested through her. Shelter's goal is to put decent roofs over the heads of the working poor and their families. A large percentage of that group is single women with dependent children. That's where my passion lies."

"With disadvantaged women and children?"

"Absolutely," she said, and would have mentioned how privileged she felt to work with them had Matt and a dozen questions about his presence not eroded her focus anyway.

A fourth reporter and camera crew of two hung back near a van parked six sedans and a couple of SUVs away from Matt's truck, all of which were lined up on the other side of the chain-link fence that separated the parking lot and tiny one-room terminal from the single runway. The man in charge of the crew appeared to be the short, baby-faced ball of energy in a backward baseball cap who bustled through the eight-foot gap in the fence and headed straight for her.

Refusing to let anyone ahead of him, Tony-the-Tactless jockeyed back into place. In the heat, his aftershave was almost overpowering.

"The Shelter Project is a nonprofit organization," he began. "Are you or your mother on its board?"

"No," she replied, not at all certain where the guy was going with that query.

"Are you friends with anyone on the board?"

"I've met the board members," she admitted, couching her words carefully. "They were all at the fund-raiser in Richmond last month. I would say I'm acquainted with them."

"What about your brother?"

"My brother?"

"Senator Kendrick."

He was fishing. For what she had no idea.

"My brother has more friends than I can count. He also has a staff that is far better prepared than I to answer questions about him. I'm here to build a house."

Taking advantage of his momentary silence, Paula popped back in.

"When do you actually start work on the project?"

"Today. I was told to arrive ready for work."

The short guy stuck out his hand.

"Ron Conway. Network special projects," he said in that terse way media people had of identifying themselves. "I'm directing the documentary. The guy in the red cap over there is Andy," he said, nodding to a young man who barely looked old enough to shave. "He's audio. The guy with the ponytail behind the camera is Steve. Just go about your business and pretend we're not here. We can pick up most conversations from twenty feet away, so don't worry about us missing anything. We'll be with you the whole way."

She couldn't begin to tell him how thrilled she was to hear that.

"I'm pleased to meet you, Mr. Conway. Just let me know what you need me to do."

"Nothing other than what you're supposed to do. We're not staging anything. Just ignore the camera."

"Ours, too." Paula gave a "cut" signal to one of the cameramen in front of them. "We want some footage at the site."

Microphones were turned off and cameras swung away as everyone headed for the open gate. But not by a single nerve did Ashley relax. Six cars down, she saw Matt straighten his long, muscular frame from where he'd leaned against his vehicle's front fender.

The uneasy thought that he was apparently her ride competed with the voices behind her. The WFAZ cameraman complained about how hot it was going to get. Someone else wanted to stop for cold drinks.

"Hey, Tony." Ashley heard the tall female reporter demand as she watched Matt emerge from the rows of cars, "what were you after with those questions?"

"A story," came the terse reply. "I want something with some meat to it. I can't think of anything more boring than covering some pampered celebrity whose trauma of the day will be ruining her manicure."

"She's a Kendrick. Ratings will be up ten points on any station that has anything on her."

With their voices low and walking several yards behind her, Ashley didn't think they knew she could hear them. Not that it mattered. She knew it wasn't really her people were interested in. It was the mystique created by her mother's royal blood, her father's carpetbagger ancestors and his own family's wealth. Few people truly knew her at all. What they knew was an image, the one she felt honor bound to maintain. There most definitely wasn't anyone on the planet who knew her the way Matt did. Not even the man she'd once considered marrying had known of her deep-seated craving for freedom, or so completely destroyed her normal reserve.

The fact that she had let her guard down so completely with him now pulled that guard firmly into place. She had never blamed the wine for what had happened that night. She'd never even considered it. She knew she had let the barriers fall because he'd made it easy to do, because something about him had made her not care about propriety or obligation to a family image. She was afraid of what he now knew about her, of how easily she'd allowed herself to be seduced. Afraid of what he thought of her because of it. And seeing him again was truly the last thing on earth she wanted to do.

The knot in her stomach felt the size of a Florida orange when he stopped in front of her.

A white T-shirt stretched over his broad shoulders and chest. Well-worn jeans hugged his powerful thighs. Beneath the windblown hair falling over his forehead, black sunglasses hid his eyes. She could see nothing but her own reflection in those concealing lenses, but she could practically feel his glance work its way from the collar of her casual pink polo shirt and over her designer jeans to her new boots before he reached over and took her bags.

"I hope you brought cooler clothes," he said, his voice flat as he headed back to his truck. Reaching it, he lifted her luggage into the pickup's bed. "We've been hitting the nineties every day. The humidity is up there, too."

"My clothes are fine," she assured him, far more uncomfortable with him than the sticky heat. "I like warm weather."

With her bags stowed, he walked past her to open the passenger door. "Then, you're going to love it here."

The documentary crew's camera had them in their sights. Aware that they were being filmed, she should have felt relieved to put some distance between the lens and the reporters. Instead, she felt more as if she were stepping from the mouth of the lion into its throat when she climbed into the truck and Matt closed the door with a solid thud.

She barely had a chance to blow out an uneasy breath before he climbed in on the other side.

Not knowing what to make of his impersonal attitude, telling herself she should probably just be grateful for it, she shifted her glance toward the floorboard. His feet looked huge in his heavy work boots. The bottom of his jeans were frayed, the fabric so worn in spots that it was nearly white. A few more washings, or one deep knee bend, and the tiny hole above his knee would become a split.

It didn't look to her as if he were dressed simply to play chauffeur.

"Why didn't you tell me you were involved with Shelter?"

"It didn't seem important."

Keys rattled as he stuck one into the ignition.

"It seems important now," she quietly replied.

The engine rumbled to life, hot air blasting from the air-conditioning vents. "All that matters right now is that we both have a job to do, Ashley. You're here to work and so am I. Let's just let it go at that."

Looking as resigned as he sounded, he put the truck into gear to back out of the space. Behind him was the white van. Its driver was clearly waiting for him to go first.

Seeing the vehicle in the rearview mirror, Matt bit back a sigh. Ahead, a blue WFAZ TV van sat waiting for him to go so it could follow them, too.

He had no one but himself to blame for the fact that they all were there.

Beside him, Ashley finished buckling her seat belt and folded her hands almost primly in her lap. Her pale pink

nails were perfectly polished, perfectly shaped. Her shining
hair was swept smoothly back from her delicate features and
caught at her nape with a wide gold clip. Her flawless skin
looked as smooth as satin, her lips lush and moist.

He knew exactly how soft those lips were, and how arous-
ing her hands could be. It was the way she smelled that got
him, though. Her light, fresh scent had been instantly familiar, its effects on his subconscious immediate, and definitely unwanted.

"I saw in the volunteer brochure that your company man-
ages these projects," she said, her voice dripping with caution. "I just didn't think you would actually be working
here yourself." Especially knowing I would be here, she
could have added, but didn't.

"I wasn't until yesterday." He'd felt frustrated even before she'd arrived. He felt even more so having to deal with
the effects of her scent on the primitive part of his brain
that clearly recalled the pleasure he'd experienced with her.
"I donate a foreman and a couple of craftsmen to each job
to work with the volunteers," he explained, forcing himself
not to growl the words. "But I had to relieve the foreman
on this job."

"I hope he wasn't ill."

Her quick, almost instinctive concern pleated his forehead. "He's fine. I'm just taking over because you're here."
And because of my big mouth, he thought, pulling ahead to
get their little show on the road. "I couldn't ask one of my
foremen to deal with you."

Her calm was as impressive as the regal arch of her eyebrow. "Deal with me?"

"And your entourage." He checked his side-view mirror
before he turned onto the road leading from the little mu-
nicipal airport. Sure enough, the news van had pulled out
right behind the one with the documentary crew. Right be-

hind that was a tan sedan that belonged to one of the reporters.

It seemed she didn't have to look to know they were leading a parade.

"You knew the press would be here," she quietly reminded him. "You knew about the documentary people, anyway. I have little control over the rest."

For a moment, he said nothing. Of course, he'd known about them. That was why he'd taken over himself rather than dumping the responsibility for this particular project on one of his men. It could sometimes be difficult enough working with untrained workers, as good-hearted and well-intentioned as they were, without having the distractions of a celebrity in their midst.

He had told himself before she'd stepped off the plane that he would do exactly as he had already asked everyone else at the site to do and treat her as they would anyone else. He would overlook the fact that she had undoubtedly never done a hard day's work in her life, just as he intended to ignore the events that had brought them both to being where neither wanted to be. If he'd learned anything in thirty-one years, it was that there wasn't a thing he could do about the past, but he could sure as hell see that it didn't repeat itself.

When it came to everything but business, he lived purely in the present.

Presently, sticking to business was all he cared to do.

"Then, we'll concentrate on what you can control," he finally said. "I didn't send anyone else to get you because I wanted to make sure you understand that I can't cut you much slack."

"I'm not asking for any."

"I didn't say you were," he defended, patiently. "But unless you've been moonlighting in maintenance at your country club, my bet is that you don't have any skills that are going to be immediately useful on a construction site.'' He frowned toward her hands. ''Have you ever used a hammer? For something other than a doorstop, I mean.''

From the faint pinch of her mouth, he doubted she'd ever even held one. It was entirely possible, he supposed, that she'd never even seen one up close.

''How about a tape measure? A level?

''My point,'' he continued, making himself behave when what he really wanted to do was remind her that he knew exactly how protected and indulged she'd been, ''is that every volunteer has to be capable of accomplishing her job. If you're going to be here, you have to work just like the other volunteers. Getting the house up is our first priority. We're on a schedule and we have to keep to it.

''I'll show you how to do something that doesn't require a lot of instruction. If you don't understand what you're doing, ask for help.''

''Is this the orientation speech the brochure promised?''

He wondered how long all that cool composure would last once she was on the job. ''I suppose it is,'' he conceded. ''Everyone else got theirs when they started a few weeks ago.''

''I thought I was supposed to do this start to finish.''

''Like I said, there's a schedule. We couldn't wait until you were ready before we started. If the weather holds, we should be finished in another three weeks.''

She opened her mouth, judiciously closed it again and glanced out the passenger window. He had a feeling she wasn't checking out the view. As intent as she seemed on maintaining that annoying unruffled poise, she was probably biting her tongue.

He'd actually liked her better when she didn't hold back, when she said what was on her mind. But, then, she apparently had to be in a rebellious mood and half-inebriated to do that with him.

He forced his tone to stay even. "Do you have any questions?"

She looked as if she had a ton of them. She also looked as if she didn't know if she should pose them to him, or save them for a friendlier face. He wasn't fooled by her quiet manners, or the composure she so diligently maintained. From the rigid way she sat, he figured she was as comfortable with him as she would have been with a water snake.

"We have to work together," he pointed out flatly. "You might as well ask."

The edge in his tone drew her faint frown. "Only if you'll answer."

"Of course, I will."

"Then, how did you get involved with this?"

That wasn't at all the sort of question he had in mind. Talking to her about his turbulent youth definitely was not on his agenda of things to discuss with her. Especially when that youth was what had set him so clearly apart from her and her breed.

"A friend told me about it," he replied, knowing he was being deliberately vague, not caring as he pulled his glance from her mouth. The nerves low in his gut tightened. So did his voice. "You shouldn't wear perfume here."

From the corner of his eye, he saw her blink at him. "Excuse me?"

"You shouldn't wear perfume," he repeated, her scent still taunting him. "Scents can attract bugs."

"I'm not wearing perfume."

Puzzled, she watched his jaw lock. Preferring only to get this ride over with, she also changed the subject.

"How far is it to the job site?"

"About half an hour. We'll drop off your bag at the motel first."

They were heading east, away from the commercial development she had seen from the air along the coastline. The few small, single-story manufacturing facilities they'd passed had already given way to little more than a flat landscape, lush with low vegetation and occasionally punctuated by majestic umbrella-like palm trees.

Matt reached over and turned on the radio. "I want to catch the weather," he muttered over the blast of the air conditioner.

What they got was the news. Specifically a traffic report for Sarasota, ninety miles northwest and an ad to be sure to visit the Cypress Slough preserve out of Fort Myers where visitors could take a mile-long boardwalk and see wetland inhabitants such as wading birds, turtles and alligators.

The thought of seeing an alligator gave her definite pause. She hadn't even considered the local wildlife when she'd thought of her trip here. But the noise from the radio prevented silence from becoming awkward, and she was pretty sure that was all Matt was really interested in, anyway.

The Cypress Motor Inn sat right off the two-lane highway on the outskirts of Gray Lake. It was flanked by a doughnut shop on one side, a field of vegetation on the other and had the nearby amenities of a two-pump gas station and a convenience store a couple of city blocks down. A pool, crystal blue and sparkling, occupied the middle of the grounds. Patches of green lawn hugged it on three sides, punctuated here and there by the same sort of tall palm that surrounded the entire building. Crushed white seashells filled in the other side and served as a parking lot.

The motel itself definitely needed a coat of paint. The tan cinder block building wrapped itself around the pool in a deep U. All doors faced center. And all doors were paired with a large window with a slightly rusted air-conditioning unit protruding from beneath it.

The Shelter office had given her the name of the motel as the one being closest to the site. Since every volunteer made her own reservation and paid her own expenses, Ashley had already been prepared for something a tad less luxurious than she was accustomed to. A person got what she paid for, and what she'd paid for was costing her $59.95 a night. She'd upgraded to get a room with a kitchenette.

Matt caught her looking with some trepidation down the long, empty breezeway. The Vacancy sign in the office window looked permanent.

"There's no place to lock up your bag at the site, so I'll leave it in the office," Matt explained, as he pulled to a stop by a row of pink plastic flamingos. "You can check in when we call it quits for the day."

"That's fine," she said, thinking it best to be agreeable. "Did you bring a hat?"

The suggested clothing list she'd been sent had highly recommended sun-protective clothing, along with the unfashionably sturdy practical boots she wore. Since a purse would only be in the way, the list had also suggested that ladies either carry what they needed in their pockets or use a very small waist pack. The little black pack on the seat beside her had been a good-luck present from her assistant. Elise had filled it with headache tablets and sunblock.

"I have a baseball cap."

Since it was in one of her travels bags, she climbed out after him and was promptly greeted by the rumble of the three vehicles pulling in behind them. A sound boom was thrust through the window of the white van even as Matt lowered the truck gate and set the bag she indicated on it.

The door on the side of the van rolled back to reveal the kid with the ponytail hoisting his camera onto his shoulder.

"Roll," she heard someone call.

"Are you going to open this?"

Matt's question had her glance jerking to his chin then to her bag a moment before she quickly unzipped it.

If Ashley knew how to do anything well, it was pack. She could get more into a suitcase that stowed under an airline seat than most people could get into a Pullman. Her technique was to roll. Everything. Everything that could be bent, anyway.

Neat little sausages of lace, mostly pale beige, shell-pink and ice-blue, nestled in a long neat row next to rows of light cottons, silks and white socks.

Reaching under her blow-dryer and makeup bag, she pulled out the white cap she'd rolled by tucking its bill into its back strap, grabbed the pair of work gloves her assistant had bought for her and shut the lid before the camera could get a good shot of her underwear.

With the bag zipped back up, she calmly met the cleft in Matt's chin.

"Thank you," she said, and headed back to her side of the vehicle with a smile and a wave for the camera.

The day would never come when she would relax around the press. Yet, caught between a lens and the man whose tension radiated toward her like heat waves, at the moment, the latter definitely seemed friendlier.

"Got it!" the guy who'd introduced himself as Ron called and gave her a thumbs-up before he motioned his cameraman to get a shot of the motel's neon sign, missing *M* and all. Fifteen seconds later, he signaled him to cut and close the door.

Matt was back from the office in less than a minute.

Less than five minutes after that, he led the little caravan through the sleepy little town of Gray Lake, with its dubious claim of being the fishing and crane capitol of Lee County, and down a residential street of small neat houses that ended with a few vacant lots, a dozen parked cars and two more TV vans.

Ashley could hear the high-pitched scream of a saw even before Matt silenced the blast of the air conditioner and the invisible talking head on the radio. The rhythmic pounding of hammers became audible an instant later.

Except for several large royal palms, the lot at the far end of the street had been cleared back to a stand of what looked like giant pineapples and primordial plants with leaves the size of turkey platters.

"Hang on a minute," Matt told her and was out his door before she could say a word.

They'd parked behind a battered green pickup truck that held construction supplies. Right behind Matt's truck came their little caravan. Her attention remained on Matt, though, as she watched him walk toward the skeletal, roofless frame rising from a cement slab.

Approaching the burly man at the saw, he made a slicing motion across his throat. A moment later, the saw went silent and several of the dozen workers scattered over the lot turned toward him.

She had no idea what he was saying. Two women had just converged on the truck, a blond cheerleader type in a tan oxford shirt and khaki skirt and an older, more seasoned-looking redhead who had tamed her wild curls by cutting them as short as possible without shearing herself bald. Ashley would have known who, or what, they were even if they hadn't clutched microphones and had their cameramen on their tail. As they simultaneously whipped off their sunglasses, she caught the determined gleam in their eyes.

Feeling like prey, making herself overlook it, she hung

her own sunglasses from the neck of her shirt, unclipped her hair so she could pull it through the back of her cap and pulled the cap on. Seeing Matt heading for her again, she opened her door before she could let dread slow her down.

"Miss Kendrick," the blonde said as Ashley's feet hit the ground, "Tahlia Bernstein, WRTX, Naples. We've been talking with the people you'll be working with. What do you plan to do now that you're here?"

"Meet them," Ashley replied, her smile engaging. "And find out what I'm supposed to do."

"Miss Kendrick," the other woman began, only to cut herself off when a sound boom slid in front of her face.

"Sorry about that, ma'am," the angular young man in the blue ball cap called. His drawl sounded pure southern Texas. "I'm just trying to get it past y'all."

Matt stopped behind them, a full head taller than the youthful-looking Andy, and totally dwarfing the women. One dark brown eyebrow arched toward her.

"May I see you for a minute?"

"Excuse me," she murmured to the microphones and slipped past the boy with the boom to get past the blockade of onlookers forming near the reporters.

She hadn't noticed the locals before. They'd apparently been sitting in the shade of the palms and cypress on the vacant lot nearby and emerged when they'd recognized her in the truck.

Ashley smiled at a middle-aged woman in a straw hat and hot pink muumuu, but most of her focus was on the group of Shelter volunteers gathering in the shade of the newly erected block walls. By noon that shade would be gone.

Looking as if he figured he might as well get introductions over with, Matt started to take her arm, seemed to think better of touching her and motioned her toward the tattooed bruiser by a wicked-looking power saw. The burly carpenter pulled his safety goggles farther up on his red bandana-covered head and gave her a nod.

"That's Dale," Matt told her, seeming oblivious to the fact that the man was missing a front tooth. "The guy by the block pallets over there is Ed. He's our lead carpenter," he continued, indicating the wizened old guy wiping sweat from his forehead with his forearm. "They're from Callaway Construction. I'll let our volunteers introduce themselves."

The ten men and women in old work clothes gave her smiles that ranged from curious to nervous to merely polite. Wanting very much to be part of their team, and knowing first impressions were terribly important, she took the initiative and held her hand out to a forty-something woman in a Shelter Project T-shirt and a slouch hat.

"Hi. I'm Ashley," she said, as if everyone there didn't already know that, and more conscious of Matt than anyone else, proceeded to work her way down the line.

Behind her cameras rolled, making some of the volunteers look nervously in their direction. A couple of others grinned and waved. A boy of about seventeen, his skin almost as red as his hair, called "Yo, Mom!" and gave his potential viewing audience a V for victory sign.

"Okay, everybody. That's it," Matt called, mercifully cutting off the last woman in line, who had just asked Ashley to autograph her lunch sack. Despite the edge Ashley sensed in him, friendly authority marked his tone. "Let's get back to it before the heat hits. Okay?

"Gene," he called to the retired engineer who had told her this was his sixth Shelter project, "do you need any help mixing mortar?"

"We've got it covered. One more batch and we're through with the exterior walls."

"How about you, Ed? Can you use her for framing?"

The craggy-faced lead carpenter squinted in her direction. "Can you use a nail gun?"

Ashley opened her mouth.

It was Matt who answered. "You can show her how."

He gave a shrug. "Sure." He waved her toward him. "Come on. I'll get you a work apron and get you started."

A nail...gun?

Ashley turned to Matt, but he was already walking away.

"Hey, Miss Kendrick," she heard Ed call. "Let's get going, huh?"

Chapter Four

Ashley couldn't help the relief she felt when she realized Matt had just handed her off to someone else. She couldn't help but notice that he hadn't wasted any time doing it, either.

Resigned to do what she must, determined to do the best job she could, she turned to Ed Wyckowski. The gravel-voiced carpenter took a long look at her, pulled the toothpick from his mouth, told her to put on her gloves and led her to a stack of wood piled inside the open walls.

"So you're here 'cause the boss bid on you, huh?"

"He told you about that?" she asked, not quite sure what to make of the twinkle in his pale blue eyes. He was amused. She just couldn't tell if it was with Matt, her or the situation.

"Wife did. She eats up all that entertainment and society stuff. She can tell you who's married to who, who broke up, who got caught doing what. She reads that *People* magazine and the *National Enquirer.* Me, I don't read much but the sports section and *Motor Trend.*

"We're going to be framing in this wall," he continued, pretty much establishing that he was through socializing for now. "We're taking those two-by-fours over there and nailing 'em to the soleplate soon as we get the plate attached."

Stuffing his toothpick into his shirt pocket, he toed the long strip of wood lying where gray block wall met cement foundation.

"You know anything about construction?"

"I can spell it," she offered gamely, looking around the totally unfamiliar spaces. White plastic pipes stuck up in three separate places from the foundation. Sawdust covered the ground under two metal sawhorses and had scattered to reach just about everywhere else. A trail of it led out the openings for the front and back doors. Lumber sat in neat piles inside and out.

"Well, you're going to be a lot more familiar with it than that by the time you finish. What we're going to do is frame out the walls with studs so down the line we've got something to nail Sheetrock to and insulate. This here's one of the easier jobs at this stage. Takes muscle to haul mortar and lay block." He glanced at her slender arms, clearly thinking her anything but sturdy. "Don't worry," he said, apparently seeing that she was, "this'll be a piece of cake once you get the hang of it."

Bending his sinewy, rawboned body, he picked up what looked like a large silver drill with a two-foot long metal strip hanging from the business end. The awkward-looking tool was connected by a thin hose to a green tanklike object on wheels.

"That air compressor supplies the energy to drive the nail. This magazine," he explained, indicating the long metal thing, "holds nails that are glued together in long strips.

"Here," he continued, pulling his safety goggles from around his neck. "Put these on. Anytime you're working around anything that can chip off and fly at you, you wear 'em. Hear?"

Ashley frowned first at the large clear plastic glasses, then at the man who suddenly looked as if he expected her to object to the decidedly unfashionable accessory.

"Safety's the rule around here, miss. Matt's a stickler for it."

"But these are yours. If I take them, what will you wear?"

The determination in the man's sharp eyes gave way to the slow arch of one bushy graying eyebrow. "There's more around here," he assured her over the conversation of the documentary people setting up shop near a trio of protruding pipes. Their camera already had them in its sights.

"Stay put and I'll get 'em. You're going to need a work apron, too. The pockets are handy for carrying your tools and such." Suddenly aware he was being filmed, looking self-conscious about it, he started off, only to turn right back. "You might as well start measuring off while I'm at it."

He unclipped a silver tape measure from his tool belt. From his faded Hawaiian-print shirt pocket, he pulled a flat yellow pencil. "We'll start with a soleplate along the length of this wall. We butt two-by-fours against each other end to end. Start from the end of this board and measure off every eighteen inches. Use those two-by-fours over there."

Popping his toothpick into his mouth, he headed through a door-size gap in the block wall, his pace unhurried in the slowly rising heat.

"What kind of preparation did you do to work on this?"

The question came from Ron, the documentary director. He stood six feet away, shoulder to ribs with his lanky, ponytailed cameraman. His soundman stood ten feet back, holding the boom over them.

With three cameras rolling—two she couldn't identify because she couldn't read their affiliation printed on the equipment and the one that would be following her all day every day—she replied that she hadn't done anything. Thinking she'd barely understood a word Ed had said, she added that she'd been told by the Shelter office that no preparation was necessary. While they appreciated skilled labor, they could find a job for nearly everyone.

Since her job at the moment was to measure, that was what she prepared to do as voices drifted beyond the opening for a doorway.

Matt was out there. She could only hear bits and pieces of what he said, but the press had him cornered, too. She would bet her box seats at the ballet that he didn't want to deal with the press any more than he wanted to deal with her. With them right there in his face, however, he pretty much had to answer their questions about how he felt about having her on his crew.

She didn't doubt for a moment that his honest response would have been that he didn't think much of her or her presence at all and that he wished he'd left well enough alone when she'd failed to return his call. Being more of a gentleman than her parents would have once thought he could be, he opted for a more politically correct reply. He told them he welcomed her support of the organization, and that he hoped her presence would heighten the public's awareness of the need for adequate housing for the working poor.

She missed whatever other questions the reporters fired at him. When she pulled out the coiled metal tape, the thing immediately snapped back into place. The only measuring device she'd ever used—that didn't have to do with cooking, anyway—was a ruler. Trying to figure out how to make the tape stay out, she also heard Matt mention to the reporters that they were all standing where wet mortar had been spilled.

A gentleman with a gray beard and glasses, Gene, she remembered, walked over and showed her how to lock the tape. After giving him a grateful smile, she measured off her first eighteen inches on the board on the ground, marked it with the pencil and listened to Matt call for someone to run yellow construction tape around the perimeter of the property to keep the spectators off the property. Beneath his surprisingly easygoing request were the murmurs and mutterings of reporters who, apparently, had just taken a look at their shoes.

Within minutes, she was doing what she'd spent much of the past month doing—trying hard to not think about Matt at all. On her knees on the cement, measuring, she was also trying to ignore the perspiration she could feel running between her shoulder blades.

She'd been on the site for all of ten minutes and she already needed a shower. Working inside the open structure had the advantage of blocking her from view of the crowd outside and, for the moment, she was in shade, but the nine-foot-high wall also blocked the breeze, negligible as it was.

Swatting at something that stung her neck, she straightened. She needed Ed. She'd reached the end of the board.

Whatever had bit her the first time either came back for seconds, or it had a friend. Another pinprick stung the back of her arm. Rubbing at it, she turned to see the tall brunette from the Sarasota station marching through the doorway.

"I'll do my intro over there," the woman said to her cameraman, heading to where sunlight could illuminate her, and stepped over the hose to take up her position. Straightening her collar, she turned to face the lens. "We can splice it ahead of the bit with the boss and what I get now."

As the reporter put on her camera face and went into her spiel about being "Paula Littleton, on site in Gray Lake with Ashley Kendrick," another power saw joined the whine of the first. In the din, the rhythmic thud of hammering all but disappeared.

Not caring to be caught doing nothing, Ashley headed for the stack in the middle of the foundation to get another board. The reporter was right behind her.

"Would it be possible to get an interview with you away from the noise?" she asked as Ashley grabbed the end of what Ed had called a two-by-four.

She'd barely lifted it when she felt the weight leave her hands. The redheaded teenager had caught it in the middle and was lifting it for her.

"I'll get it," he insisted, his voice surprisingly deep. "Where do want it?"

"By that one over there," she replied, smiling as she motioned to where she'd left the tape measure. "Thanks so much."

As ruddy as he was, she didn't think it was possible for him to turn any redder. Still, he managed to do just that as he hoisted the long, narrow strip of wood onto his skinny shoulder and headed past the documentary crew.

"How about down by the news van?" the reporter persisted, one finger pressed to her ear. "That saw is interfering with our audio."

"I'm sorry. I can't." Ashley's expression looked sympathetic, but felt more like relief that she could avoid playing twenty questions for now. Every time she opened her mouth in front of a mike, there was danger of saying something that could be misquoted. "The gentleman who's showing me what to do will be right back."

"Do you want some more of these?" the teenager who'd introduced himself only as Kenny called.

"That's okay. I can do it."

"It's no trouble."

"I just want a couple of minutes," the reporter insisted.

"I really can't."

With the cameras following her, she headed back to line up the board Kenny had brought her with the one already there. She was on her knees again, measuring, when her back started to prickle.

It wasn't sweat this time. The sensation had to do with the big man walking toward her. From the way her stomach jumped, she didn't have to look up to know who she would find there.

"Hey, Kenny," Matt called as the rangy teenager started to pick up another board. "I thought you were helping Dale. Let's stick with one job, okay?"

Matt hadn't heard what Ashley had said. But he'd caught her easy smile as she chatted with the reporter and seen how she'd made the kid blush when she turned that smile on him. For someone who looked totally out of her element surrounded by studs and sawdust, she seemed awfully comfortable with the attention.

Stopping to stand over her, he watched her remeasuring the marks she'd already made.

"Twice is enough." She didn't look at all as if she belonged there. Even dressed as casually as she was, an air of refinement surrounded her. Or, maybe, that air was just an unmistakable atmosphere of privilege. "You can go ahead and nail."

Reminding himself that he was going to ignore who she was, afraid the thought was going to become his mantra, he watched her body go still a moment before she glanced up. A pair of safety goggles hung around her neck. Rising, she brushed at the sawdust already caked on her knees.

"I don't know how to use the nail gun."

"Ed didn't show you?"

"He gave me his goggles so he went to get some for himself. And an apron."

Ed, he knew, had just been sidetracked by one of the other volunteers. He could be two minutes or twenty.

Determined to make progress before the real heat of the day set in, he flipped a switch on the compressor. With the drone of its gasoline-powered engine joining the scream of the saw, he picked up the gun and crouched down beside her.

Her scent drifted toward him, warm and taunting.

"You have to be careful with these things," he said, aware of a twinge low in his gut. "It won't fire until it's pressed against something. That pushes back this catch release and triggers the nail," he explained, dutifully ignoring the instinctive reaction. "The problem is that if it's pushed against your leg or you bump someone with it, it'll go off then, too. That's why you're to keep this safety on here and use the pull trigger every time you want to drive a nail. We try to make as few trips to the emergency room as possible around here."

Her glance moved up from the tool he held between them, her eyes barely meeting his. "I'll be careful," she promised.

"I mean it. These things can be dangerous."

"I said, I'll be careful."

She met his eyes then, the blue of hers as clear as a summer sky and filled with restraint. If she could have stepped back from him, she would have, he thought, except she was blocked by boards and a wall.

Beyond that wall, other boards clattered.

"Put on your goggles," he told her, and pulled his own from the tool belt he'd retrieved on his way over.

Bracing himself on one knee beside her, goggles in place, he picked up the gun again to show her how to use it. Wishing he didn't have to breathe, he pressed the barrel to the strip of wood on the foundation.

A quick pop later and Ashley was staring at a nail head.

"Your turn," he said, rising, and handed it to her.

The awkward object felt even heavier than it had looked. Grasping it with both hands, Ashley, still crouched, turned to face the board.

"Brace your weight and get over it this way."

Her heart jerked against her ribs at the feel of his strong hands closing around her upper arms. He turned her sideways. Since the gun was too awkward and heavy for her to hold as easily as he had and with the block wall in the way of her head, it was the only way to get her weight straight down over the gun.

She could have sworn his hands were still on her when she glanced up and saw them on his hips. Unnerved by the sensation, by him, she pulled the trigger.

He caught her before the slight buck could throw her off balance.

"You need to be over it more."

She frowned up at him. "You weren't."

"I don't have to use both hands to hold it, either." His glance raked over her. His tone sounded amazingly even. His eyes looked knowing, and as hard as flint. "I know for a fact that I have more upper-body strength than you do."

Ashley felt herself flush. Caught totally unprepared for his blunt reminder of how well he did know her body, she turned her head away, blinked at the gray wall and hoped fervently that no one had caught that.

"Here." He reached to position her himself.

His arm ran the length of hers, skin to skin, his hard chest to her back. The contact clinched her stomach, nudged hard at memories.

Matt remembered, too. Pressed against the curve of her slender back, her head bent as she looked down, he remembered how he had turned her in his arms and pushed the hair from her neck. How his lips had teased the sensitive flesh behind her ear. How his hands had curved her sides, slipped over her flat belly and skimmed up to cup her high, firm breasts.

He remembered her groaning at that exquisite contact.

He could recall far more than that.

"Get your finger on the trigger," he said, his voice suddenly trip-wire tight. "Thumb through here."

He positioned her hand, profoundly aware of her soft skin, her fragile bones. "Keep your weight over it."

She swallowed. "I am."

She felt as stiff as a plank. Feeling stiff in places himself, Matt muttered, "Squeeze."

A quick pop and the nail was in.

The moment it was, he slid his hand from where it had closed over hers and pulled away from her body as if it had just turned to hot coal.

A flash had them both looking up.

"I couldn't get your faces." A new addition to the media circus lowered his camera. He was either newspaper or freelance. Since there wasn't a microphone in their faces, she strongly suspected the latter. "Could you turn this way a little more and hold that thing between you?"

Matt looked as if the only place he wanted to hold the nail gun was to the stocky guy's dark, curly head. "I don't think so," he snapped, and sent that same steely glare to a television technician raising a light reflector on a tripod. A cable from another piece of photographic equipment ran around the lumber in the middle of the gray cement and through a window opening at the far end of what would eventually be a very modest three-bedroom house.

"Hey, buddy." The tightness in Matt's voice made its way to the muscles of his neck as he motioned for the guy to move. "This isn't a sound stage. That's got to go. There can't be any cords around here that don't belong to a power tool. Those shoes have to go, too."

His irritated glance slid from low pumps on a budding Barbara Walters picking her way toward them to the sandals on the documentary guy with the ponytail.

"This is a construction site," he informed them all. "You want to be here, you wear boots or running shoes. And I don't want any of you inside the structure. We need room to work here. You want to hang around, you do it on the other side of that tape out there."

Ron twisted the bill of his hat around on his head so the word Fox was visible. Lifting his five feet eight to five feet nine, he stepped in front of the man everyone else was backing away from. "We have a contract to follow Miss Kendrick...."

He knew all about that blasted contract. "Except you." He motioned toward his cameraman's sandals. "But he goes until he gets some boots.

"Ed," he said, seeing his lead carpenter approach with a white canvas apron and a pair of old goggles, "make sure these guys stay out of everyone's way. I'm going to call the supplier and make sure that order of two-by-sixes gets delivered this afternoon."

A lot of grumbling joined the shuffle of feet as Ed gave his boss a faintly puzzled look, then ushered the reporters back to where the crowd was fanning themselves beneath umbrellas. Ashley kept her focus on the gun, determined to master it if for no other reason than she didn't want Matt to show her how to use it again. Not that that was likely to happen. Not the way he'd behaved just now.

She felt badly that he'd taken his dislike of her out on the reporters. As she heard Ron hand over his keys to his cameraman and tell the guy to do as the man said, she felt bad simply about being there. She had truly found an upside in the awareness her participation would bring to Shelter. But Matt had made it clear that he had a schedule to maintain, and her presence clearly disrupted the work of the volunteers also donating their time to the project.

One of the burlier volunteers had been relegated the task of keeping reporters and cameras out of the structure and keeping an eye on the documentary crew. From what she could hear on the other side of the wall after Dale cut the saw, Gene and another volunteer had been enlisted to keep an eye on the crowd.

That was at least three people whose productivity would be down.

Then, there was Matt. Dealing with her, he obviously wasn't getting a whole lot accomplished himself. Neither was Kenny, who kept abandoning his job hauling wood for Dale to haul wood for her.

A couple of the reporters hung around for the rest of the day. So did the curly-haired guy with the camera, who totally ignored Matt's directives and camouflaged himself in the foliage, snapping pictures of Ashley through a window opening.

When Matt noticed him, he didn't bother to rout him out. It wasn't like him to take his frustrations out on strangers. Not anymore, anyway. But Ashley had his nerves stretched paper-thin, so he figured he'd let nature take care of the persistent press. The bugs would run the guy off, sooner or later.

He also figured the heat would take care of the other

reporters and the crowd. And it did. By noon, fewer than a dozen people were still hanging around hoping for a glimpse of the woman hidden by the walls. By three, only two die-hards remained. The only problem now was that work had slowed to nearly a crawl.

Kenny and the masons kept rushing to help Ashley whenever she picked up a board or looked at all puzzled by what she was doing.

Even in jeans and a ball cap, wearing a work apron and safety goggles, she still managed to look like a lady—something that seemed to bring out the latent chivalry of every male member of the crew.

She seemed to lap up the constant attention. When she would turn her smile from one man to the next while they held boards in place for her, or they ran off like besotted suitors to get more nails when she ran out, it was almost as if she expected someone to be there for her the instant she needed help.

Even the female volunteers deferred to her, letting her go first at the water cooler, cautiously asking if she would pose for a picture with them or sign something for one of their children. She seemed delighted to meet their requests, even if it did mean taking time from what they were all supposed to be doing.

Since he suspected he wasn't being totally rational where she was concerned, he made himself keep his mouth shut for now.

Every worker was a volunteer. Good-hearted people came and went from these projects as their own valuable time allowed. Many were quite skilled. For all of those reasons, he hated to pull rank on any of them. As annoyed with himself as he was, he didn't even try suggesting that they might want to get on with their own jobs. Add heat and the frustration of dealing with a supplier late with a delivery to the mix, and he figured he'd be light-years ahead of the game by staying out of everyone's way.

He left Ed in charge and climbed into the sweltering cab of his truck to drive to Fort Myers. He couldn't let a late delivery hold them up, so he'd pick up the toe plates and brackets the framers needed himself. By tomorrow, the novelty of having her around should have worn off. He hoped.

"That's it, miss. Let's get things cleaned up and call it a day."

Ed wiped his forearm over his forehead and turned off the air compressor, removing the noise from the stifling air. The whine of the saw had quieted half an hour ago. Five minutes ago, so had the hammering.

Ashley wiped off the layer of dust coating the face of her watch with her finger. It was four-thirty and everyone around her was putting tools either into their own cars or Dale's pickup and heading for home.

Pressing her hand to her back, she straightened from where she'd just nailed the last stud to the soleplate and said she'd see them tomorrow when they said the same to her. Dale, the red bandana on his head soaked with perspiration, shouldered in one last load of lumber and eased it onto the cement with a clatter. The carpenter, who had come from Matt's crew in Maryland, was a big barrel of a man with a tattoo of barbed wire around one biceps and an inordinate amount of chest hair visible around the edges of his tank top.

He was also surprisingly soft-spoken, almost shy, Ashley decided as he dragged the bandana off his head to wipe his forehead and gave her a friendly nod.

He had just replaced the pile she and the other framers had worked from.

Wiping her own face with a damp tissue from her pocket,

she forced back a groan. She was hot and tired and that pile was a decidedly unwelcome reminder that she would have to repeat her entire performance tomorrow, unimpressive as that performance had been. Even with help, she'd only nailed a dozen studs, a few cripple studs and a couple of trimmers into place.

She'd picked up the terminology in no time. Becoming proficient with the physical aspects of the job was going to take her a tad longer.

Mercifully, Matt hadn't been there to witness her lack of progress.

Ed tipped the compressor onto its wheels and rolled it toward the door. "Bring the hose and the gun, will you? You can ride to the motel with Dale and me.

"There's a barbecue place not far from the motel," he continued, frowning at the documentary crew tagging behind them. He still seemed self-conscious having them there. Every time he'd look up to see the camera aimed at him, he'd start scratching at his chin or his head and turn away. He scratched at his chin now. "We're going there after we clean up. You're welcome to join us if you'd like."

She was starving, and just the mention of food threatened a decidedly unladylike grumble from her stomach. But, at that moment, with the cameras still behind her, knowing they'd be everywhere she went, privacy felt far more important. She was exhausted from having to watch every word she said, every move she made. And it was only her first day.

"Would you mind if I take a rain check on dinner?" Settling the hose on her shoulder, she coiled it as she would a horse's lead rope. "I'm not all that hungry right now," she said, lying through her teeth, "and I'd like to just turn in early."

"Suit yourself," he muttered, frowning at the lack of

meat on her arms. "Want me to bring you back something in case you get hungry later?"

"Would you?" she asked, hoping she didn't sound as eager to jump on the offer as she felt. "If it wouldn't be too much trouble, I mean."

"Less trouble than having you pass out from hunger on the job. What do you want. They got pretty much anything that can be thrown on a grill. Can't say it's fancy, but it tastes pretty decent."

"Anything on the menu will be fine."

"Sure you don't want to change your mind and come with us?"

She told him she was sure. And thanked him again, even though going with them would fill the void in her stomach that much sooner.

Ron, his hat backward again, hustled up beside her. "You're not going anywhere but to the motel?"

His crew of two, one sporting a pair of stiff new boots, moved in. The one with the camera swung around in front of her, walking backward as easily as most people could sit or stand.

"I'm in for the night," she told him.

"Well, let me know if you do leave, will you? We're supposed to capture your whole experience here. I'm at your motel."

He told her his room number, then motioned to his men. "Okay, guys. That's a wrap. What time are you leaving in the morning, Miss Kendrick?"

She looked to Ed.

"Matt likes to be on the site by five-thirty," Ed mumbled. "Don't lose any daylight that way. We'll probably leave about five-fifteen."

The thought of having to be up at the crack of dawn nearly made Ashley groan. Not wanting to be impolite, what she did instead was draw a deep breath, smile at Ron, who groaned for them both, then headed for Dale's truck while the documentary crew headed for their van.

Twenty minutes later, she had checked herself in to the Cypress Motor Inn with a minimum of fuss. Wanda, the clerk working the desk, couldn't have cared less what her last name was. But then the muumuu-wearing woman with the cigarette-husky voice and a pink foam curler anchoring a curl above each temple gave the impression that she wasn't impressed by much of anything.

"No room service here," she informed Ashley after she'd asked. "Gianetti's Pizza delivers. Stay away from the clam special, though. I wasn't right for a week last time I tried it."

"Do you have a laundry service?"

"Laundromat's on Third Street. There's a cleaners on Crane."

Ashley bit back a sigh. Reaching for the key the woman pushed at her, she smiled, said, "Thank you," and dragged her bag, which the woman had charged her five dollars to stow, down the cracked concrete breezeway to room 108.

The relief she felt to be inside, alone, immediately met with hesitation. Her accommodations for the next three weeks—or however long she lasted—were the polar extreme of what she was accustomed to. Her own two-bedroom condo was actually quite modest in size. Miniscule compared to the mansion where she'd grown up, the family home she still loved. But every inch of her own private space was decorated in soothing creams and taupes, rich fabrics, vibrant paintings and deep, inviting furnishings. It was a place filled with books, family photos and music. She loved listening to music—classical, alternative, bluesy jazz. She had been told before that a person could walk into her condo and immediately feel comfortable, which was exactly how she wanted her friends to feel in her home and at her table. Her one true indulgence was in her kitchen. She loved to cook and owned nearly every gourmet gadget and style of sauté pans on the market. She'd even brought her favorite with her.

She just wasn't sure she wanted to subject it to the chipped electric two-burner stove she could see on the far side of the room.

She hadn't expected anything resembling her home. For $59.95, she had also known she wasn't getting anything even remotely similar to the hotel suites to which she was accustomed. The sort with six-hundred count Egyptian cotton sheets on the bed, Godiva chocolates on the pillow and French milled soap in the bathrooms. But as she leaned against the closed door and let go of her bag, she couldn't honestly say, either, that she'd been prepared for something that looked as if it had been due for renovation in 1960.

The carpet was pea green. The double bed with its nearly flat pillows and blond Formica nightstands, sported an aqua spread with huge green philodendron leaves. Matching prints of pink whooping cranes framed in faux bamboo hung above it. So did a moth with gray wings.

Leaving her bag by the door as if subconsciously preparing for a quick escape, she ventured past a television bolted to a long low dresser, avoided looking in the mirror next to it, gave the kitchenette with its dubious-looking stove and narrow refrigerator a skeptical glance and guardedly decided that nothing about the place mattered as long as it had a shower.

Next to privacy and food, a shower was the thing she craved most.

Within minutes, the moth was part of the sewer system and she was in the tiny bathroom with its yellowed mirror and shower that ran like a kinked garden hose. In the other room the air conditioner blasted away, trying to move the heavy sticky air.

She had no idea how long she stood under the trickle that teased with occasional surges of something that actually resembled water flow. She just knew that when she'd left Virginia that morning, she hadn't counted on the draining humidity, how truly physical the work would be, or the mosquitoes that had sent out a couple of stray scouts for her earlier in the day and returned with their troops for the actual attack closer to evening.

Scratching at the back of her leg twenty minutes later, she resolved that she would just have to handle the bugs, along with whatever else nature and her stint on the project threw at her. The red marks where the goggles had dug had faded from her cheeks, but she had splinters in her fingers despite her gloves and, in the sticky air, she still felt wet even though she'd dried off twice with the tissue-thin towels. Since she'd committed to the project, she would simply look at this entire experience as her own version of *Survivor*. Bugs simply seemed to be part of the endurance test. As long as she didn't have to eat them, she would be fine.

She just wished she could muster a little of that bravado toward Matt.

The thought had her empty stomach churning. In the overall scheme of things, she really knew so little about him. Before the one night they'd shared, she'd thought of him as mysterious, rebellious, as a man who played by his own rules and who pretty much ignored everyone else's. Between the arrogant stunt he'd pulled at the auction and his clear dismissal of her the day he'd brought her the check, it also seemed pretty apparent that he didn't like not getting what he wanted when she hadn't called him back. What threw her completely, though, was how generously he donated his time and his men to Shelter. It took no effort to give money. Time was different. Ed had mentioned that Matt had worked these projects himself for as long as he'd known him. And that had been nearly ten years.

She left her hair wet because it was cooler that way and pulled a short silk robe on over fresh underwear. With her feet in a pair of beaded flip-flops, she carried her dirty work clothes to the closet of the white block-walled room and pushed back the folding door.

Matt was the other reason she hadn't gone to dinner with Ed and Dale tonight, she admitted, taking the white plastic bag from the shelf holding an extra pillow. Ed hadn't said a thing about him joining them, but the possibility of Matt showing up where his men ate wasn't exactly remote.

Stuffing her clothes inside the white plastic laundry bag, she dropped it in the back of the closet and forced a mental change of subject. Thinking about Matt upset her stomach. What she needed to think about was how she was going to keep it filled, which meant figuring out how to get groceries to stock the little refrigerator.

She was thinking about calling Wanda when a knock had her turning toward her door.

Anticipation of food had her spinning toward it. She would have thought for certain that it would have taken Ed longer to clean up and eat. But as she edged back a corner of the aqua drape to make sure it wasn't some overzealous reporter rather than the man she could cheerfully hug for being so thoughtful, her anticipation evaporated like steam.

Matt stood outside her door. She could only see his profile, but his jaw was locked tight enough to shatter his back teeth.

Chapter Five

Ashley unlocked the chain and cautiously opened the door. Matt held a white paper bag in each hand.

"I know you're used to servants and staff," he said before she could even say hello, "and I expected the day to be a waste as far as work went, but my crew doesn't need to wait on you after work, too. From now on, I'd appreciate it if you'd get your own dinner just like everyone else."

He held the smaller of the two bags toward her. The shadow of sandy evening stubble shading his jaws made him look rugged. The way his gray eyes were narrowed simply made him look annoyed.

Ashley couldn't remember having done a consciously rude thing in her life. But with Matt making it sound as if she were some sort of prima donna who had actually expected all the unsolicited assistance she'd received, she was sorely tempted to go for a personal first and close the door on his handsome face.

Instead, deliberately refusing to let him make her react so childishly, she said, "Come in," and stepped back so he could. If there was a camera out there somewhere, she'd really rather not risk it getting a shot of her having a disagreement in the doorway in her robe with wet hair and no makeup.

"Just for the record, I didn't ask anyone to do anything."

Hoping she didn't sound as defensive as she felt, she took the sack and quickly closed the door behind him. Public image wasn't on her mind nearly as much as the feeling she always had around a camera. The feeling of being exposed—which is exactly how she felt, anyway, when she looked over to see Matt's glance move over her bare legs.

"Everyone was just being helpful," she explained. "And Ed offered to pick up something for me for dinner. I accepted. That's all."

A muscle in Matt's jaw jerked. "You could have gone with him and Dale and saved him the trouble. He said he invited you."

"I could have," she agreed easily enough, "but I chose not to."

She had no idea how he'd intended to respond to that. Whatever he would have said was bitten back when his glance settled on the navy silk crossed between her breasts. A slice of pale blue lace bra peeked from one side.

Giving the thin fabric a self-conscious tug, she set the sack on the long dresser supporting the television. Uneasy with the tension that had come in with him, totally unfamiliar with the edginess it caused, she blew a calming breath and forced a guarded smile.

"I certainly didn't mean for you to get stuck bringing that." Unconsciously scratching the side of her neck, she nodded toward her dinner. "But thank you for it. I was starting to get a little hungry."

It appeared that he didn't quite know what to do with her attempt to play nice. He was displeased with her and her presence and he seemed to want to stay that way. But faced with her attempt to be reasonable, or maybe just too tired to waste energy arguing, he backed down enough for his jaw to unlock.

"I ran into Ed and Dale at The Pit," he finally said, "Ed ordered it while I was waiting for mine and asked me to take it."

"I honestly didn't mean to impose on anyone's time." Certainly not yours, she thought, wishing rather desperately that they could somehow go back to the moments before he had answered her brother's door.

It took her aback to know that he so obviously considered her spoiled and self-centered. And she hated not knowing what he might say in irritation with others around. She just didn't know how to ask a man she had literally run from to please not let on that they had been intimate because her one-night stand with him wasn't the sort of thing she wanted the world, or her parents, to read about. She didn't know, either, how to ask if he really had called her the next day because he'd truly been concerned about whether or not she'd made it home all right.

He was probably right about the self-centered part. She'd been so wrapped up in her embarrassment over her encounter with him that his concern hadn't even registered until long after he'd walked out her office door.

"I'll be happy to get my own food and cook it myself as soon as I can figure out how to get groceries delivered. I just got here," she reminded him, an itch high between her shoulder blades demanding attention, "so I haven't had a chance to accomplish much. I haven't had time to unpack, much less go through the Yellow Pages."

"The Yellow Pages?"

"To find a grocer who delivers. And a cleaners," she reminded herself, thinking she needed one that picked up, as well. "I'll be organized by tomorrow night," she promised, "so you don't need to worry about me taking up anyone else's time, either. The only thing I'll need from anyone is a ride to and from the site. If you'd prefer, I'll arrange for a rental car and drive myself. I was told that wouldn't be necessary, but if it will help, I'll be glad to do it."

"You won't need a car."

"Then, I'll need the ride," she concluded. "Everything else, I'll handle."

She was unwilling to give him anything else about her to criticize. She was perfectly capable of making her own arrangements for whatever she needed. She would also obey his rules on the project and do her job to the best of her ability. If everyone would just let her.

She might have told him that, too, had he not been frowning at her.

"What?" she asked, when *what now?* was more what she was thinking.

She dropped her hand, only to have two little bumps on her arm take their turn.

Matt watched her hand snake around to her back again. The motion pulled at the silk of her short robe, tugging it against the high firm shape of her breasts, accentuating the slenderness of her hips, her waist.

The robe was actually quite modest. Except for the flesh at her throat it covered her from elbow to knee. It was being intimately familiar with what was under the expensive fabric that had him tightening his hand on his sack.

"Did you bring anything for those bites?"

"I wish I had. It wasn't on the list, and I didn't think to add it."

Her hair looked darker wet, her eyes softer, her features

even more delicate. Without makeup, she didn't look anywhere near as sophisticated as she usually did. She looked
almost...sweet.

Matt reached for the door. He could handle her coolness.
He had defenses for that. It was that vulnerable, open look
he found so dangerous. It was what had gotten him into
trouble with her in the first place.

A half dozen angry red spots dotted the smooth skin of
her legs and arms. Not caring to think about how many more
there were, or where, he pulled back on the latch. "I'll be
right back," he muttered, resigned, and left her working on
a bite above her ankle.

He headed for his room, his boots heavy on the cement
walkway, oblivious to the leggy pink plastic birds lining a
planter of low palms.

He wondered if she had even considered going to the
grocery store herself rather than having someone bring groceries to her. Sincerely doubting it, he opened the door two
down from hers and dropped his dinner next to the laptop
and files covering the table by the window. Except for the
kitchenette, his room looked just like Ashley's, right down
to the crane prints above the bed. Hers smelled better,
though. Like soap and the shampoo he had mistaken for
perfume.

Knowing he would smell a whole lot better himself after
ten minutes under the shower, he grabbed a small pink bottle
from his shaving kit and cranked the air conditioner on to
High on his way back to the door.

He'd be eating alone in his room tonight, the same as he
had the last two nights he'd been in Gray Lake. As much
as he would have liked to spend an hour or two with a cold
beer and his men, he simply couldn't afford the time. Be-
sides the multimillion dollar project for Kendrick Investments in Newport, he was breaking ground for a sports

arena in Jacksonville. Normally, he enjoyed the week or two a year he could put into a Shelter house. The time he spent working on their projects was hands-on, a chance to do something physical, to stay in touch with the bones of his work and, in a way, to pay back the chance he'd once been given himself.

This year, though, the project seemed only like another obligation. The timing was lousy. The weather reports were becoming more ominous. And the woman who'd gotten under his skin years ago and sat there festering would be sleeping two doors down from him for however long she lasted.

The thought that she might fold after a few days cheered him considerably. At least it did until he headed back to her room and found himself inside alone with her once more.

If he were a nice guy, he supposed he would offer to treat the bites on her back that she couldn't easily reach, but he wasn't feeling particularly nice at the moment. He wasn't feeling particularly masochistic, either. Just getting as close to her as he had that morning had left his body feeling as taut as finely tuned piano wire. If he had his hands on her again, he'd never get any sleep at all.

"Keep it," he said, handing over the small bottle of calamine lotion. "I need to buy a bigger bottle for the first-aid kit, anyway."

"You don't need it yourself?"

"I haven't so far." Ignoring the quick concern in her eyes, refusing to be seduced by it, he stepped back. "Ed said he'd told you what time we need to be at the site. There's a doughnut shop next door if you want breakfast. Just be at my truck at a quarter after five."

Ashley made it to his truck with a minute to spare, no mean feat considering how she'd felt when she'd wakened. She'd slept the sleep of the dead, something that had truly surprised her considering the sag of the mattress, the underlying rattle in the air conditioner and the dampness in the air that seemed to permeate everything, including the sheets.

She hadn't realized the toll the day before had taken on her. At least she hadn't until her travel alarm had gone off. One swat at the offending little instrument and she'd come awake with a gasp and a groan. Her arm felt as if she'd been lifting hundred-pound weights.

When she'd propped herself up on her other elbow, she'd discovered that that side ached, too. So did her thighs, though it took her until she'd put on a coat of mascara, lip gloss with sunblock, moisturizer with sunblock and sunblocked her arms and the tips of her ears, to figure out that the soreness there was from all the squatting, rising and squatting she'd done nailing studs to soleplates.

The achy arms took no time to figure out at all. Every motion as she pulled on an older, thinner pair of jeans that looked worn but had cost a fortune, and the thinnest T-shirt she'd brought with her made her curse the eight-pound nail gun that had strained muscles she hadn't even known were there.

Her underarms ached. She'd also discovered a blister on her trigger finger last night where her glove had rubbed. But she kept all her little aches and pains to herself when she heard Ed crunch his way across the shells in the parking lot and she looked up to see Matt approaching with him.

Matt's focus seemed to be on the clouds that had moved in overnight. That blanket of gray added yet another layer of humidity to air already heavy with it.

The thermometer she'd passed on her way by the office read seventy-three degrees. With the damp air, it already felt more like eighty. Yet, warm or not, she would have given up her shiny new BMW for a cup of the coffee the men were carrying. Had she not been loathe to keep them waiting, she would have headed for the doughnut shop herself. Had she not been moving so slowly when she'd first awakened, she could have been there and back by now.

"Mornin'," Ed called, brushing bits of powdered sugar from his old work shirt.

"Good morning," she called back as the door of the van beside her rolled open.

Ron-the-director poked out his head. "Hey, Miss Kendrick. We thought you'd be heading over there with them." An obscenely cheerful smile stretched his boyish features. "Are you going over now?"

A pink doughnut box sat beside him on the seat. In the front seats, his crew sipped coffee. It seemed that they had been some of the shop's first customers.

"We're going to the site."

"Got it." Giving her a thumbs-up, he rolled the door closed again. They had obviously been lying in wait, not wanting to miss a moment of her little adventure.

Before she could do more than wonder if there were any other reporters she should be aware of, Matt's glance met hers. For a moment, she thought he might say good morning, or ask if her bites were better.

"Glad you're on time," was apparently his idea of a cordial greeting.

"I told you I would be."

His response was to dig his keys from the pocket of jeans even more faded than those he'd worn yesterday. That pale denim molded his powerful thighs. A white Shelter Project T-shirt clung to his broad shoulders, the fabric stretched taut and looking far more worn than those she'd seen on the other volunteers.

She chose to focus on Ed. "Is Dale not coming?"

"He's already gone. He went into Fort Myers to pick up some drill bits."

Matt lifted his cup toward the truck. "Let's get going, okay?"

Ignoring the hint of impatience, or maybe just not hearing it, Ed motioned her ahead of him and reached to open the door.

"You think anything's going to come of this?" he called to Matt. He looked toward the sky, much as his boss had done only moments ago. "Not sure I like the sounds of what that guy in there was saying about how they're due for a big one here."

"Due for a big what?" Ashley asked, as conscious of Matt as she was of the smell of his coffee when she slid across the bench seat.

Ed pulled a wrapped toothpick from his shirt pocket and poked it through the white paper. "We got us a couple of tropical storms building out at sea." He squeezed her more toward the middle. "It's too soon to know if they're going to turn into anything. This here's hurricane season, so it could go either way."

"Hold this." Matt held out his cup. Arching an eyebrow at her when she hesitated, he nudged his coffee closer. "I can't hold it and shift."

She was sorely tempted to remind him that he could say "please." With Ed right there, it seemed best just to let it go.

The scent of his coffee filled her lungs as she took it. Thinking it cruel and unusual punishment to have to sit there and hold his cup when she wanted a cup of her own so badly, she looked back to Ed's craggy, but friendlier face. "How soon will we know if we need to worry?"

"Not for a day or two. Might not need to worry at all. These things can peter out to nothing in a matter of hours or keep building until they turn into a problem. We'll just keep an ear on the radio.''

Rather like Matt had been doing yesterday, she thought. Her glance fell once more to the cup.

From the corner of his eye, Matt caught what he could swear was longing in Ashley's expression. She wanted coffee. Craved it, he was guessing from the way she swallowed when she looked up. Yet she said nothing about stopping to get herself some. Not even when they approached, then drove past, the doughnut shop.

A tiny sliver of guilt poked his conscience. It was possible, he supposed, that her silence had something to do with his comment last night about imposing on people's time. He knew she had no food in her room and while her room had probably come with a coffeepot because she had an equipped kitchen, the Cypress Motor Inn was so cut-rate that its patrons were lucky to have soap to wash with, much less complimentary coffee to brew.

Not sure if she was being stubborn or considerate, deciding he didn't want to bother figuring it out, he caved in and dipped his head toward what she held.

''Go ahead.''

Her glance darted to his.

''Go ahead,'' he repeated. ''Help yourself.''

For a split second he thought she was going to say *Really?* It was that kind of gratitude in her eyes. But all she did was smile, murmur, ''Thank you,'' and close her eyes to inhale the aroma of freshly ground French roast.

As she did, his glance skimmed from the ponytail she'd pulled through the back of her white ball cap to the white pearl studs in her ears. Sunglasses of the designer variety dangled from the V of her white cotton shirt. A tiny Ralph Lauren emblem embellished one short sleeve.

With her fingernails still perfect, thanks to the gloves lying in her lap, the subtle sway of her shining hair and the luxurious sweep of her dark lashes, she practically screamed high maintenance.

He couldn't imagine any other woman who would wear pearls to a construction site. Nor could he imagine any other woman who had been raised as she had who wouldn't have called it quits after yesterday. She had been born into the lap of luxury. She'd grown up on an estate with its own private lake, tennis courts, stables and riding paths. Maids made beds, answered doors and kept chandeliers gleaming. Her family had a cook and a chauffeur, groundskeepers and a stable master.

He hadn't been inside the condo he knew she now lived in; the one he'd driven by a few weeks ago out of what he'd assured himself was nothing but idle curiosity. But the address was one of the most exclusive in Richmond. Knowing how well her brother lived from the proceeds of his trust fund and his salary and perks from the Kendrick companies, he felt certain that Ashley could have pretty much anything money could buy.

That was why he wouldn't have been surprised at all had she found fault with the decidedly low-rent accommodations. At the very least, he'd expected her to balk at the lack of room service and having to handle her own care and feeding. Last night, he'd expected to hear complaints about the dirt, the heat, the inevitable splinters, blisters and the ever-present bugs—some of which didn't bite, but were as long as his thumb and ranked about a nine on nature's ugly scale.

She hadn't said a word about any of it. She'd looked a little uneasy about a lot of things, but she hadn't voiced a single word of complaint. Not to him. And not to Ed. He knew. He'd asked his lead carpenter last night just how much of a problem she was and Ed had said that, except for the people following her around, she wasn't a problem at all. Compared to their regular volunteers, she actually caught on pretty quick.

She may have won Ed over, Matt thought, but she was definitely moving more stiffly than she had yesterday. He noticed that within a minute of arriving at the site. But the instant she noticed him watching her, she straightened her shoulders and, smiling at the other volunteers and the reporters who'd been waiting like a pack of hungry wolves, picked up where she'd left off last evening with the framing.

The moment she did, Kenny, wearing a bandana around his head the way Dale did, started bringing her the boards she should have been carrying herself.

Matt decided it was less annoying to let the boy work where he wanted and put another volunteer to work helping Dale. He had fifteen workers today, the full contingent that had signed up for the job. Still, with the heat, progress proceeded at the pace of a geriatric slug.

By midmorning break, the higher humidity had gotten to one of the older women and she'd decided to go home. Five of the other volunteers had only signed on for half days, so they headed off to their other obligations while everyone else cooled off in the air-conditioned luxury of The Hamburger Shack for lunch.

When the remaining crew returned to work, the pace remained exasperatingly unhurried. But Matt knew that hustling in the heat would only bring on dehydration headaches or heatstroke, so a nice easy pace, along with frequent shade-and-water breaks were what made it possible for work to continue.

He also knew that the physical discomfort of the heat contributed to bad moods and tempers. Specifically his own when he climbed down from a ladder where he'd been driving bolts through top plates and saw that Pete, one of his framers, and Gene, his veteran volunteer, had started catering to Ashley, too.

He swore that every time he turned around yet another worker was at her side. All the woman had to do was look puzzled and three guys would drop their hammers to go see if they could help out.

With the saw buzzing in the background, he wiped the sweat from his face with the tail of his T-shirt and headed for where Ed had her framing an interior wall that would help support the roof. He couldn't do a thing about the people who had gone. There was nothing he could do about the heat. But he could make it clear to Ashley that she needed to discourage all the ''help'' she was getting. At the rate they were going, it would be Christmas before the roof went on.

With the threat of a storm looming over his deadline, he needed this house up in two days.

''Hey, Gene. Kenny. Pete,'' he said, hands on his hips and his smile as friendly as he could make it. ''We have two bearing walls that need to go up. How about you three working on that one over there and let Ed finish up here with Ashley?''

''I don't mind helping here,'' Kenny announced. His deep voice cracked, sending a rush of red over his cheeks. ''You don't mind me helping, do you, Ashley?''

Lowering the safety goggles to dangle around her neck, Ashley daintily wiped the perspiration from beneath her eyes with her index finger. ''Of course I don't.''

The retired engineer with the neat gray beard and glasses held a level up to the stud he'd just nailed in. ''I've been telling Miss Kendrick about all the projects I've been on. This is my sixth, you know.''

''I know, Gene.'' Patience fairly dripped from his tone. ''That's why I could really use you to oversee building that

wall. I'm a little short of skilled help today, so I need someone who knows what he's doing to take over down there.''

Gene's chest didn't puff, but he did stand a little
straighter. ''Be glad to,'' he replied, adjusting the brim of
his tan bush hat. Or, maybe, he was tipping it. ''Enjoyed
the visit, Miss Kendrick.''

''Come on, Kenny,'' he said and grabbed the blushing
boy by his shirtsleeve.

Kenny didn't protest. But Matt didn't doubt that the
young man who was putting in his community-service hours
for one too many speeding tickets wanted to as he was
hauled past Ed by the lumber pile and handed a nail gun of
his own.

With her gun dangling from one hand, Ashley gingerly
rubbed her biceps and watched them go.

The thin white shirt she wore sported a V of sweat between her narrow shoulder blades. The top of her white cap
had a smudge of dirt where she'd apparently scratched at
an itch under it.

''This isn't working.''

Her ponytail swayed as she turned to look up at him. A
fine sheen of perspiration glowed at the base of her throat.
''What isn't?''

The documentary crew's sound boom had swung to follow Gene and Kenny. Lowering his voice anyway, Matt
looked into her all-too-innocent eyes and tried not to clench
his teeth. ''I need you to do your job and let everyone else
do theirs. I told you before, everyone has to pull his own
weight around here. If you can't, you have to go.''

He didn't know how she did it, but in one slow blink of
her feathery lashes, the expression in her eyes went from
incomprehension to ice. The rest of her features remained
remarkably even. ''I'm not going anywhere, Matt. When I

make a commitment, I stick to it. Will you excuse me, please? I need that level.''

She bent, reaching past him to pick up the yard-long device with the bubbles that could indicate perfect horizontal or vertical.

He stayed right with her, his voice as low as he could make it without dropping to a hard whisper. ''You're going to have to go if this keeps up,'' he insisted. ''Do you know how many people it usually takes to frame a wall?''

''I have no idea.''

''Two,'' he said flatly. ''Do you know how many you've had here?''

''No,'' she replied, the patience dripping from her tone making it sound as if the heat might be getting to her as well. ''I'll bet you're going tell me, though, aren't you?''

Damn right he was. ''Over the course of the day, six.''

Beneath the bill of her cap, her perfectly shaped eyebrow arched. ''Does that include Ed?''

''He's supposed to be working with you.''

''But he's not,'' she pointed out ever so reasonably.

''That's because there isn't room for anyone else over here!''

''In that case,'' she concluded, her voice now even lower than his had been, ''I guess this is something we're both simply going to have to deal with. And by the way, as for doing my job, I would love to do it if everyone would just let me. I don't need all the help I'm getting, but I don't want anyone to think I don't appreciate their offers. Everyone is being very kind, and I don't want to be rude.''

An arm thrust itself toward them. Staring down at a microphone in a very feminine hand, Matt bit back a curse and glanced at the tall brunette in a blouse, skirt—and tennis shoes.

"Is there a problem here?" the woman asked, her voice dripping with anticipation.

Ashley's reply was immediate. "Not at all." The coolness vanished, unmasking what looked like genuine consternation. "I was just telling Mr. Callaway that I don't want to be rude, but I really don't understand his concept of crew distribution. He was about to explain it again."

Looking as if she might be doing a little mental scrambling, consternation eased to a smile. "I had no idea what all went into the construction of a house," she said to the woman who'd spent a fair amount of time watching from her air-conditioned car. "Did you?"

The reporter blinked like an owl. "Ah, no," she replied, clearly more accustomed to asking questions than answering them.

"So," the woman continued, turning to Matt. "How would you explain something like that to someone with no construction experience?"

It was as clear as the camera lens over his shoulder that Matt had no interest whatsoever in enlightening this meddlesome female about the finer points of personnel management. It also seemed to Ashley that he wasn't terribly pleased with her implication that perhaps the problem wasn't solely hers and that he needed to manage his crew more efficiently.

Needing to remove that telltale frown before he said something she might come to regret, she surreptitiously nudged his foot, silently begging him to go along with what she had said.

All that did was deepen the scowl.

"I was about to tell Miss Kendrick that I don't have time to explain it to her…again," Matt emphasized, going along with her simply because it was the easiest way to escape the microphone. "We all need to get back to work."

Fighting the urge to push the camera out of the way, he took a step back. The press had become as pesky as the bugs. ''There's a storm brewing off the coast,'' he continued. ''If it decides to land anywhere around here, I'd rather have all this lumber nailed into place than sitting here for the wind to scatter halfway to the highway.''

News of a potential storm appeared to be news to the reporter. At least as far as it affected her present story. Latching on to the new slant, she trotted off after Matt, asking how a storm would affect the project here and what they would do if it did hit.

Ashley had no idea what Matt said that had the woman frowning at him before she headed back to her nice, probably downright chilly, air-conditioned car. As she turned back with a sigh for all the work left to do, she didn't care. She wasn't a carpenter. She hated what she was doing. Hated the heat. Hated Matt for getting her into this. And hated herself for not having handled the entire situation with him differently.

She shared as much blame for their current situation as he did. If she hadn't simply disappeared that morning, if she had just taken some time to consider what it was about him that had made her drop her guard so completely, they could probably have avoided all of this.

Sex had proved itself a lousy way to start a relationship.

Feeling every bit as edgy as Matt had looked, she knew for certain that she couldn't handle another day like today. The heat was hideous, but if she paced herself and stayed hydrated she could manage it. Between the aches she could still feel and the queasiness she battled most of the morning since she'd had only coffee for breakfast, she'd been tempted to leave more than once. Lunch had taken care of the slight nausea and as long as she didn't have only coffee for breakfast from now on, she felt certain she would be okay on that front, too.

What she wouldn't suffer—what she refused to suffer—was another day of working with Matt acting like a bear with a thorn in its paw.

They needed to talk.

Alone.

And they needed to do it tonight.

Ashley waited until the digital numbers on her travel alarm hit seven-thirty before she left her room. It took her that long to shower, put away the two sacks of groceries she had ordered last evening from the local Piggly Wiggly and bribed the assistant manager to deliver at 6:00 p.m., eat and figure out exactly what she was going to say to Matt.

He was perfectly capable of listening to reason. She knew he was because, while he had little patience for most of the press, he seemed infinitely understanding with other members of the crew. With them he was reasonable, logical and fair. Beyond that, he had once listened to her. Really listened.

The fact that he had, undoubtedly played a huge part in why she'd so easily dropped her guard with him. That night at her brother's, Matt had truly heard what she'd said about wanting to break free. Even if only for a while. Had she told any of her friends or her family that she wished she had the nerve to do something outrageous, they would have laughed the idea off as a joke, or whisked her off for an emergency spa session to relax her obviously stressed mind. But Matt hadn't just listened. He'd encouraged.

Granted, he'd ultimately encouraged her straight into his arms, but it wasn't as if she hadn't wanted to be there.

The blunt honesty in that admission made her brace herself as she picked up the key to her room. The sooner she got this over with, the better off she would be.

It was dark as she moved past the bugs clustered around the glowing yellow door lamps. The mosquitoes were worse in the evening. So were the gnats. Robbed of the opportunity to take her time, she sprinted from her room to Matt's and quickly knocked on his door.

Light leaked around the aqua drapes, but she couldn't see inside. She knocked again, wondering if he'd gone out, and was about to leave when the door opened.

He wasn't wearing a shirt.

Her glance met the snap on his jeans and the washboard ripples of his stomach.

"Do you have a minute?" she asked, the nerves in her own belly tightening as her eyes jerked up.

Not looking at all surprised that she was there, or maybe just resigned to the fact that she was, he stepped back so she could let herself in.

Without a word, he headed across the room. His bare feet made soft thuds on the green carpet as she stepped inside and closed the door. Blueprints and files nearly obliterated the bedspread. The glowing screen of his laptop on the table beside her held a complicated graph.

It seemed he'd done as she had and eaten in his room again tonight. An empty red-and-white box with the smiling face of a white-bearded gentleman occupied the only part of the table that wasn't also covered with work.

"I'm not going to keep you," she began, watching him pull a T-shirt from a black-leather duffle. The beautifully defined muscles of his back and arms shifted with the movements, his tanned skin golden in the light of the lamps he'd turned as bright as they would go.

Pulling the clean shirt over his head, he turned and yanked it over the equally hard muscles of his chest.

"I won't keep you long," she murmured, rather grateful for what he'd just done. He stood on the other side of the room, twenty feet of tension separating them, yet her body had reacted immediately to the sight of his. The flutter low in her stomach felt exactly the same as it had when his chest had curved to her back yesterday. Exactly the same as it had the first time he'd kissed her.

"I just want to keep what happened today from happening again," she said, disconcerted by the insistent tug of her body toward his. "With the reporter," she clarified. "They thrive on controversy. So please don't give them any more of a story than they already have by getting upset with me in public.

"I know the press is causing problems with your schedule," she hurriedly continued, fighting the urge to back up as he approached. "But the best way to get rid of them is not to give them anything to write about. They're bound to get bored with the routine sooner or later."

His hair looked as if it had been combed with his fingers. Plowing them through it again, looking a tad exasperated as he did it, he stopped an arm's length away.

"You think so?"

"I can't imagine that they won't."

"They're not there to watch the routine, Ashley. They want to watch you."

"I can't imagine that they won't get tired of that, too."

"I wouldn't count on it," he muttered. "There doesn't seem to be any logic to what some people regard as entertainment."

At least they agreed there. "Look," she murmured, thinking this would be so much easier if he would stop scowling at her. "I know you don't want me here. I don't want be here, either. And I wouldn't be if you hadn't done what you did at the auction," she reminded, her tone as reasonable as she could make it. "But arguing isn't going to change any of that. Especially if we do it in front of a camera."

The air conditioner gave a wheeze and a rather ominous click. In no mood for the thing to go out again, Matt sent a warning glare in its direction. Dealing with Ashley was dead last on the list of things he wanted to do tonight. He had the daily-activity report on the Shelter job to complete, a dozen e-mails from his site managers to answer and a subcontractor with a shipment of conduit hung up in a shipyard that was holding up electrical installation on the Newport job.

He also had no desire whatsoever to have her stand there looking as if she'd just walked in from a day under a beach cabana in her little coral shift and dainty sandals and tell him he couldn't feel frustrated with her if he wanted to.

"I'm quite aware that I'm responsible for you being here," he informed her tightly. "It's a fact I've reminded myself of on more than one occasion, and something I sincerely regret."

She blinked as if she'd been punched.

True to her refined roots, it was only a moment before her cool control kicked in. Her tone even, she tipped her chin. "Then why did you do it?"

Hands on his hips, jaw working, he glanced away.

"No, Matt," she insisted. "You just said you regret it, and I'm having to live with your aversion to me, so let's get it out and done with. Why did you do what you did at the auction?"

He wasn't about to tell her that he'd just wanted her to acknowledge him. No way on God's green earth would she ever know that she'd once made him feel as if he wasn't good enough, refined enough, monied enough for her to associate with the likes of him.

Lifting his head, defense fairly leaking from his pores, "How about, I was bored."

"Bored?" The delicate arches of her eyebrows shot up. "You were…bored?"

"It happens."

"Bored," she repeated, as if she couldn't believe something so common could possibly be the cause of her present discomforts. "As in 'there wasn't anything all that interesting going on so you thought you'd break the monotony'?" She shook her head, swiping her hair back when it brushed her face. "Haven't you outgrown that yet?"

His brow slammed low. "Outgrown what?"

"Your need to cause trouble like this."

"What could you possibly know of my needs? Until we wound up in bed a month ago, we'd never had a single conversation that got past 'hello.' Every time you'd see me coming, you'd turn the other way or walk by so fast I damn near got windburn."

Ashley had held her ground until he mentioned bed.

Stepping back, his big body far too close, she glanced to his chest. "There was a reason for that."

"I'm surprised you'll admit it."

"Well, it's not like I knew what to do about it." Her chin came up. "You were…"

"I was what?" he insisted when she cut herself off.

She shook her head once more.

"I was what?" he repeated, canceling the step she'd taken. A fist of frustration clenched in his gut. This woman had been eating at his peace of mind far longer than he should have ever allowed. "You brought this up, Ashley. You're the one who doesn't like the way I'm treating you. Maybe we should just go ahead and clear the air here," he conceded. "Maybe you should tell me why it is that you'd see me coming and run."

She didn't seem to think that was a very good idea at all. "I didn't 'run.'"

"What you did was close enough."

"That was years ago," she insisted, wariness creeping into her eyes. "I don't understand why it's even important now."

"Humor me," he growled.

"Matt—"

"Why, Ashley?" His tension radiated toward her, into her. "It's the same reason you ran from my bed, isn't it? The same reason you wouldn't return my call."

"Yes," she shot back. "It is. Was," she amended, because her reasons now were so much more complicated. "I was afraid of you. Okay? You were big and male and I…" Her voice caught, losing its force. "…I'd never met anyone like you."

For a moment, the only sound to be heard was the clank and whir of the air conditioner. Matt stood over her, her admission seeming to echo in the sudden, deafening silence between them.

With a disbelieving blink, the accusation and anger carved in his face melted to what looked an awful lot like confusion.

She had no idea why he'd wanted her to admit what she had. As she stood there watching his eyes search hers while her heart felt as if it would pound right out of her chest, she just hoped he couldn't tell how wary she still was of him. There was so much about him she didn't know, so much about him she hadn't given herself a chance to understand. Everything about him provoked a reaction from her at some level. She wasn't accustomed to anyone affecting her as strongly as he always had.

She watched him step back, slowly releasing her breath as he did. The effects he'd had on her in the past month were light-years beyond anything she'd felt around him as a naive young girl.

His confusion now looked far more like disbelief.

"You were afraid of me?" He shook his head as if trying to comprehend. "You thought I might physically hurt you?"

Her eyes widened. "No. No," she repeated. "Nothing like that."

"Then, what?"

"You were…what I said. You…intimidated me." She shook her head, not knowing how else to explain how he'd affected her all those years ago. "And I didn't know how to act around you," she concluded, looking very much as if she really just wished he would let the whole thing go.

Matt was actually more than willing to do that. He felt as if he'd been poleaxed.

Until that moment, he'd had no idea how big a chip he'd once carried on his shoulder. Or, how that chip had weighted his attitude and perceptions. It had never once occurred to him that he was the one who had held the power with her. She was the one with the status, the money and the bloodlines that ran back to European kings. He'd been a mongrel the system had pulled off the streets. The one nice mothers didn't let their nice children associate with. Especially nice girls.

And she had avoided him because she'd been afraid of him.

Fear was the last hold he would ever want over anyone. In any form.

The thought that she was still fearful of him somehow had him taking another step away in the suddenly heavy silence.

The quiet warble of his cell phone had her looking as relieved as he felt at the interruption.

He nodded toward the phone by the laptop, took a tentative step toward it. "I'm expecting calls about the other sites." The soft summons sounded again. "I need to get that."

Totally confused by his reaction to her admission, shaken at having made it, Ashley gave him an uneasy nod. "I should go, anyway."

"Hang on."

He snatched up the phone with a brusque, "Callaway. Yeah, Don," he said, his eyes never leaving her face. "Hold on a minute, will you?"

He lowered the small instrument. With it facing the side of his thigh, he watched her move to the door.

Ashley saw the heavy slashes of his eyebrows merge over the disquiet in his eyes. For a man who had been quite insistent about clearing the air, it now seemed he didn't quite know what he wanted to say.

Finally, all he said was, "See you at five-fifteen?"

"I'll be there."

"Okay."

"Okay," she murmured. Feeling as confused as he had looked moments ago, she turned to let herself out.

She had no idea what she had accomplished. She hadn't a clue if he had grasped the concept of keeping a lid on any action or reaction he didn't want to risk seeing on the six o'clock news.

All she knew for certain was that, by noon the next day, the strain between them had an entirely different edge to it.

Chapter Six

She had been afraid of him. It hadn't been disdain or disapproval that had colored her actions toward him after all. It had been some combination of female wariness and timidity he didn't understand and never would have suspected her to possess.

Twelve hours later, the knowledge still jarred Matt. That knowledge taunted him, too. Ashley had felt shy and susceptible around him all those years ago, and it did things to a man to know he affected a woman in such a way. Especially when he could easily recall how beautifully she had responded to his touch.

The thought had made for a very restless night.

It also put an entirely different perspective on just about everything she'd ever said or done around him. It definitely put a different perspective on everything she did around him now.

The staccato beat of pounding hammers melded with the

voices of men unloading roofing trusses from a flatbed truck. The crowd that had gathered today had been roped back even farther, resulting in a fair number of the curious becoming rather creative in their attempts to glimpse Ashley. Or, better yet, get a picture or an autograph. He'd caught more than one Kendrick fanatic slipping past the yellow tape wearing a tool belt and work apron—and more than one reporter trying to use the construction ladders to get a different angle on a shot.

It wouldn't matter that it was their own fault for ignoring barriers and safety warnings. If someone tripped over construction debris or fell and broke a body part, they'd still probably sue.

The thought of legal hassles, however, wasn't his first concern as he looked to where Ashley worked near Ed and another group of framers.

He'd watched her like a hawk all day. Just as he had yesterday and the day before. Only now, rather than watching to make sure she didn't cause any problems or get herself and someone else into trouble with her inexperience, he realized he was keeping an eye on her more to make sure people weren't causing trouble for her.

He didn't know if he hadn't let himself see it before, or if the stress was just beginning to show, but as the afternoon wore on he noticed little signs of strain creep into her smile. They were there as photographers persisted in photographing her at the water cooler, wiping sweat from her neck, trying to pull her weight. The hard work and the draining heat were clearly getting to her as much as they were everyone else. Yet, even in safety glasses, a ponytail and a ball cap, she still had the photogenic quality the cameras loved. It was in the tilt of her head, the delicacy of her features, her soft appealing smile as she continued on. She seemed determined to work as hard as the next person, and just as determined to keep any complaints she had to herself.

Not, he thought, his muscles bunching as he helped hoist a massive roof truss into place, that she was likely to complain with a sound boom right over her head catching nearly every word.

Balanced atop the wall of a future bedroom, he pulled his hammer from his battered leather tool belt and nailed through the metal connectors to fix the truss in place. Except for the man doing the same on the wall opposite him and the one below who tilted up the cumbersome wedge-shaped supports with a long board, the area below had been cleared of crew. Ashley worked at the opposite end of the structure, framing in a kitchen wall.

At least, that's what she had been doing. At the moment, he was aware of her handing a bottle of water to one of the women she'd been working with and pointing to the blue canopy the workers all used for shade.

He'd noticed her doing the same sort of thing yesterday, watching out for the person next to her, taking care to see they weren't getting overheated. At the time, he'd figured she was doing the Good Sam routine for the benefit of the cameras. Now, remembering when he'd taken her the lotion for her bites and how quick she'd been to make sure he wouldn't be in need of it himself, he suspected her concern would have been there even without an audience.

A twinge of guilt hit with the downswing of his hammer. Catching the corner of his thumb, he jerked it back. A split second later, he grabbed the truss to keep his balance, swore at himself for not paying attention, swore at the throbbing pain and grabbed his thumb to make it stop hurting. Had he hit the thing dead-on, he'd have cracked the nail in half. As it was, a red bruise was already forming under one corner of it.

Making himself focus, he edged himself along the narrow ledge to slide another of the heavy trusses into place.

Sweat trickled past his temple to his jaw. Ignoring it along with the pulse in his thumb, he muscled the prefabricated roof support upright and waited for the crew member on the other side to get his end in place.

From the corner of his eye he caught a glimpse of Ashley's pink shirt and ponytail. The documentary crew had circled for a new angle—and a reporter he didn't recognize had a microphone practically in her face.

A new crop of press had shown up, along with most of the batch from the day before. The new guy, though, was already proving more aggressive than the others. From what Matt could suddenly hear, it seemed he'd gotten so close that he'd nearly encountered her nail gun. Ashley looked to either be apologizing profusely or asking if he was hurt.

He held his hand out to the man working opposite him. Over the pounding and the buzz of a saw, he hollered out to make sure the beam was secure and headed for the ladder.

He had blamed the strain he'd seen in her smile on work and the heat. As his boots hit the ground and he crossed the concrete pad, he had the feeling there might be more contributing to her stress than that.

She had gone straight to her room both nights she had been there. She had declined offers from Dale and Ed to join them for dinner, and she had refused to go to the grocery store herself. He had thought at the time that she was just being antisocial and spoiled, that being who she was she wouldn't condescend to something so common as stocking her own cabinets or sharing a meal with people who worked with their hands for a living. He had ignored the fact that she'd been working with her hands herself. Since she had been pressured into that, he'd figured it didn't count.

Yet, now, as he watched two more reporters duck under

the perimeter tape, both apparently feeling that if the new guy could get a quote, they could, too, it occurred to him that he might have read her wrong there, as well. Instead of thinking she was better than everyone else, she'd just been protecting herself. Or trying to. Her room provided the only escape she had. It was the only place she could get away from people who seemed bent on watching her every move.

"What's the problem?"

Four reporters turned at his quiet demand. The only one who held any interest for him was the reporter he now recognized from the airport, a *GQ* sort with unnaturally white teeth and a fake-bake tan that seemed rather redundant in Florida.

"She nearly tripped me with the thing," the guy muttered, motioning to the cord leading to the air compressor. "I'm Tony Schultz. *Sun Daily News.* And you are?"

"The boss."

"Do you have a name?"

"You answer my question first."

The man looked annoyed. Or maybe he was trying to look important. "Fine. The problem is this whole operation. What are you doing letting a novice handle a tool like that?" he demanded, looking every bit as self-righteous as he sounded when he motioned toward what Ashley still held. "She said herself when she got here that she didn't know a thing about construction and you turn her loose with a nail gun? That thing could be dangerous," he pronounced, holding the microphone so his recorder could pick up everything he said. "Does OSHA know about this? The Unions?"

"We're volunteers here," Matt replied, his tone deceptively even. "Union agreements don't apply. And we're in full compliance of safety standards. Or, would be, if you weren't compromising them."

The cameras that had caught Ashley apologizing were

suddenly trained on Matt. Aware of the quiet plea in Ashley's worried eyes, ignoring it, Matt looked from the microphone the reporter held.

"Is that thing on?" he asked, his expression deceptively, dangerously calm.

The guy with the teeth had totally overlooked Matt's accusation. "You bet it is. It just came over the wire that Cord Kendrick is getting serious about the daughter of an ex-Enron executive. I want family comment."

"You won't get any here. We're trying to build a house and you're in the way."

"Miss Kendrick," the reporter began, ignoring him, "your brother has caused your family embarrassment on more than one…"

"Excuse me," Matt cut in, patience thin, tone still even as he turned to Ashley. "Miss Kendrick," he said, his smoke-gray eyes steady on hers. "Do you have anything you want to say to this man?"

"I already told him I don't."

"You're sure?"

She gave him a barely discernible nod. "Quite."

Aware of others now joining them, Matt fixed his attention on the man who stood nearly eye level with him. "Did you get hurt when you walked into her nail gun?"

The reporter's forehead pinched at the abrupt change of subject. Or, maybe, Matt thought, it was his phrasing that brought the swift frown.

"I didn't think so," Matt concluded as the man opened his mouth. "And, by the way, she's getting the same supervision as every other volunteer. Her supervisor tells me she's getting quite proficient, too. If anyone is creating a safety hazard here," he informed him, "it's you."

He nodded to a couple of the cameramen behind him.

"Can you guys get a shot of him standing on the compressor hose?"

A hint of hesitation diluted the smirk on the reporter's square-jawed face as the cameras panned down. Another camera flashed a moment before he jerked his foot off the dull gray tubing.

"Got it," his own cameraperson acknowledged, only to have his smile killed by his co-worker's quick glare.

"Good." Matt gave a satisfied nod. "Nothing like a photo for evidence.

"You asked who I am," Matt reminded him. He gave the man his name, his hands loosely on his hips, his failure to offer his hand deliberate. "I'm the person responsible for this project, and you're not authorized to be here. There's a reason that construction tape is out there. It's to keep people like you from hurting themselves or causing an accident like you almost did with Miss Kendrick."

He nodded to the tool she'd eased onto a pile of bracing. "The gun she's using fires nails at about fourteen hundred feet a second. If it had gone off in your leg, it would have driven a three inch nail straight into your thigh. I understand that's painful. Especially if it goes into bone. And by the way," he added, gratified by the way the man flinched, "that would have been your fault. Not hers. Now, unless you want me to call your newspaper and report you for trespassing, I suggest you get back behind that tape.

"All of you," he said, his glance pure steel as it swept over the more familiar reporters who'd joined them. "I've asked you before to stay back and I really don't want to have to do it again. Nothing is going to happen here that you haven't seen already. Go home. Let us work."

"But Callaway, we have a…"

"I know," he muttered, all but sighing when the director of the documentary piped up. "You have a contract. The three of you just stay back and out of the way. And you're going to have to figure out some other way to get your audio. You can't use that sound boom in here once the trusses are up. The rest of you. Go. Now.''

There was no mistaking the finality in his voice. Ashley suspected that the same decisiveness also marked his features as she stared at the line of sweat down the back of his shirt.

She had no idea how Matt would react if he knew she had been the one to bump into the reporter and not the other way around. She hadn't done it on purpose. She'd just been trying to avoid the guy when he'd come up on her other side and startled her so much that she jumped and bumped the gun into him. The moment she'd seen him, she'd known he wasn't there to ask if she planned any tours of the area while she was there, what her typical day was like, or what sort of sunscreen she used. She remembered him from the airport. He was looking for juice, meat, a scandal.

There hadn't been anywhere she could go to escape him.

Matt turned toward her as two of the burlier workers escorted the reporters away. Reaching past her for the gun, he checked to make sure that she had kept the safety on.

''That was my fault,'' she confessed, her voice nearly a whisper.

''No, it wasn't. He shouldn't have been here.'' His voice was quiet, too. It was his expression she couldn't read. He hadn't said much to her all day. Nothing that hadn't been necessary, anyway. But the antagonism that had underscored his attitude toward her had totally failed to surface.

''If he comes back again,'' he said, handing her the gun, ''use this thing on his foot.''

Ashley would have bet her next shower that Matt had chased off the reporters solely to allow everyone to get back to work.

The faint curve of his sensual mouth told her he'd done it for her.

The last thing she would have expected from him was a rescue.

Embarrassingly grateful for what he'd done, touched by it, she wondered if he had any idea how it felt to have someone intervene for her when she'd felt so helpless to escape herself.

"Don't tempt me," she murmured, unable to imagine him ever feeling helpless about anything. "I know they're just trying to do their jobs. And I'm sure there are some who are fair and less cutthroat. But some of them can be such—"

"Jerks?"

Her smile came easier. "I've called them worse."

"Probably not in mixed company."

"Actually, I have," she quietly confided. "Just not around my mother."

One corner of his mouth kicked up again, his smile as unexpected as his kindness had been as his glance eased over her face.

"I don't imagine you would have done that," he admitted. He took a step back. "Tell you what, you get to work and I'll do what I can to keep them away from you."

She gave him a nod, her eyes cautious on his. "Thank you."

She could have sworn she sensed that same caution in him. She just wasn't sure why it was there.

"No problem."

"Matt?" she said as he started to turn away. Since he didn't seem nearly as antagonistic as he had before, there was something she needed to know. "Did you know about Cord's girlfriend?"

"I can't say that I did." In deference to the documentary

people fiddling with their sound equipment a few yards away, his voice dropped. "But I won't be surprised to read that the Feds are now investigating his holdings."

"And probably our family's," she concluded, just as quietly. "Dad's going to kill him."

Matt shrugged. "Cord never does things the easy way."

Ashley had the feeling that Matt didn't, either. Even with the careful distance she sensed in him now, there was that edge that spoke of hidden scars and lessons learned through conflict and confrontation. There was just no time to wonder what those conflicts had been.

The deep buzz of one of the power saws died, allowing them to hear the quick commotion that had them both scrambling through the maze of upright studs. The alarmed sounds led them to where Dale, Ed and a half dozen others hovered over the bearded man seated near the metal legs of the big saw.

"What happened?" Matt called as he jogged the last few yards.

Dale looked up, his blunt features worried beneath the red bandana on his head. "Hit a knot in the wood. Board bucked and the blade got his thumb."

"Did it take it off?"

Ed's head came up. "Still attached. But he's going to need stitches."

Matt crouched next to where Gene held his hand with a blood-soaked handkerchief. From where Ashley came to a halt beside him, she caught the quick tightening of his jaw an instant before he cupped Gene's shoulder.

His deep voice sounded amazingly calm. "Can you keep pressure on that long enough to get you to a hospital?"

The retired engineer looked about as gray as his beard. Mostly, he looked as if he was about to get sick. "I think I can."

The less-than-certain reply wasn't good enough for Matt. With his hand on the man's shoulder, he glanced up. "I need someone to ride with us and hold pressure on this. Not you, Ed," he said, when the older man opened his mouth. "I need you here."

There was an awful lot of blood. Crouched beside Matt, her hand on Gene's leg and her eyes on his pale face, Ashley swallowed. She was the most expendable person there. "I can do it," she said, an instant before cameras appeared over everyone's shoulders.

Gene gave her a weak smile. Matt, however, murmured a quiet, "No," before he looked up at a volunteer with a dark moustache and a sunburn. "How about you? Can you help us out?"

The guy she knew only as Bert looked uncertainly at the blood dripping to the sandy ground. He was clearly squeamish. Being male, he also wasn't about to admit it. "Yeah. Sure." His Adam's apple bobbed when he swallowed. "Just tell me what to do."

"Here's some paper towels." One of the women had torn several from the roll by the water cooler and folded them into a thick pad. She thrust it between them. "Take the roll, too," she added, shoving that toward Bert, as well.

Suddenly aware that she was now only in the way, Ashley edged back. As she did, Matt glanced toward her.

"Thanks for the offer," he finally said, voice low as he helped Gene to his feet. "But there'll be less confusion if you just stay here."

Her help would be more of a liability than an asset. Matt hadn't needed to say the words for Ashley to know exactly what he'd meant. If she went with them, the media would be right behind. Reporters would follow her right into the emergency room, hot on the trail of whatever slant they decided to put on her part in the poor man's misfortune.

As she watched Matt and Bert lead Gene away and heard Ed encourage everyone to get back to work, she silently conceded that Gene and the E.R. staff were definitely better off without her help—no matter how much she would have been willing to give it.

The thought left her feeling oddly disheartened. It also did nothing to make her feel a part of the people working the project. Or to alleviate the sense of isolation she felt, even surrounded as she was by the crew and the crowd and the cameras. The very reason the crowd and the cameras were there set her apart from everyone else, and made it impossible for most people to regard her simply as one of them. They didn't even seem to care that a man had just been hurt.

"Ashley! Look over here!" The face of a woman in a fuchsia sun hat was hidden behind a camera. "I want a picture for my daughter!"

"Ashley!" Over the head of an older gentleman in a bright shirt, Bermuda shorts, dark socks and sandals, she saw a book being waved in the air. "Would you sign this? It's Monte Morison's biography of your family!"

Oh, yes, she mentally muttered, as the throng that had swelled to nearly a hundred continued calling out. The infamous biography. The three-year-old unauthorized one that had detailed her parents' controversial courtship and the scandal that had rocked a small nation when the woman next in line to be queen had given up her claim to the throne to marry a wealthy American politician. The sensationalized biography had recounted all of Cord's public aggressions to that point, uncovered a few their parents and the public hadn't known about and implied that her health nut of a little sister, who wouldn't even allow caffeine past her lips, had an eating disorder.

It had also gone into great detail and speculation about

Ashley's sudden obsession with privacy a few years ago. The release of that voyeuristic exposé had started the rumors about everything from a nervous breakdown to having gone into seclusion because she'd been brokenhearted after her breakup with an actor she'd never even dated. As for her desire to escape from constant public view, all that had ultimately accomplished was to make her a more attractive target for the press.

Just grit your teeth and smile, she reminded herself, recalling what her mother had ultimately advised her, *and don't give them anything to criticize.*

"Come on," Ed said to her as she waved amiably at the lady with the camera and a few others who'd eagerly lifted lenses in her direction. If the owner of the book wanted it signed, she could track down its author. Ashley wasn't about to endorse the blasted thing. "Matt said he'd let us know about Gene as soon as he has anything to report."

"Gene isn't going to lose his thumb, is he?"

Ed shrugged. "Hard to say. Didn't look too good, though." Shaking his head, he stuck one of his ever-present toothpicks in the corner of his mouth and headed inside the skeletal structure.

With a new appreciation for the roof over her own head, specifically for those who'd labored to build it, Ashley batted away a bug and dutifully followed.

Matt called Ed on his cell phone an hour later. Word was that the veteran of six Shelter projects wouldn't lose his digit and that he hadn't needed a transfusion, news that relieved them all, but Gene had come close enough to serious harm to put the fear of God in every single volunteer about the importance of paying attention around power tools. The object lesson wasn't lost on the press, either. Especially after Matt's lecture to the journalist who had grudgingly taken his photographer and disappeared. For the rest of the day, the only media who came anywhere near her were the three guys doing the documentary, who, she decided, had to have the most boring job on the planet.

Now that she could stop worrying about Gene, Ashley decided she couldn't think of anything worse than hanging around day in and day out watching one person do the same thing over and over. Unless it was being the person doing the same thing over and over while she was being watched.

"Hey, Ron," she called, toeing the switch on the compressor to turn it off. The noise level dropped by half. "Do you know how to rough out a door?"

The director in the backward ball cap and sunglasses straightened from where he lounged in the shade of a wall near a new portable fan he'd plugged into his own newly purchased generator. Aside from moving the sticky air, it blew away the bugs. "I can't say I've had that pleasure."

"You want to learn?"

He glanced over one shoulder, then the other. "Me?"

"Sure. It would give you something new to film."

As if a lightbulb had suddenly popped on, he pulled off his glasses and gave a bobbing nod. "I see what you're getting at," he mused, mental wheels clearly spinning. "We get footage of you passing on what you've learned. Good angle. I like it." Satisfaction with the idea fairly glowed in his eyes. "But it would be better if we used one of the other volunteers. One of the locals."

"They already have jobs to do. That's why I asked you." She tipped her head, smiling at his reluctance. "You're not really doing anything else," she pointed out. "And what about Andy?" The twenty-something soundman in the red cap looked bored out of his mind. "If he can set a mike somewhere around here, you can both do this."

"Group lesson. Better yet. Hey, Andy," Ron called,

heading toward him, "let's get that mike on a stand. We need it stationary."

From the corner of her eye, she saw Ed walk up. Frowning, he pulled his toothpick from the corner of his mouth and scratched the stubble on his jaw. "What are you doing over here?"

"Helping us all out." She didn't want to tell Ed that after only two days, she felt ready to crawl out of her skin being so on display. She had agreed to allow it. She knew that. And she reminded herself at least once an hour that what she was doing was for a good cause. More homes could be built because of the money the network had paid for the dubious privilege of having her name and face on an hour-long special. But it just seemed easier to have the guys usually behind the camera in front of it with her.

Her voice dropped to nearly a whisper. "Since we're down one of your best men, I thought I'd get us a couple more volunteers. I overheard Andy say he used to help his dad build furniture, so we know at least one of them can use a hammer." She hesitated. "Matt won't mind, will he?"

"Matt never minds help on these projects. But you're going to teach them?"

"As much as I know," she offered, not offended at all by the hint of doubt in his question. She was far from expert. Three days ago she hadn't known a casing from a crowbar. But she'd proven herself to be a quick study and had picked up the basics of her job well enough to pass on. "I just need you to double-check me."

Ed's mouth formed an upside-down U as he slowly nodded. Light danced in his eyes. "You might be on to something here," he murmured, sizing up the potential addition to his crew. They were both healthy young men. If he could get even a few hours worth of work out of them each day the time he spent with them now would be worth it. "Ge them safety glasses. We've got about half an hour before we start cleanup. That'll give us a start.

"Oh, and Miss Kendrick," he said as she started away, "Matt won't be coming back to the site today, so we'll be riding back to the motel with Dale. Matt's staying at the hospital until Gene is stitched up, then he'll take him home."

"That's very nice of him."

Ed shrugged. "That's just Matt."

That's just Matt.

Ed's easy conclusion stayed with Ashley the rest of the day. He had offered it as fact, as if he had never known Matt to be any other way. But the more she thought about the quiet conviction in his simple statement, the more she realized the statement wasn't actually all that simple.

It implied that Matt was a kind and caring man. A thoughtful man who considered the needs of others as well as his own and who went out of his way to see that those needs were met.

She supposed she'd already known that about him, simply because of the time, money and men he donated to Shelter. But she was also beginning to see how his men respected him, and how dedicated he was to his obligations. A man didn't accomplish what he had by spending his spare time causing trouble as she'd accused him of doing. Considering the size of the other jobs she knew he'd undertaken, and based on what she had seen in his room last night, she doubted he had any spare time as it was. After working all day at whatever was required of him, he probably tackled his paperwork long past the time everyone else had gone to bed.

The man she'd once shied from had never struck her as being so tireless, so conscientious, or anywhere near so... responsible.

But back then, he hadn't been, she reminded herself as she sat propped against her pillows in her motel bed that evening, staring at the pages of a bestseller she'd been dying to read and getting nowhere. Back when she'd first met him, he hadn't been responsible, reliable or any of the other redeeming things he seemed to be now. The only trait he'd seemed to possess beyond a talent for trouble was the raw masculinity that had made her feel like a young mare around a wild stallion.

In some ways, he still made her feel that way.

The admission had her trying one more time to concentrate on the book. But she got no farther than rereading a paragraph she'd already read twice when she heard the heavy thud of footsteps outside her room. The beat of her heart skipped at the sound, then went into double-time when the sound passed her drape-covered window and abruptly stopped.

She had listened all evening for Matt to get back from taking care of Gene. Part of her wanted very much to know how the man was doing. Another part, a less sensible and purely instinctive part, simply wanted to see Matt. She wasn't entirely sure why, either. It was possible that she just needed to let him know that she appreciated what he'd done for her with the reporters that afternoon. Or maybe she just wanted a chance to understand who he really was. She didn't even know what she would say beyond asking about their co-worker.

Thinking she'd figure it out when the time came, she slipped from the bed, pulled her short robe over her shorter sleep shirt and peeked out the corner of the drape to make absolutely certain it wasn't someone else lurking outside her door. Twice in the past two nights, she'd started to slip out for ice from the machine in the alcove three rooms down. Both times, she had spotted the paparazzo with the dark curly hair watching her room from one of the walkway pillars across the motel's center pool area and promptly closed the door.

Going without ice was merely an inconvenience. Feeling as if she were one step from being stalked made her infinitely more uncomfortable.

She cautiously nudged aside the end of the fabric. Even as she did, she saw Matt already moving away, his broad back to her and his footsteps once again heavy on the walkway.

Her first thought was to go after him. The thought of the paparazzo promptly cancelled it. As she slowly closed the tiny gap in the drapes, doubled-checked the locks on the door and the position of the chair she'd pushed under the knob, she considered that going after him wouldn't have been a very good idea anyway. It seemed he wasn't all that certain about talking to her, either.

That uncertainty was the last thing on her mind when she wakened three hours later, her heart pounding. It took a moment for her to be certain she wasn't dreaming and the rushing pulse in her ears made it difficult to discern the sounds, but something had just wakened her. She wasn't even certain what it was that had snapped her awake with such a start, but there was no mistaking the shift of shadow outside her window before that shadow suddenly disappeared.

Her first thought was that the paparazzo was out there up to something.

Her second was that it could be just about anyone.

The latch on her door moved.

Her heart lurched against her ribs. The flow of adrenaline jerked her bolt upright, her mind scrambling to remember what her parents and the security people she'd often been surrounded with had told her and her siblings to do should they ever find themselves pursued by an overzealous fan— or someone looking to make a small fortune by holding one of them for ransom. She knew it was entirely possible that the shadow only belonged to a common thief, but the thought hardly eased her mind. She was totally unprotected there.

The sliver of light that cut across the foot of her bed from the bathroom gave her just enough light to see the phone on the nightstand. To call another room, all she had to do was dial seven and the room number. She knew Matt was in number one-sixteen.

Quietly picking up the receiver, it never occurred to her to wonder why her first instinct was to turn to him.

Chapter Seven

"Matt?" The soft voice crowded into his consciousness, its tone whispered and urgent. "There's someone outside my room."

Matt rolled to his back, dragging the phone cord across his bare chest, the receiver pressed to his ear. Even wakened from a dead sleep, he knew that voice. It had haunted his restless dreams far too many nights.

"Ashley?"

"Can you see who it is?"

The panic in her plea jerked him conscious. It also pulled him upright. "Hang on."

Pale light seeped around his nearly closed bathroom door. Dropping the receiver onto the bed, he snatched his jeans from the chair across from it.

He'd barely zipped them when he reached the door. With the flip of the latch, he stepped into the tropical night air before he even considered who he might encounter farther down the long walkway.

"Hey!" he called, scowling at the trio of skinny teenage girls outside Ashley's door.

A light hovered over every room number along the column-lined and covered corridor. In that pale yellow glow, he watched all three spin toward him. Mischievous smiles died on the way. The little blonde who'd just reached toward the door handle, her hand tentatively extended as if she'd just been dared to touch it, went as red as her long-haired, navel-ring-wearing counterparts.

Matt started toward them. "What are doing out here?"

Three sets of eyes widened on his unsnapped jeans and bare chest before they collided with the glare darkening his sleep-creased face. Not waiting to reply, or, more likely, not having a valid one, the girls backed up, turned in unison and ran, giggling, for the parking lot.

It wasn't worth the effort to go after them. He'd been in enough real trouble himself years ago to recognize kids who were harmless and those with a mean streak. He was more concerned with the woman on the other side of the door, anyway.

Walking past the crickets jumping on the concrete, he knocked lightly below Ashley's peephole.

"It me," he called quietly. "Open up."

The door remained closed.

"Ashley?"

He didn't know if she didn't believe it was him, or if she'd closed herself into the bathroom and couldn't hear. Rather than pounding harder and waking any other guests who might have been trying to sleep, he headed back to his room.

Closing his door with a muffled click, he crossed to his bed and flipped on the nightstand lamp. The receiver still lay on the sheet. He absently held it to his ear, expecting a dial tone.

The line was still open.

"Ashley?"

"Is he gone?"

The anxiety was still clearly there.

"It wasn't a he. It was just some kids dinking around."

"Kids?"

"Girls. Teenagers. It looked like they were daring each other to touch your door or something." Or, maybe, they were just wanting to touch something she had touched. He barely understood full-grown women. What went on in their minds in the adolescent stage was totally beyond him.

"It wasn't that guy with the dark curly hair?"

Matt's brow slammed low. "What guy?"

"That guy with the camera and all the big lenses. He was at the airport and the site the first day. And he's been hanging around here the last few nights." She hesitated, her quiet voice suddenly quieter. "I thought it might be him."

It was Matt's turn to pause. "He's been here the last few nights?" Like everyone else, he'd heard stories of how bold paparazzi could be, and the lengths to which they'd go to get a shot the tabloids would pay serious money to publish. But the thought of some sleaze trying to take pictures through her drapes to catch her dressing or naked had him going dead still. "Why didn't you say something?"

The instant the question was out of his mouth, he would have given just about anything to pull it back. "Never mind," he murmured. He already knew the answer. She hadn't said anything because he'd made it clear he didn't want her asking for his or anyone else's help.

"It wasn't him." Sobering possibilities and consequences began to sink in as he forced assurance into his voice. "It was just kids."

He turned to the window, taking the phone with him to nudge aside his drape. His room was at one corner of the U-shaped building, which made it relatively easy to check out the other long corridor angling from him and the corridor across the dark and deserted lawn and pool. As late as it was, and as visible as Ashley was during the day, he'd never considered that anyone might be skulking around at night. But then he hadn't expected what he'd just encountered with the girls, either.

He definitely hadn't expected the fear he'd heard in Ashley's voice.

"They're gone now. There's no one out there."

For a moment, the only sound on the line was the unmistakable rush of an uneasy breath being slowly released.

Guilt joined a massive dose of concern as he turned from the window. He had never considered what coming here would mean for her. He had never given any thought at all to what treating her only as another worker would mean. He hadn't intended to extend any special treatment to her. Not in her job assignments, nor in her accommodations. And she had asked for none. But she wasn't like the other volunteers. She was someone the public loved to see, to know about, to encounter. Considering the wealth of her family, she was also someone who could be a target should some less-than-upstanding individual or organization decide they needed to make a quick million.

The possibility of being kidnapped would never occur to most people, and would sound crazy to the rest. He wouldn't have thought of it now himself, except for what Cord had once requested of him. The request had been made years ago, back when his friend had barely been speaking with his family. But Cord had asked Matt that he notify the Kendricks if he ever went for over a couple of weeks without hearing from him.

That was the first time Matt had realized that his often reckless, thrill-seeking, fun-loving friend could feel vulnerable.

He had never given any thought at all to how much more endangered a woman in such a position would feel.

"Are you all right?" he asked, sitting back down again.

"I am now."

"Do you want to come here to sleep? Or have me go there?"

The question was out before he even considered the wisdom of it.

Her response was just as immediate.

"I don't think that would be a very good idea, Matt."

Of course she didn't, he thought. There was only one bed in either room. If she would even let him in it, he would want her right where he'd had her before. In his arms, under him, moving with him and making him crazy with the feel and scent and taste of her.

He wanted her there even now.

If he were to be honest, he'd wanted her ever since he'd seen her step off the plane.

"It wouldn't be good for you to be seen coming into my room so late," he heard her murmur. "Or, leaving so early in the morning. Thank you, though." The line hummed quietly. "Really."

Her first concern hadn't been about being with him. It had been with appearances and rumors.

He hadn't thought about that, either. "Do you have your bolt on the door?" he asked, when what he really wanted to know was if she would have let him into her bed had publicity not been an issue.

"The bolt and the chain. And I have a chair under the knob."

Matt closed his eyes, blew a breath himself. She'd barricaded herself in. Wondering if she'd done that every night, suspecting she had, he opened the drawer of the nightstand. Next to the Gideon bible was a phone book.

"You don't have any other outside doors in there, do you?" he asked, taking the book out and dropping it on the pillow. "There's nothing to the back or connecting to another room?"

"Except for the kitchenette, my room is just like yours."

One door. One large picture window. "You should be okay, then."

"I will be. I'm sorry I woke you, Matt." Apology filtered over the line. "I just didn't know who else to call."

"Don't worry about it." He had been her only port in the storm. The thought had his voice turning quiet, too. "Get some rest."

"You, too. And, Matt?" she said, sounding the way she had after he chased off the reporters. Truly grateful. And a little guilty for having been a bother. "Thank you," she whispered, and quietly broke the connection.

Matt slowly lowered the phone. He didn't bother to question the concern he felt, or the sense of protectiveness he passed off as obligation. It was his fault she was there. Therefore, he would do what was necessary to make sure she stayed safe.

He looked up the number of the local police. What he wanted was hardly a 911 situation, so he called the main number, explained to the dispatcher what had happened with the girls and that he'd like a patrolman to stop by the Cypress Motor Inn a couple of times on his patrol tonight if possible to make sure no one was hassling Miss Kendrick.

The dispatcher had sounded half asleep when she'd answered. Hearing who was in need of assistance, she'd been wide awake by the time she assured him that the Gray Lake police department would be happy to be of service to a member of the Kendrick family.

In the morning, he would call Cord and see who his family used for bodyguards. He knew they had them. Or, at least, that they had used them in the past. One had followed Cord around all through prep school and college. He assumed now that his other three siblings had borne similar shadows.

He shoved the phone book back in the drawer, threw his jeans onto the chair by the file-covered table and crawled back into bed. Ditching his bodyguard had turned into one of Cord's favorite sports. As Matt lay staring at the shadows on the ceiling, he wondered how Ashley had handled being followed by muscle everywhere she'd gone. It was easier than thinking of her in her bed, alone and frightened.

Ashley overslept.

She hated being late. She especially hated to keep people waiting. But since she'd arrived in Gray Lake, she craved sleep almost as much as she'd started craving orange sickles from the ice-cream truck that came by the site every afternoon.

Obviously, the physical exertion took more out of her than she'd first realized.

Being awake in the middle of the night hadn't helped, either. It had taken forever for her to get back to sleep.

She didn't have time to eat breakfast or make coffee, so she stuffed a granola bar in each back pocket and settled for a glass of orange juice while she slathered on moisturizer with sunblock and tried not to stab herself in the eye with the mascara wand.

Matt would already be at the truck. Hopefully, he wasn't pacing. As kind as he'd been last night, the least she could do was be on time.

A solid knock on her door preceded a deep, "Ashley?"

The sound of Matt's voice had her jamming the wand back into the tube, grabbing her white cap and pressing her hand to her stomach.

The orange juice didn't seem to be settling all that well. The queasiness was hardly surprising, though. Her stomach was otherwise empty, she'd been rushing since the moment her feet hit the hideous green carpet, and, even with the air conditioner turned up full blast, the room was warm and sticky from the outside humidity and the already climbing heat.

The blast of heavy, eighty-degree air when she opened the door promised that the day would be even more miserable than the last.

"Are you okay?"

She couldn't see the concern in Matt's eyes as she looked from the print on his snug gray T-shirt that proclaimed it to be property of the MIT athletic department. His dark sunglasses hid them. It was in his voice, though, and the pinch of his brow.

"I'm sorry. I didn't hear my alarm." The upside to having overslept was that she hadn't had a whole lot of time to think about what had kept her awake last night long after she'd hung up the phone. She'd wanted badly to accept the offer he'd made to stay with her. Once he'd assured her that there'd been nothing to worry about, much of the apprehension she'd felt not knowing who'd been outside her door had actually faded. It was the unexpected realization that she very much wanted to feel his arms around her again that had kept her staring at the shadows on the ceiling long past the numbers on her clock had registered 3:00 a.m.

He hadn't offered his arms, though. After the hands-on demonstration with the nail gun, he had gone out of his way not to touch her at all.

She couldn't see his eyes, but that didn't mean he couldn't read hers. Feeling totally disadvantaged by him, she glanced from her reflection in his glasses. "I had a little trouble getting back to sleep."

Matt watched her pick up her room key, ID and a few folded bills by the television and push them into the front pocket of her jeans. The shirt she wore today was pale apricot, the color almost as fragile as she looked as she pressed her hand to her stomach and picked up her sunglasses.

Hooking the glasses over the neckline of her shirt, carrying her cap, she stepped out the door and closed it behind her.

"I should have told you last night that I called the police," he confided, wishing now that he had. She looked tired as she looked up at him, and as pale as milk. "You might have slept better."

She tipped her head, her expression suddenly cautious. "You called the police?"

"I wanted them to put the motel on their patrol. They'll be checking to make sure no one bothers you while you're here. But just to be safe, I'm asking Bennington's to send a man."

Ashley's caution promptly turned to consternation.

Bennington's was the security agency her parents had used for years. From what she had learned from her father and the various guards she'd had off and on over the years, everyone in the company's hire was either an ex-cop, ex-military or ex-CIA. Everyone had been highly trained, could be as visible or invisible as a client needed them to be and not one that she had ever met had a neck. None of the men anyway. The three female guards who'd rotated shifts with her during her four years at Bryn Mawr and the Sorbonne had looked pretty normal. They'd just been all muscle.

The agency was also as exclusive as its clients. Only people who had need of them knew of them.

"How do you know about Bennington's?" Her already quiet voice dropped to nearly a whisper. "You didn't call my parents, did you? They'll be on me in a heartbeat to come home if they think there's a problem. You said it was just a few teen—"

"It was just teenagers," he assured her. "And a problem is what I want to prevent. I didn't call your parents. I called Cord." He'd been around her brother long enough to know that parental influence was still huge. As intensely as he valued his own independence, he couldn't imagine anyone having any power at all over his personal decisions, much less enough to make him change his plans the way the Kendricks apparently could hers.

"He gave me the name of a guy he uses once in a while." Mostly when he's gambling heavily in Vegas, he could have told her, but didn't. "I'll call him this morning to see if he's available to park himself outside your door at night. If he isn't, I'll get someone else."

He was getting her a bodyguard. "You don't have to do that."

"Yeah." A strange note of apology in his tone. "I do. If you want one during the day, that can be arranged, too."

Her response was a quick and definite, "No! Please," she added, instantly softening her abruptness. "One at night will be...fine," she concluded lamely. Being able to sleep securely would be a godsend. "But one during the day will only set me further apart from everyone else." She glanced up, then glanced away. "I really don't want that."

It wouldn't have surprised him at all to hear that Ashley wouldn't want to be shadowed by a guard during the day because a guard would be yet another person watching her every move. He hadn't suspected at all that would make her feel different.

"Hey, you two! Are we working today, or not?"

At Ed's good-natured demand, Matt stepped back. His best carpenter from his Florida operations had planted his bandy-legged frame halfway down the breezeway. He now motioned for them to hurry up.

"We're working," Matt called back and watched Ashley lift her shiny ponytail to pull it through the back of her cap as she fell into step beside him.

The ends of her hair caught under the band.

He lifted his hand to release them. Catching himself, disconcerted to find how easy it would have been to touch her, he pushed his hands into his pockets instead and watched Ed give her a nod.

"Morning, Miss Kendrick. Say, Matt," he continued, before she could do anything more than smile, "how was Gene last night? He going to be able to come back by next week?"

"We'll have to wait and see." Ed's footsteps joined theirs. "He asked if he could come back just to supervise, but I don't want him on the site until he's off his pain medication. We don't need another accident because his reaction time is impaired."

Concrete gave way to crushed shells as they headed into the open parking lot. Ahead of them was the white van that followed them everywhere. The side door hung open, exposing the crew lounging inside. Parked among the empty cars directly opposite were two cars full of middle-aged women who had apparently arrived to watch Ashley leave for the site.

"Next week will be a lousy one for him to be gone," Ed grumbled.

"Any week would be a lousy one," Matt concluded absently. Beside him, Ashley politely ignored her audience as they continued toward his truck. There were no cameras, no requests for an autograph. Just stares.

"Yeah, well, next one in particular. I'm taking the seventeenth and the eighteenth off. Remember?"

For a moment, Matt didn't say a word. He just stared at the cowlick on the side of Ed's head before Ed disappeared around the end of the truck and came to a halt by the door. Ashley offered a quick and friendly hello to the guys in the van and moved ahead to join him.

He had totally forgotten that Ed had asked to take his weekend early. They were working seven days a week to stay on schedule, so schedules for him, Ed and Dale varied to make sure that at least two of the three of them were always there.

With Ed and Ashley climbing in from the passenger side, he slid behind the wheel and turned the key in the ignition. As he did, the engines of three other vehicles kicked in.

"Do you really have to take time off now?"

"Only if I want to have another wedding anniversary. It's my thirtieth."

Ashley's head swung toward the man by the far door. "Your thirtieth? That's wonderful, Ed. Congratulations."

"Thanks. I'll pass that on to the missus."

"Two days?" Matt asked, frowning at the lineup in the rearview mirror when he pulled out.

"We're going to have dinner and spend the night at a new hotel outside of Jacksonville." Jacksonville was his home, several hours' drive north. "I told Doris I wouldn't be gone on this job for more than five days at a stretch, but I've already been gone over a week. I can't tell her I'm not coming home for this.

"If you were married, you'd know how important such things are to a woman. Birthdays and anniversaries," he pronounced with a profound shake of his head. "Any man with a sense of self-preservation learns those are dates you flat don't forget." He turned to Ashley. "Isn't that right, Miss Kendrick?"

A faint smile touched her mouth. She liked Ed. She especially liked that he wanted to do something romantic with his wife. "I would say it's definitely advisable to keep them in mind."

"See?"

Beside her, Matt's features folded in a frown. "I understand what's important to women," he muttered.

"Sure you do," Ed teased. "That's why you're still single."

"That's exactly why I'm single." What Ed saw as a handicap, he seemed to regard only as an advantage. "What women want most is for a man to be there when she thinks she needs him. Not when it's…"

The word Matt bit back was *convenient.* Ashley felt absolutely certain of that in the moment before he muttered, "Anyway," and moved on before he said something intended only for another male's ears.

"Your time isn't your own," he concluded.

"Well, you do have to share it," Ed agreed easily enough. "You can't just come and go. Especially the way you do when you get a burr to go skiing at the spur of the moment, or kayak rapids, or…"

"Or dangle over the side of a cliff on a rope," Ashley offered, when Ed couldn't seem to come up with anything else.

The older man turned a curious frown on her. "How do you know that?"

"Because my brother instigates the trips Matt doesn't come up with himself. The two of them have come up with vacations that have been turning my mother gray for years."

"I take it your brother's not married, either."

Matt made a sound that was half laugh, half choke. "Cord? Not hardly."

"So what about you?" Ed asked, as she adjusted a vent to get some air. "What are you waiting for?"

That was easy. "The right man."

From the corner of her eye, Ashley caught Matt's quick and curious frown. "You want the whole home and family routine?"

He sounded surprised, almost as if he hadn't figured her for the type.

"Very much," she admitted, uncomfortably aware of what type he might think she was. The impression she'd left him with couldn't possibly have been good. She'd spent the night with him, then refused to return his call. It wouldn't be out of line for him to think her loose. And easy.

"I can't think of too many things I want more," she admitted, feeling awful at her thoughts. She wanted very much for him to know she wasn't like that at all. At least, she hadn't been like that with anyone but him. It seemed terribly important that he know that. Yet, saying anything with Ed there was impossible.

Her glance fell to her lap.

"You sort of struck me as the domestic type," Ed admitted, his graying head bobbing. "Can't exactly put my finger on why, but it's nice to know I'm right."

He grinned.

She smiled back. "Maybe it's because I'm so not the construction type."

He chuckled, but he didn't deny her conclusion, either.

Matt didn't say a word.

Ed didn't seem to notice his silence, or her unease with it. He was right about her, though. She was a homebody to the core, and she couldn't imagine wanting anything more than a home and family of her own.

From what she'd just heard, Matt didn't want anything beyond what he already had.

She couldn't believe how disappointed she felt knowing that. Mercifully, there wasn't much time to dwell on why that unexpected disappointment ran so deep. Matt had driven past the doughnut shop and, a mile down the road, pulled into The Hamburger Shack's drive-through.

"What do you want, Ed?" he asked, looking over the breakfast menu on the board outside his window.

"Black coffee and two of those bacon-and-egg breakfast sandwiches."

He looked to her, his dark glasses still hiding most of his expression from her. "How about you? If you overslept, you didn't have time for breakfast. Did you?"

She told him she hadn't and leaned forward to see the board. Still aware of the orange juice working at her stomach, and totally discomfited by the thoughts Ed's comments had so unwittingly raised, she leaned right back. "I'll have one of those sandwiches, too, without the egg and the bacon."

"You want a plain bagel?"

"Please."

He shrugged, the motion brushing his arm against hers. "What do you want in your coffee?"

Amazingly, coffee didn't even sound good to her. "No coffee."

She couldn't fault the skepticism that slashed his features. Not after the way she'd practically inhaled half of his French roast the other morning.

"Are you sure?"

She was positive, she told him. Aside from that, it was too warm to drink anything hot. The air conditioner was busy moving the air, but it hadn't done much to cool it yet. "The bagel will be plenty."

It actually was. And after she'd finished it on the way to the site, the queasiness vanished, which left her wanting the coffee after all. Iced and whipped into a frappé. But, she would have settled for anything cold, actually. Especially if she could slather it over herself somehow. Or dip herself in it.

By one o'clock the temperature had reached the mid-nineties. So had the humidity. As she had for the past three and a half days, she tried to ignore the heat, even though its effects today seemed almost debilitating. It drained the energy from her muscles, making it hard to lift, carry and breathe. She wouldn't allow herself to admit it aloud because it wouldn't have sounded very sporting in front of the cameras, but she wanted very much to drop the nail gun right where she stood, walk off the site and never see another two-by-whatever for the rest of her life.

Instead, with the gun seeming to grow heavier as the intermittent sun sapped more of her strength, she switched to a hammer.

The problem there was that, while the hammer felt infinitely lighter, it actually required more energy to use. As if sensing her plight, Ed finally asked her to just hold studs for him so he could nail them into place.

With a long two-by-four braced upright against her shoulder, she tugged down her goggles and wiped at the perspiration that had pooled on her cheeks. The wide plastic safety glasses with their closed bottoms and sides made her feel even hotter.

"Where's this storm you were talking about?" Great blasts of wind sounded like pure heaven to her at the moment. "Any chance it'll hit soon?"

From his position near her feet, he popped another nail into place. The edges of his beige cap were soaked with sweat, the band across the bill was dark with it. "Last I heard, it had stalled somewhere south of the Keys."

"We don't even get any rain?"

Rain would have brought blessed relief, if only until the sun came out and turned everything back into a sauna, but any respite would have been welcomed just then.

Ed must have heard the disappointment in her tone. "Heat starting to get to you?"

"Maybe. A little," she conceded.

He glanced up, frowned. "Why don't you take yourself a break?"

"Because it's not break time," she replied, and crouched to position another metal bracket for him. "I can do these shorter pieces," she told him, and picked up her hammer again.

His mouth thinned at her, but dealing with the heat himself, his only response was to hand her the nail gun. "Use this. It'll take you all day to drive those in with a hammer."

Ashley stifled a groan as she took the unwieldy tool and went to work with it again. She knew it was only her imagination, but she could practically see heat waves rising off the sawdust-covered cement. Every time she bent or rose, it felt as if those waves washed over her, making her almost dizzy with their intensity and adding another layer of perspiration to her skin and her clothes.

She reminded herself not to move quickly. To pace herself the way she had heard Matt instruct them all to do. There were a dozen other people working under the same conditions, and since they weren't calling it quits, she wasn't about to, either. Or so she was thinking when she looked over and found Matt's size-eleven boots where Ed's had been only a few minutes ago.

"How are you doing over here?"

His worn jeans had a hole in the knee. She glanced past it, past the creases in the fabric that fanned out low on either side of his zipper and past the brown leather tool belt slung low on his hips. He'd rolled the sleeves of his sweat-stained T-shirt, exposing the corded muscles of his biceps. Like Dale and every other male worker who wasn't wearing a cap, he'd tied a bandana around his head to keep the sweat from dripping in his eyes.

He had looked totally comfortable wearing Armani. He looked totally overwhelming in torn denim.

Resting back on her heels, she dragged the back of her hand beneath the brim of her cap. Beneath the white cotton, her hair felt stuck to her head. "I'm doing fine."

He crouched down next to her. Without safety or sunglasses, his eyes were easy to see, easy to read. She was just a little surprised by the concern she saw as his glance swept her face. "Ed seems to think you need a break."

"Why?" Behind her, a power drill competed with the incessant pounding of hammers. "No one else is taking one right now."

Matt felt himself frown as he looked at her more closely. Her skin was pink from the heat, her lips oddly pale. Ed hadn't mentioned that. All he had said when he'd come to him a moment ago was that he thought the heat might be getting to Ashley because she seemed to be swaying a little when she'd stand up. He'd also said she'd refused to go rest when he'd mentioned it.

Had the documentary camera not been right there, Matt was pretty sure Ed would have taken care of the situation himself. But the cameras seemed to intimidate the normally unflappable carpenter and he probably hadn't wanted to get pushy with her in front of one.

Matt had no problem getting pushy. Especially now that he'd seen her.

"Take a break."

"After I finish this."

"Now."

She wiped a trickle of perspiration from her neck. "It's not necessary," she said, sounding utterly determined to stick out her stint for the afternoon to the bitter end. "I can finish this, then I'll go get some water. Okay?"

This was his fault, he thought. He was the one who'd harped at her about everyone pulling their own weight. He was the one hell-bent on staying on schedule. What she didn't seem to realize was that a couple of the workers had already gone home because they couldn't take the oppressive heat. Those who'd remained were all accustomed to living and working in it.

Preparing to point that out, he reached over and took the gun from her.

Knees cracking, he rose. Looking annoyed at what he'd done, or maybe just annoyed that she'd have to expend energy taking the gun back, she rose, too.

The moment she did, he saw the pink in her face drain to match her pale lips. The moment after that, her knees buckled.

Chapter Eight

Ashley's peripheral vision had gone gray. She'd felt the ground tilt. For a moment there had even been silence. Then, she felt herself being lifted, heard a low curse above her, a quick shout behind her and the gray cleared to reveal a patch of blue in a sky of clouds and the hard line of Matt's jaw.

He was carrying her, her side against his chest, one arm beneath her knees and the other across her back. Bewildered, she lifted her head, pulled a breath and drew in the scent of warm musky male.

The motion of bringing her head forward brought another wave of dizziness. But she was conscious enough for confusion to give way to embarrassment and an acute need to be on her own feet. She wasn't quite sure what had happened, but she didn't want to waste time asking now.

"Put me down." Her voice sounded oddly distant. "Please."

"No."

"Really." She lifted her hand to her forehead and bumped the brim of her cap. "I'm fine."

"That's what you said before you passed out."

"I didn't pass..."

"Be quiet, Ashley." She saw a muscle in his jaw jerk. As close as she was, she could also see a vein throbbing in the side of his strong neck, the fine baby-fuzz hair in front of his ear and the beginnings of the golden-brown stubble that would shadow his jaw by evening. "Ed! Get me some water."

"Got it right here, boss."

"Get the door of the truck, will you?"

Ed looked worried. "Is she okay? You okay, Miss Kendrick?"

Ashley opened her mouth.

"She just needs to cool off," she heard Matt say, his long strides carrying her toward the twenty some die-hards who'd turned Ashley-watching into an art form. Beach umbrellas, beach chairs and coolers dotted the area on the other side of the construction tape.

Reporters bolted from their cars.

"What happened? Is she hurt?" a female reporter asked as Matt swung his leg over that tape, and kept going.

"Where are you taking her?" another voice called.

Ashley saw Ed reach for the door of Matt's truck. A moment later, Matt had set her on the seat and pulled a white handkerchief from his back pocket. Taking the bottle of water Ed uncapped for him, he doused the handkerchief with water, nudged her head toward her knees, lifted her ponytail and draped the sopping, deliciously cool cloth over her neck.

"Keep your head down. It'll help keep you from passing out again," he insisted, his voice gruff, his touch on her shoulder steady and reassuring.

Ignoring the reporters, Matt slammed the door and turned

to Ed. "Have everybody take a break. And make sure everyone's drinking plenty of water."

"You got it."

He turned to see a photographer taking a picture of Ashley through the window.

"You guys are unbelievable." He pushed his hand in front of the guy, flattening it on the glass. "Leave the lady alone."

"Hey, man. I'm just doing my job."

"Well, do it somewhere else."

"Are you taking her to Emergency?" someone called.

He was taking her to the motel. At least that was his plan when he swung himself behind the wheel of the stifling cab and pulled out with more cameras flashing behind them.

Beside him, Ashley had lifted her head. She held it with both hands, her elbows resting on her knees.

He hit Max A/C on the dash and swore at the even hotter air that first blew out. "Here," he said, handing her one of the two bottles of water that had been thrust into his hands. Ed had pulled them from the ice chest they kept under the break canopy. Moisture beaded the plastic bottle.

With a murmured thanks, she took the bottle and pressed it to her cheek.

"I meant drink it. You need to cool off from the inside."

She said nothing. After rubbing at a heat cramp in her leg, she untwisted the cap and drank deeply. Recapping the bottle, she pressed it to her cheek once more.

"How are you feeling?" he asked, wondering if her color looked marginally better, or if he was only wishing it so. "And don't say 'fine.'"

She cast him a sideways glance. "How about 'better'?"

Her color hadn't improved that much, he decided. But the faint arch of her eyebrow told him her spirit was alive and well and doing fine.

Not caring to consider why she felt so compelled to mask that spirit, not sure at all why she'd once chosen to let it free with him, he watched her push the bottle between her legs and slowly pull her cap from her head.

As she did, he caught sight of a familiar car in his rear-view mirror. It belonged to one of the female reporters who'd been at the site for at least an hour each day. Right behind her was the white van.

The motel suddenly didn't seem like such a good idea.

He practically ran the traffic signal at Crane and turned left instead of right. With the other vehicles caught at the light, he continued past the road he figured everyone else thought he would take—the one leading to the hospital—and headed for a spot he'd discovered when he'd met with the Shelter board last year to buy the property they were building on now.

It took a couple of minutes for Ashley to realize she had no idea where they were. Between the cool cloth on her neck and the cold water in the bottle, she focused only on the bits of relief they offered, the still-warm air blasting against her face and the watchful silence of the man beside her.

She still didn't understand what had happened in his room the other night. She had replayed that encounter a dozen times and couldn't come up with a thing that would explain why he'd backed down so abruptly when she'd admitted how intimidated she'd felt by him. But she figured that was actually the least of what she didn't comprehend about him. He'd become almost protective of her, and she didn't understand that at all.

"Where are we?" she asked, when he turned onto a narrow rutted road in a dense grove of trees and foliage.

"At the lake. You need to cool down and I didn't think you'd want reporters pounding on your motel-room door."

He glanced into the mirror centered between the visors. "I know of two we lost back at a light."

She sat up straighter, pulled the wet cloth from her neck. She still felt shaky inside, though she was only now realizing how shaky she truly had been. Suspecting the trembling she felt now might have as much to do with the way he'd so easily carried her as it did with the sweltering heat, she watched the vegetation open up to reveal glimpses of rippling water.

They went another quarter of a mile before he cut the engine and climbed out. She'd barely reached for her own door when he pulled it open and planted his hands on his hips.

His eyes narrowed on hers, searching, assessing.

"How steady are your legs?"

He had no business looking as attractive as he did. He'd pulled the handkerchief from around his head, leaving the sides of his sun-bleached hair flat and damp where it had been tied. A trickle of sweat had left a clean path through the construction dust on his neck. His clothes were as damp and flecked with sawdust as her own and he smelled like sweat and hard work. Yet, there was no mistaking the uncompromising strength in his body, and the quiet nobility in the carved angles and planes of his face.

The darker slashes of his eyebrows merged over his quicksilver eyes.

"If it's taking you that long to figure it out, I might as well carry you."

"Oh, that's not necessary. I'm fine," she insisted, and felt herself being swept out and up into his arms.

Turning, he bumped the door with his hip and the door slammed closed.

"You don't listen very well," she accused. She had his wet handkerchief in one hand, the bottle in the other. Draping the arm with the bottle around his neck, she frowned at the hard line of his jaw.

"I listen just fine. You're just stubborn."

Not nearly as light-headed as she'd felt a while ago, she muttered back. "I am not."

The patient look he gave her as he headed for the water told her she could argue all she wanted, but he wasn't changing his stance. Lacking the energy to argue anyway, and thinking it best to concentrate on something other than the feel of his arms and what the totally unrefined scent of warm male did to her nerves, she was about to tell him he could put her down when he did just that.

They had reached the edge of the lake.

Easing his arm from beneath her knees, he let her feet hit the ground. Apparently not trusting her not to crumple on him again, he kept his other arm snug across her back, his touch sure and surprisingly possessive as he guided her to a lichen-spotted log. Tall slash pines and low palms surrounded them. Blue-gray water lapped a foot behind her. An empty fishing pier jutted into the water fifty yards away.

The humidity felt even thicker surrounded by all the foliage. She could swear she saw steam rising from the broad leaves of something that looked an awful lot like the rubber plant in her foyer.

Matt crouched in front of her. "You are stubborn," he insisted, his fingers busy with the ties on her boots. "At first I just thought you were going along with all of this because you had to. But after watching you, I decided it's not just duty pushing you after all. You're actually downright mulish."

"Mulish?" She blinked at the top of his head. Mulish? she mentally repeated. "How flattering."

"It's not my job to flatter you."

His job? "Maybe I'm just...determined."

"I don't think so." Tugging loose her laces, he grasped her boot by the heel and pulled it off. He stripped her thin white sock off right after it, revealing her pink, perfectly pedicured toes. "I definitely know the difference between stubbornness and determination."

"How can you be so sure?"

"Because stubborn is what I was for the first eighteen years of my life. No one could tell me what to do. Kind of like you now," he pointed out, working on the other lace. "You were told to take breaks, drink plenty of water and head for the shade if the sun was getting to you. And I know Ed has told you more than once that you don't have to redo something because your nail holes didn't line up or the grain of the wood didn't match.

"You haven't listened to any of it," he informed her, his voice tight as he pulled off her other boot and sock and rolled up the legs of her jeans. "You could have made yourself even sicker trying to keep up. Heat exhaustion isn't a joke. And you're going to drive yourself nuts trying to do everything perfect."

Ashley opened her mouth to tell him that getting everything perfect wasn't at all what she was trying to do. But her conscience kept the words from forming. She knew she was guilty as charged. She had spent years obsessing over details so no fault could be found with anything she did.

"I just wanted to hold up my end of the job," she defended, not that crazy about being on the receiving end of a lecture. "And to do it right."

"You can't do everything right all the time, Ashley. No one can. Cut yourself some slack, huh?"

His hands closed over her upper arms. "Turn around," he muttered, and turned her to face the opposite side of the log.

The delicious shock of her feet hitting the surprisingly

cool water had her pulling in a deep breath. The sight of Matt yanking off his shirt when she glanced behind her, stalled that breath halfway down her throat.

The log rocked a little when he sat down beside her. Faced the opposite way, he wiped his shirt over his face, down his chest and dropped it on the log between them.

The tanned skin of his arms and thick shoulders was slick with perspiration. His corded muscles bunched with his movements. His body was hard and honed and with him sitting only two feet away, she could easily see little nicks and scratches through the golden-brown hair on his forearms.

No Roman sculpture could compare with the male perfection of his body. And she couldn't deny the tug of awareness she felt in her own. But seeing the little injuries he'd earned working alongside them all moved that tug from low in her stomach up toward her heart.

Lifting her limp ponytail, she pulled the handkerchief from her neck, gave it a shake to cool it, and draped it over his.

"You look warm, too," was all she said, before she handed the bottle over, as well.

He looked from it to her. "Your color is better," he said, taking it.

She'd had men tell her she had pretty eyes. She'd had a man once tell her over the two-dozen roses he'd brought that she reminded him of an angel. Jason had told her she was beautiful. But sitting there with Matt, squishing her toes on the muddy lake bottom and being buzzed by something after her blood, none of that seemed to matter as much to her as the way Matt smiled when he told her her color was better.

Either the heat had affected her more than she'd thought,

or he was getting to her on levels he had never touched before.

"Thanks," was all she could think to say.

The cords of his neck convulsed as he tipped back his head and drained all but the last few swallows.

"So," she murmured, turning her glance to a bug turning circles on the water a few feet out. "Do you mind if I ask what you meant before?"

"About you being a perfectionist?"

"I'm afraid I already understand that one," she murmured ruefully, splashing water over her calves. "About what you said about your first eighteen years." Her tone was casual, her interest was not. "You said no one could tell you what to do."

Matt planted his elbows on his thighs. With his feet spread and the clear plastic bottle dangling between his knees, he guardedly glanced toward her.

A few days ago, he couldn't have imagined confiding anything about his past in her. There were so many things about himself he simply wanted to forget, things few people even knew. But he now recognized the insecurity in Ashley that he had once battled himself. The reasons that uncertainty existed for each of them were poles apart, yet they still shared it. Hers had first manifested itself in the timidity he'd mistaken for snobbishness when she'd been younger. Now he could see it in the way she pushed herself to gain everyone's approval. She tried to please her family and the public and totally stiffed herself in the process. He knew she did. She'd as much as told him so herself at her brother's.

He, on the other hand, had dealt with his insecurities by letting everyone know he couldn't have cared less about their approval and thumbing his nose at anything that might have helped him gain it.

"I had a little problem dealing with authority," he replied, understating considerably.

"When you were in prep school," she concluded, because it had been so blatantly obvious then.

"Actually, I had a problem a long time before that." He kept his focus on the bottle between his knees, absently picking at its wrapper. "There wasn't a social worker or a cop I trusted, and I tended to bolt from whatever foster home I was in. By the time I was thirteen I was pretty set in my ways."

Ashley stared at Matt's profile. For a moment, what he'd said didn't seem to want to compute. He was speaking of a childhood that had been light-years from her own.

"Foster homes?" she asked, questions piling up like cars in a train wreck. "Where were your parents?"

"I have no idea who my dad is," he said, still picking. "And they took me from my mom when I was ten. She had a little problem with alcohol."

"Where is she now?"

"Dead."

"Oh," she murmured, turning to watch the methodical way he peeled a strip of the water-bottle label halfway down.

She wanted to tell him she was sorry. Fearing sympathy might make him withdraw, suddenly desperate for him not to do that, she tried to keep it to herself.

The quick, sharp ache she felt for the motherless little boy made it impossible. "I'm sorry, Matt." He tore another strip. "I really am."

"It was a long time ago," he replied, making it sound as if it hadn't mattered, hadn't hurt. "It wasn't long after that anyway, that the principal of the school I kept skipping made me an offer I couldn't refuse."

"How old—"

"Thirteen," he said. "I'd been arrested for shoplifting a six-pack and Mel, Mr. Hughes," he amended, identifying the principal, "went with me before the judge. Everyone in school had taken some sort of aptitude test a few weeks before and I happened to ace it. He wanted the judge to know about it."

He had always liked to read. He'd devoured sports and adventure magazines and novels like candy, and math had been a no-brainer for him. He'd just hated being told what to do in school. Just as he'd hated being told where he could live and with whom after his mom's drinking had put them on the streets and the authorities had taken him from her.

He didn't mention that latter part to Ashley. The part about being on the streets. Part of him was already wondering if he would see aversion in her eyes were he to look at her. Another part wondered why what she thought mattered so much.

"You were in a foster home, then?" she asked.

Insisting to himself it *didn't* matter now, he made himself tell her just to prove it. "I was probably on number four or five by then. We'd been on the streets for about six months when they put my mom in detox and me in the first home. I sort of lost track."

Steeling himself, his gut oddly tight, he looked to where she sat toying with the sleeve of his abandoned shirt.

All he saw in her expression when she lifted her eyes was quiet interest, and an odd sort of empathy.

"I know it's hard when you feel everyone else is running your life. Even if they're only doing what they think is best for you." She tipped her head, ducking it to catch his eyes when he glanced away. "So, what happened with the judge?"

The tightness eased. She had accepted what he'd said

without a trace of judgment—and caught him completely off guard with her understanding.

He had never considered that she would have any idea how it felt to be locked into a system she couldn't escape. He realized now that she had been trapped as surely as he had, and that she had been all of her life. The cage had just come with a different lining.

Time and fortune had allowed him his freedom. But she would never escape who she was.

"This was my third offense at that point," he admitted, unable to deny a certain empathy himself. "He told me I could either go into a juvenile detention home for the next four years, or take the principal up on an offer he'd made. Mel had been offered a position as headmaster at a private school in Virginia. St. Ives," he identified, fairly certain that by now she had to be wondering how an angry, incorrigible ward of the state had become enrolled in one of the more exclusive boys' college preparatory schools on the East Coast.

"He and his wife didn't have any kids," he continued, "and he seemed to think I had potential. He was convinced that a chance and a change of scenery were all I needed."

"They became your guardians?"

"Yeah. And I gave them a helluva time. I hadn't wanted their charity," he confided, his voice quiet, his thoughts clouded with the old memories, "but I didn't want to spend four years locked up, either."

So he'd gone with them, he told her. He knew they felt sorry for him, and he'd hated that. He'd actually hated pretty much everyone and everything about then. He hadn't a thing of his own but his pride, and he'd felt that if he buckled down and followed their rules, that those with authority over him would have taken even that and he would have nothing left at all.

He had quietly defied Mel and Linda Hughes at nearly every turn, broken their rules, broken the rules at St. Ives and pretty much followed his own code. Still, they had refused to give up on him. Even when the police brought him home the night he'd hot-wired a car, which Cord happened to help him with, the Hughes hadn't sent him away. All they had done was ask if he needed a vehicle of his own badly enough to steal one. Deciding he apparently did, Mel told him he would find him a job so he could earn one himself.

He had put him to work the next day with a construction crew on a Shelter project. The job itself didn't pay, but Mel paid him and between the foreman on the job who taught him the hands-on skills, and the project architect who recognized his curiosity about how everything went together, he ultimately found his career.

"I loved watching a building go up," he mused, shaking his head. "It was like this giant 3-D puzzle and I couldn't imagine anything I wanted more than to take an idea for a structure and make it happen from the ground up."

From the pensive lines in Matt's carved features, it was amazingly easy for Ashley to see that the thought of creating something with his own hands completely fascinated him. Or, maybe, it was just being responsible for its creation that completely captured his imagination. Even battling those who had wanted only to help and, undoubtedly, himself in the process, his heart had hungered for a way to channel his intelligence and his drive, and latched on hard when it had found that route.

His broad forehead furrowed as he tugged another strip of label. He suddenly looked very much as if he hadn't intended to mention anything about what had mattered to him, what he so obviously cared about now. Seeming surprised that he had, he set the bottle with its skirt of shredded paper on his shirt and muttered, "Anyway. That was when stubbornness gave way to determination. And you," he said, clearly preparing to shift the focus from him, "are just plain stubborn."

"I'll concede that I'm…persistent," she decided, because she was about to prove just that. She wasn't ready for him to change the subject. There was too much she needed to know. "Did you eventually go to work for Shelter?"

"No."

"Then, how did you start your company?"

"I got good at economics," he said with a shrug. "I started investing every spare dollar I earned in tech stocks. By the time I was twenty-four, I had an engineering degree, practical experience and enough money to hire good men who knew what they were doing to work for me." He nudged the bottle. "You should drink the rest of this water."

He didn't want to talk about himself anymore. That seemed as clear to her as the rings of silver around his smoky-gray eyes.

"Do you still see the Hughes?" she asked, rubbing at an itchy spot on the side of her face.

"Yes," he said flatly and reached over to turn her face so he could see what she'd scratched. With his blunt-tipped fingers under her jaw, he pulled the wet handkerchief from his neck. "It's just dirt," he pronounced.

If it was his intention to distract her, he was going to have to try harder.

"Where do they live now?" she asked, conscious of his touch, more conscious of the concentration etched in his face when he drew the damp cloth from her cheekbone to her ear.

"Melbourne."

"Australia?"

"Florida."

"They retired here?"

His glance cut to hers as he lowered the cloth. "About five years ago," he said, not bothering to drop his other hand. "That's how we started building houses down here. There are other programs in the country, but Shelter had been only in Virginia. We wanted to expand it."

"So you work these projects to give back what you got," she quietly concluded.

"Something like that." With profound patience, he met her eyes. "Are you through now?"

He wanted to know if she was finished with her questions. He couldn't deny the odd relief he felt at how easily she had accepted what he'd told her. It was the reason that relief felt so profound that bothered him. It hinted at something unfamiliar, dangerous and far more complicated than he had any desire to deal with.

Especially with her watching him so closely with those big blue eyes.

"Are you?" she asked quietly.

"Am I what?"

"Finished with what you're doing."

His glance drifted over her face, the gentle, delicate lines of it. There was nothing wrong with her color now. The glow of her skin looked as inviting as it felt beneath the tips of his fingers. Her lush lips were again a soft seductive shade of peach. "It won't come off," he said, referring to the spot on her cheek. "It's pitch."

"Pitch?"

"From the lumber. You got it on your hands and wiped it on your face." His fingers drifted up, touched the spot he'd thought to wipe away. "You'll need soap to get it off."

Ashley swallowed.

She knew she'd been pushing to get those last bits of

information out of him. But something in her had needed to confirm what she had begun to suspect; that the work he did for Shelter came out of a sense of gratitude for the chance the project and his guardians had afforded him. Matt had a good heart. He was loyal to the people he cared about. Knowing how loyal he was to her brother, she didn't doubt that for a moment.

Her thoughts stalled there. With the brush of his thumb to the corner of her mouth, he finally accomplished what he'd set out to do. She was now distracted. Completely.

They were alone, surrounded by nothing but the tranquil sounds of the water and the foliage that hid them from everything but the motorboats that bobbed like toys farther out from the shore.

Ashley was barely conscious of anything beyond the intent way Matt carried his touch along the fullness of her bottom lip. He brushed it gently, his touch exquisitely light, his expression growing taut with concentration. It was as if he was memorizing the feel of that soft, plump flesh. Or, maybe, testing it to see if the feel of it was what he remembered.

His own lips parted with a slowly drawn breath. Suddenly wanting him to do exactly what he seemed to be thinking about doing, her own breath grew thready. She knew how soft his mouth could be. She knew how deliciously demanding it could become. She knew how free she'd once felt in his arms.

She touched her fingers to the back of his hand, felt the warmth of his skin enter hers.

His eyes went dark at her unspoken invitation. Turning his hand, he captured her fingers, slipping them through his. Hands clasped palm to palm, he brushed the backs of his work-scarred knuckles over her cheek.

"It sounds as if we're about to have company." He murmured the words, his eyes never leaving hers as he drew his knuckles to the underside of her chin.

Caught in the seduction of his touch, his words made no sense. He seemed to realize that in the moments before he tipped his head toward the road.

It was then that she heard the distant sound of a car engine.

"It could be anybody."

"Could be," she quietly echoed, and thought her heart would pound out of her chest when he drew her hand toward him. For a breathless moment, she felt certain he was about to put her arm around his neck and ease her into his arms. The pull of his body already had her leaning closer, its magnetic effect scrambling her mental radar, robbing her of the sensibility that should have had her moving away, looking to see who might see them. Or, more importantly, looking to see if a camera was about to capture the moment on film.

The thought that she truly didn't care if she wound up on the cover of a tabloid with him collided with the warmth of his mouth on her palm when he opened her hand and pressed a kiss there.

"Come on," he murmured, easing back to pull her around. With a soft splash, her feet left the water. "I need to get another shirt and get back to the site. I'll leave you at the motel."

She ducked her head, fervently hoping he couldn't see the disappointment she feared burned on her face. Or the bewilderment she felt at herself over her totally unfamiliar lapse in judgment. Heaven only knew what headlines would accompany a shot of the two of them getting up close and personal. Her brother Gabe and his wife had only been friends when a shot of the two of them had fueled rumors that they were having an affair. Considering that she and

Matt already had been intimate, speculation over the two of them would actually have credibility.

"I'm going back with you." Head still down, she glanced at her watch. "It's only for another hour," she pointed out, as intrigued as she was disturbed by his ability to dissolve constraints. "It'll be easier if I go back now, anyway. There will be questions and I'd rather answer them at the site than at the motel."

The protectiveness surging through Matt wasn't at all familiar. It felt almost as dangerous as the pull he'd felt toward her moments ago. But he was a man who had learned to pick and choose his fights and he didn't argue with her now, especially not knowing who might appear through the trees any moment. Despite the incident with the girls last night, Ashley had managed a degree of relative solitude at the motel. Except for the paparazzo she'd seen hanging around and the documentary crew who were supposed to be there, the media had respected at least that much of her privacy.

The minute that changed, however, he would haul her out of there. In the meantime, he had a bodyguard from Maryland arriving at seven o'clock.

That evening, Ashley was a thirty-second spot just before sports on the local news. After years of having bits and pieces of her life pop up heaven only knew where, she gave no thought to how the story of her dropping in the heat had made it all the way to Virginia when her mother called wanting to make sure she was all right.

"I'm fine, Mom. Honest. It's just this humidity. Being here is like living in a sauna." She stood in front of her little stove, preparing her dinner. The turquoise terry shift she wore was actually her bathing suit cover-up. She found it served just as well to cover her matching bra and French-cut underpants. "I don't think I've been dry since I arrived here."

Her anxious mom didn't seem interested in the analogy. "Well, you didn't look fine, Ashley. You looked limp. The newscaster said he didn't know which hospital you'd been taken to. If you hadn't answered just now, I wouldn't have had any idea where to call. I was worried sick."

"Oh, Mom." The pat of butter in her sauté pan had just melted. Holding her cell phone in one hand, she set the cutting board on the edge of the pan and slid sliced mushrooms into it with a knife. "I had no idea you knew about this. I would have called if I had. It really is nothing," she assured her, hating that her mother had worried. She could cheerfully choke the newscaster her mom had seen. She just had no idea which one it had been. She hadn't turned on the television herself that evening. After she'd showered off the dirt, she'd filled the tub to her chin with cool water and bubbles and lain with cold aloe pads on her eyes enjoying the goose bumps. "It's just hot here. I'll take more breaks and get into the shade more often. I'll be fine."

"You're sure?"

"Positive."

"You're going to see this through, then."

The cultured tones of Katherine Kendrick, born Katherine Teresa Sophia Renaldi of Luzandria, held motherly concern. They also bore a distinct note of foregone conclusion.

"Of course I am," Ashley replied, smiling. "This isn't all that different from that time in the sixties when you went to Alaska to bring attention to the slaughter of baby seals. Except it was freezing there. You had to stay in an igloo and nearly wound up with frostbite," she reminded her. "I saw the pictures." She set the knife aside, gave the pan a shake. "You didn't think about not seeing that through, did you?"

"Of course, I thought about it." Her mom's voice held a smile, too. "I never got warm, the polar bears terrified me and I still can't stand the thought of yak meat, but that's what separates strong women from the weak. We think about retreating when a situation becomes difficult, rail about it to ourselves, then buck up and do what we know we have to do."

Duty, Ashley thought. There was no escaping the desire to see it through. That need to do what her heart knew was right was right there in her genes.

"Just make sure you don't push too hard, dear. I know how you are when you take something on, but you're not accustomed to the demands of physical labor. In all honesty, I can't picture you doing what you're doing," Katherine confided, sounding as if she was shaking her perfectly coiffed head at the thought of her refined offspring working up a sweat, "but the cause is truly a worthy one.

"By the way," she continued, as if she wanted to mention something before she forgot, "in that news clip, was that Matt Callaway carrying you?"

So that was what her mother had seen. Matt hauling her off. Wondering if a similar image would appear in the morning paper, thinking it a senseless waste of newsprint if it did, she murmured, "It was. He's overseeing the project."

"I didn't know he was involved with Shelters." Genuine surprise hummed over the line. "I'm certain I didn't see his name among the officers or directors when we did their fund-raiser. I would have noticed."

"He stays more at the hands-on level." Ashley set the knife and cutting board in the small sink and absently reached into the sparsely equipped utensil drawer for a spatula. She wanted to ask if her mother had been aware all those years ago of what Matt had been going through, what he'd been up against. She wanted to know if her mom knew there had been understandable reasons for the anger and disillusionment that had caused him to lash out as he had.

She couldn't ask, though. If she did, she might have to explain how she had come by the knowledge herself, and she couldn't do that. Part of her wouldn't betray what he had shared because she sensed that he had said far more than he'd intended. Another part, a more private part, wanted to horde those moments she'd spent with him that afternoon, to keep them to herself simply because they felt too personal to share.

"He donates some of his men to every project," she finally added. "He's actually been involved with the construction end for years."

That seemed to be news to her mother, too. "Is his involvement why he bid on you at the fund-raiser? To get this publicity for it?"

He'd said he'd done it because he was bored. Ashley still didn't know what to make of that. "He's a friend of Cord's," she said instead, absently poking at the contents of the pan. "Who knows why he did it."

The sound her mother made was something between a sigh and a tsk. "It's possible he doesn't even know. I know Cord doesn't understand why he does what he does," she admitted, exasperation competing with sadness over her son's scandalous behavior. "And they're very much alike. At least, they used to be," she qualified. "From what I hear about Matt these past few years, he's outgrown the unruliness I recall and made quite a success of himself.

"I don't know if you remember," she continued over the sound of a quick double knock on Ashley's door, "but there was a time when your father and I didn't want him anywhere near your brother. Now, I have the feeling he's the only person who can keep him on track. Those properties they're developing are the best thing that ever happened to Cord.''

The knock sounded again, demanding Ashley's attention when she would have much rather not interrupted her mom. She didn't want to ask questions about Matt herself, but she was more than willing to listen to anything her mother offered on her own.

''I'm sorry,'' she said, interrupting anyway. ''There's someone at the door. Will you hold for just a second?''

''Oh, that's okay, Ashley. I have to go. Now that I know you're all right, we won't cancel meeting the Meyers at the club for dinner tonight. I need to change. Call me tomorrow, will you?''

Holding her phone to her ear, Ashley headed past the little table she'd carefully set for one and skirted the bed. She knew her mother worried about her. Her mom worried about all four of her children. Her quiet concern had followed Ashley and her siblings every time they had left the estate when they were younger. Even though they were all now grown, Ashley knew that concern still existed. She suspected it would continue to exist as long as her mother still breathed.

''I'll call,'' she promised and was saying good-night when she peeked out the corner of the drape to see who'd knocked on her door.

Matt stood in the fading evening light, his hands on his hips, his head lowered, his jaw working.

He hadn't touched her since those moments by the lake. Though she'd been aware of him watching out for her when they'd returned to the site, he seemed to have gone out of his way to avoid physical contact.

It was almost as if the message she'd tried to deliver about the media's presence had finally become clear. When she'd gone to his room the other night to ask him to please not give the press anything to print, she had been thinking only in terms of him getting upset with her in front of them. Remembering how he had been the one to pull back at the sound of a car at the lake, she had the feeling he was now just as aware as she was that any interest he showed in her could be of interest to the press, too.

When she opened the door and saw his head come up, she had the feeling he was no more certain than she was how he felt about that.

Chapter Nine

Ashley opened the door and was about to step back when Matt's glance darted down the walkway. She'd thought he looked distracted. Now, he simply looked annoyed.

She didn't have time to wonder why that annoyance was there.

The eager face of a college-aged young man suddenly appeared beside him, all smiles and anticipation. Right behind him came the jerk-of-a-journalist with the teeth and the tan, microphone and recorder in hand. Ashley figured Tony Shultz of the *Sun Daily News* must keep a stack of freshly laundered blue shirts in his car, along with a gallon of his cologne. His collar looked as crisp as the other man's did limp. He also reeked of something that needed to be applied in much smaller doses.

"We're following up on Miss Kendrick's fainting spell today," the younger reporter replied. "Our readers want to know how Miss Kendrick is doing. May we have a minute,

Miss Kendrick?'' he asked, turning to her. ''We just have a couple of questions.''

His wire-rimmed glasses and bright eyes made him look just as eager as he sounded. He appeared to be an intern. Or, possibly, a buffer. Tony Schultz hadn't been around since Matt had tossed him off the site yesterday. He didn't appear too eager to be where he was now, either. Probably, Ashley assumed, because he didn't want to be covering her at all. She still remembered the comment he'd made the day she'd arrived, the one about how he wanted to cover a real story, not one about a spoiled celebrity who'd be worried about her manicure, or something to that effect.

''It's all right,'' she said to Matt since it looked as if Matt was getting ready to toss Tony and his little tiger off the motel property, too. ''I don't mind.''

Just because the one reporter was rude didn't mean she had to be. Tony hadn't liked her before he'd even met her. That meant he'd be looking for anything negative he could find to print. Familiar with his sort, she wasn't about to provide him with fodder.

''What are your questions, Mr.….?'' she asked the young man who was apparently so new he hadn't yet learned the identification protocol.

''McGraw. Lewis,'' he added.

''Sun Daily News,'' she supplied, helping him out.

''Right. Lewis McGraw. *Sun Daily News.*''

''And the questions?'' she reminded him. She liked that he'd been polite enough to ask if he could ask them, rather than forging ahead the way his partner did. If he needed more than a minute, she'd be happy to give it to him.

''Were you treated at a hospital today?''

''That wasn't necessary,'' she replied, telling him the same thing she'd told the reporters who'd found their way back to the site that afternoon. ''Mr. Callaway just took me where I could cool down. I wasn't the only one who had problems with the heat today,'' she explained, wanting him to know the problem hadn't only been hers. "A couple of our other volunteers had gone home earlier in the day because of it. Our supervisors are very aware of our working conditions and are great about making us take water and shade breaks,'' she added for Tony's benefit. "I just hadn't paid attention to them.''

"So you've suffered no lasting effects?'' the junior reporter asked.

"None at all. I went back to work this afternoon and I'll be at the site tomorrow.''

Tony stepped forward, sounding earnest, looking calculating. "Is there anything else you can tell us about your episode this afternoon? Have you ever fainted before?''

"No, Mr. Schultz. I haven't.''

"Is there any history of epilepsy or stroke in your family?''

Oh, for Pete's sake, she mentally groaned. "I'm perfectly healthy,'' she replied, seeing no point in answering something that could lead heaven only knew where.

"If you're in good health, could there possibly be a reason other than the heat for you fainting this afternoon?''

It took only moments for Ashley to realize how precisely he'd phrased his question. That was also about how long it took for the younger reporter's eyes to widen at the subtle, but entirely personal aspect of the man's insinuation, and for Matt's jaw to lock.

Her own expression immediately cooled.

He wanted to know if she could possibly be pregnant.

Ignoring the man as well as the query, she turned to his more civilized protégé before Matt could jump in and tell him he was totally out of line—which would have only given him something to print. She wasn't about to justify the uncouth question with any sort of response.

"I believe I've answered your questions, Mr. Lewis. If you will excuse me now?"

"Yeah. Sure. Thanks," he said, lifting his hand.

"Just one more—" Tony began, only to cut himself off when Matt, his eyes as hard as flint, stepped forward.

"It sounds like she's finished," he said as Ashley slipped inside.

"What are you now? Her bodyguard?"

"Actually, he's in another room," Matt replied, motioning vaguely behind him. "I'd be happy to get him, though."

Matt's voice held deceptive calm. He had the feeling, though, that his expression didn't appear quite so accommodating in the moments before the younger man gave him a nervous little smile and the more jaded one turned away, muttering that his underling was going to have to work on asking the tough questions rather than the obvious ones if he wanted to survive in the business.

Matt had no idea what junior said in reply while they walked off. As he pushed the door to Ashley's room wider and stepped inside, his only concern was with the woman who'd hurried across her room to rescue something buttery from her stove.

"You didn't have to talk to them," he said, shutting out the heat and the intrusions. The radio on the nightstand played quietly, so quietly he could barely make out the strains of Celine singing about life going on.

"Yes, I did." Using the end of a hand towel for a hot pad she slid a large pan onto the back burner and flipped a knob to turn off the heat. "I tried avoiding reporters and all it did was make them more determined to get to me. It's almost easier to give them what they want so they'll go away.

"I'm just grateful he didn't come right out and ask what he was insinuating," she murmured, tossing the towel on the aqua Formica counter. "And that he didn't have a cameraman with him the way television reporters always do. The way sound bites can be manipulated, who knows what would have wound up on video."

"Or in the headlines."

"Exactly."

Matt watched her turn to where he'd remained by the door and thread her fingers through her loose hair. The vibrant, animated woman standing in the middle of the shabby kitchenette bore little resemblance to the wan and wilted woman he had watched himself carry on the six o'clock news while he'd bolted down a hamburger and talked to his site manager in Newport. The chic woman in the short sleeveless cover-up and the matching turquoise sandals with their little silver beads, didn't look as if she'd ever set foot near a construction site, much less held her own on one.

The overhead light caught strands of silver and gold in the shining hair tumbling to her shoulders. She looked totally out of place in the rundown accommodations. She also appeared totally oblivious to them.

"I don't know how you do it," he confessed as she moved toward him. He was only now beginning to appreciate that she lived in a fishbowl. He was also only beginning to understand what the expression meant. She could seek the privacy of the castle nestled in the middle of that bowl, hide among the feathery ferns, but she couldn't come out any side without being on full display. "I'd either go crazy or wind up in jail if I had to live like that."

The delicate wing of one eyebrow arched as she stopped an arm's length away. "In jail?"

"I'm afraid I'd be tempted to hurt people with microphones or cameras."

A faint smile glowed in her eyes. "There's nothing wrong with temptation. It's acting on it that causes problems."

She had a point, he thought, thinking she looked pretty tempting herself just then. When she smiled, she seemed to light from within, even when that smile was restrained. And whenever she smiled, he found his eyes inevitably drawn to her mouth. As enticing as her lips were glossed and shiny, he found them even more so as they were now, totally natural and free of anything but her softness.

Pushing his hands into his pockets, he reminded himself that he hadn't come there to act on temptation. "So have you thought about it?" he asked, wanting to ignore the way his body reacted to it anyway. "Hurting someone with a camera?"

"I've actually fantasized about it." Absently kneading the tight muscles in her neck, she watched him smile. She liked that she could admit such a thing to him and not have to explain why it was so. She liked the way he championed her when the press was around, too. She'd never had a man do that for her before. They usually just stepped back and disappeared. "But mostly I just live with it."

"Because you can't escape it," he concluded.

"Something like that. Like I said, I've tried avoiding them. I dropped out for almost a year, but all that did was make things worse."

"When did you do that?"

"I'm sure you didn't come here to hear about my failed attempt to gain control over my life." The quick certainty in her expression faded to curiosity. "Why are you here?"

"To talk to you about changing rooms. But that can wait," he decided. "What do you mean, you dropped out?"

"Why do I need to change rooms?"

"Because this doesn't have an adjoining door and I don't like the idea of Bull not being able to get in here if he needs to. He said adjoining rooms will make it more secure for you.''

"Bull? He introduced himself as Jeffrey Parker."

"Bull is how he was introduced to me a couple of years ago. It's what your brother has always called him."

The rather large, bald and extremely courteous man who had presented himself at her door an hour ago then left for dinner did look a bit like a bull, she conceded. Stocky. No neck. And she knew her brother had recommended the man, which went a long way in making her comfortable with her temporary bodyguard. But then, she'd never been uncomfortable with any of Bennington's people. She just hadn't realized that Matt had met him before, himself.

"Anyway," he continued, even as she realized that his knowing Jeffrey Parker put her even more at ease, "when did you do this?"

"After I graduated. I wanted to live the way everyone else did. I wanted to sit down in a restaurant without half the patrons staring. I wanted to lie on a beach without fearing that the world's most unflattering shot of my backside would wind up on tabloids in supermarkets all over the country. Since that hadn't seemed possible," she said, starting to shrug, the twinge in the muscles stopping her, "I moved back to the estate and worked by computer for the foundation. I never left except to go to my grandmother's."

"For a year."

"Thirteen months actually. That last month was when the tabloid speculation went from the ridiculous to the damaging."

"By the ridiculous you mean…"

"Alien abduction."

He lifted his chin. "Ah, yes. So how are the little green people?"

"I couldn't understand a word they said."

"And the damaging?"

"The one that bothered my mom the most was that I was in an institution following a breakdown. Reporters were hounding my family and friends because I'd become this big reclusive mystery no one could solve and speculation was getting completely out of hand.

"All I wanted was to be left alone." Self-recrimination entered her voice as she sat down on one of the platter-size leaves printed on her bedspread. "I just didn't realize how selfish that was until I considered what the rumors were doing to my family and its reputation. I'd always been afraid of doing something that would cause the wrong kind of publicity and that's exactly what I'd done.

"So," she said, spreading her hands, "five years later, here I am."

She looked far more accepting of the intrusions into her life than he would have been, Matt thought. Or maybe, she was just resigned.

"Do I have to change rooms right now?"

He pushed himself away from the door. There wasn't much he didn't recall about the night they'd spent together—most of it having to do with them being horizontal. But what he recalled now was the wish she had professed to do something outrageous. He had dismissed the first thing she had mentioned as not shocking enough. And it hadn't been. What she had sought to do was simply sail away. To escape. Considering what she had just told him, that need had obviously been there for a very long time.

"Just sometime this evening," he replied, stopping in front of her. "There are two adjoining rooms on the other side of mine. I've already arranged for you to have them."

Her glance slid from his belt buckle to his eyes. "Thank you," she murmured, rubbing the back of her neck as she looked around the decidedly neat but impersonal space. "It won't take me long to get my things together. I'd just like to eat first.'' She nodded toward the stove. ''Have you had dinner? I was just going to make an omelet, and I have plenty of eggs.''

He'd thought she might balk at the hassle and inconvenience of moving, especially considering the day she'd had. He realized now that he should have known better. Ashley did what she had to do. If not with a smile, then at least, without complaint. And if she had to change rooms so her bodyguard could do his job, she would do it with all the grace she could muster.

''I already grabbed a burger.'' He wished he hadn't, then immediately thought it best that he had. Had he been hungry he wouldn't have hesitated to accept her offer. He would have had an excuse to stay. As it was, now that he'd done what he'd come to do, he had none. ''But thanks for the invitation.''

''Sure.'' Disappointment flickered in her eyes, only to give way to an easy smile. ''I just thought you might be getting as tired as I am of eating alone.''

She didn't want him to know how much she wished he were staying. That seemed as apparent to Matt as the invitation he'd seen in her eyes at the lake that afternoon. That invitation had preyed on his mind, taunted him as much as the remembered feel of her body, the sweet seductive taste of her mouth, her skin.

It would be so easy to take her up on what she seemed to silently offer. And had she been anyone else, he wouldn't have hesitated to go along for the ride. They were both adults. As long as there were no expectations beyond enjoying each other's company for a while, as long as things stayed uncomplicated, he would have had no qualms about a temporary relationship with her. But she wasn't someone else. And he couldn't shake the feeling that things were becoming complicated already.

The wisest thing to do would be to simply keep his hands off her. The only problem was that he wanted her so badly he ached.

"I am getting tired of it," he said, holding out his hand and pulling her to her feet. "So how about I take a rain check. I'd stick around now to keep you company, but then it would just take you that much longer to do what you need to do and get into your other room. Bull said he'd be available at seven-thirty to help move you over and make sure you're in and secure for the night. That's less than an hour."

He had thought he would let her go. Now that she was upright and could walk with him to the door and bolt it behind him, he had no reason to keep hold of her hand. But the feel of a rough spot beneath his palm had him turning her hand in his.

She had an adhesive strip wrapped around her index finger. Picking up the hand he'd held earlier that afternoon, he saw that she'd replaced the two he'd noticed then, too.

A faint frown creased his forehead.

Ashley thought he was looking at her chipped nails. Even wearing gloves most of the time, her manicure hadn't survived.

"They're a mess," she murmured, and started to pull her hands away.

"Don't." His mouth thinned at one of the strips on her right hand. "Cut or blister?"

"That one's a splinter."

"Can't you get it out?"

"I'm right-handed. I couldn't get a good grip on it with the tweezers."

"Where are they?"

He smelled of soap and citrus and the clean scent of laundry soap that clung to his fresh T-shirt. Even though the air conditioner moved the warm air, she could feel the heat radiating from his body. "Where are what?"

"Your tweezers." He lifted her hand, frowning. "How long has the splinter been in there?"

"A couple of days. And they're in the bathroom. In my makeup bag," she concluded on her way past the bed since he was already tugging her to the door of the tiny bathroom.

From among the bottles of lotions and creams on the postage-stamp-size counter, she picked up a beige zippered bag with a designer's initials stamped all over it.

Digging out the small silver tweezers, she handed them over.

Between the various itches and aches each day brought, she would be more than happy to be relieved of one. The splinter didn't hurt unless she rubbed or pressed something against it—which she seemed to do at least a dozen times a day. It would be a relief not to feel the needlelike bit of wood poking into her flesh.

The light in the bathroom wasn't the best, but it was as good as any available. Leaning against the small counter, his shoulders seeming to take up half the room, Matt tugged her between the V of his legs.

Ashley barely noticed the reddened skin near her knuckle as he carefully removed the little bandage from her finger. She was far more conscious of his powerful thighs, his broad chest; much more interested in the concentration etched in his undeniably handsome face and the incredible gentleness in his strong, capable hands.

He was an amazing man, she realized as he caught and eased the tiny sliver from her tender flesh. He was a man who had beaten the odds through sheer determination and drive. A man who had succeeded beyond many people's wildest dreams, yet who remained humble enough to keep giving back to those who had opened the gates to his goals. A man whose touch she was beginning to crave, and one she had no business being attracted to at all.

The more she knew of him, the more drawn she was by him, the more aware she became of how very wrong he was for her. Only minutes ago, he had made it clear that he wouldn't want to live as she did, that he would hate not being able to go outside his own walls without the possibility of being recognized, photographed, intruded upon. And only days ago, he had made it just as apparent that he wanted his personal freedom as much as she someday wanted marriage and commitment.

She blinked at a hook-shaped scar on his thumb. A much fresher injury colored half of his blunt-tipped nail. It seemed easier to focus there than on how wrong they were for each other.

Paper crackled as he opened a fresh bandage from the box she'd left open beside a tube of antibiotic cream. "Hold this."

He handed her the bandage, reached for the tube. With the efficiency of a man who'd performed the task before, he tossed the wrapper into the wastebasket, smeared cream on the little pad of gauze, and wrapped the bandage gauze-side down over her little wound.

She touched below the angry bruise on his thumb. "What did you do?"

"Hit it with a hammer."

"Ow," she mouthed in empathy.

"Occupational hazard," he said, trying to focus on what he was doing rather than the gentle concern in her eyes. Not focusing is why he had the bruise to begin with. "I'm used to it. You're not. There," he pronounced, holding her hand up for her inspection. "Now, what's wrong with your neck?"

She didn't seem to realize she was rubbing it again. Realizing it now, her hand fell. "It's just sore from looking up to nail top plates. Occupational hazard," she explained, eyes smiling.

His glance slipped to her mouth. Before that glance could linger, he took her by the arms and turned her around.

His hands skimmed under her hair. With his fingers curved over her shoulders, his thumbs slid down either side of her upper spine.

"Is that where it hurts?" he asked, pressing his thumbs inward as he eased them toward the base of her skull.

The exquisite pressure on the sore, achy muscles almost made her knees buckle.

She drew a deep breath, fighting the urge to sag back against him. "One of the places."

"Where else?" he asked, circling his thumbs back down.

"Pretty much everywhere."

She heard him chuckle, the sound rich and deep. "I'm not surprised. I'm just surprised you'll admit it."

"Are you accusing me of being stubborn again?"

"Not stubborn." Matt watched her hair slip over the backs of his hands, wondered at the silken feel of it. She smelled of her soap, shampoo and powder. The whole room did. "Strong."

Beneath his hands, he felt her body go still.

With her back to him, her head bent slightly forward, he couldn't see her expression. All he could sense was hesitation.

"I'd like to be," he heard her quietly say. "But I'm not. Anything that looks like strength is just me faking it."

His palms slipped along her shoulders, his fingers still kneading. "And if you fake something like that long enough it becomes real. Stop underestimating yourself, Ashley. You're already there."

She turned, her expression oddly pensive as she looked up at him.

"What?" he asked, his thumbs now resting on her collarbone.

It wasn't fair, Ashley thought. It wasn't fair that this man kept drawing her closer when she should be backing away. She shook her head, unwilling to retreat just yet. When she was with him she didn't feel as if she had to be all the things everyone else expected. She could just...be.

She lifted her hand, laid her palm on his hard chest. "If I was really strong, I'd turn around and walk away right now." Beneath her hand, she felt the heavy beat of his heart. "But I really don't want to do that."

Her own heartbeat felt a little too rapid as the gentle massaging motion of his fingers slowed to a stop. His eyes held hers, his thoughts quietly turning to a struggle in the moments before they drifted to her mouth.

The struggle lasted only long enough for him to frame her face with his big hands. "I'm having the same problem myself," he confessed, and slipped his fingers up into her hair.

His head descended, blocking the light, blocking everything but the feel of his breath entering her lungs when he settled his mouth over hers.

The faint sound she made could have been a moan. It might have been a sigh. All she knew as she opened to him and felt the slow, gentle intrusion of his tongue was that she had ached for this. She just hadn't realized how badly until she felt her arms wind up around his neck and she edged herself closer.

She had longed to be kissed the way he kissed her. As if he had all the time in the world and he intended to take it to savor everything about her. He didn't demand so much as he encouraged. He sipped and teased, angling her head to increase the pressure of his mouth, then eased back, causing her to seek him, to explore as he did.

She loved that about him. She loved that he emboldened her to touch him as freely as he touched her when he drew her closer, slipping his hand down her back to press her more firmly between his thighs. Threading her fingers through his hair, she stretched her body against his, loving the solid feel of him. He made her body feel fluid, boneless with a need that softened parts of her, tightened others. She loved that, too. The way she felt in his arms.

It would be so easy, she thought, her mind fogging, to simply love…him.

The realization caught her with her head back, his breath warm on her neck as his lips traced toward the pulse hammering at the base of her throat.

His hand slipped down her back, bunched the soft fabric of her cover-up in his fingers. He bent, drawing her closer, slipping his hand farther down so he could touch bare skin. With his palm, he cupped the firm flesh of her bottom, felt the slash of lace that cut high and bared her hip. He edged her closer, pressed her stomach to the thickness behind his zipper.

Matt hissed in a breath, eased her back.

Thoughts of her had made him feel as restless as a panther in a cage. The feel of her had him ready to bay at the moon. In less than a minute, he would be backing her toward the bed, stripping her to her skin and burying himself inside her.

He was trying to remember why he shouldn't do just that when he felt her hand on his cheek, stilling his progress toward the gentle mounds of her breasts. As he looked up, she pressed her forehead to his chest.

Her breath trembled out.

"Yeah," he murmured, realizing what she was doing. At

least, thinking he did. Slowing down was an excellent idea. "I suppose I should let you go." He drew his hands up, locked his arms around her. "Bull will be here soon."

Ashley nodded, her forehead brushing soft cotton. Letting her go was the last thing she wanted him to do.

She felt his lips brush the top of her hair, her heart squeezing at his tenderness. She was falling in love with him. She knew it. She even knew it wasn't wise, sensible or even sane considering that he would probably bolt if he even suspected how she was beginning to feel. But as she looked up and met the desire still glittering in his eyes, she had no idea what to do about it, either.

"I'll see you in the morning," she murmured.

He slipped his fingers through hers, brushed his lips over her mouth. "Walk me to the door," he said, easing her back. "And lock it behind me."

Ashley overslept. Again.

She'd never had this problem before, but at least she'd gotten the hang of throwing herself together in about ten minutes flat. Of course, she had a lot less to do than she would have at home. Her makeup was minimal, mostly because it would melt off anyway, and her hair took no time at all. She simply scraped it back, whipped it all into a ponytail and stuffed it under her baseball cap.

That's what she was doing when she knocked on the adjoining door and nudged it open a crack. Across the dim room the television was on, volume low, a chase scene in full progress.

"I'm leaving, Mr. Parker," she said. "See you this evening?"

"I'll be here," came the disembodied assurance. The television went off, apparently by remote. "You have a good day."

She told him she would, told him to sleep well because he would have sat up all night, one ear cocked for any sound that shouldn't have been there, and closed the door to head for the one that lead outside.

She hoped to catch Matt coming from his room, or to see him before Ed joined them at the truck. He had admitted to being tired of eating alone, and tonight seemed as good as any for him to cash in on his rain check. She just didn't want to mention it with anyone else around.

She couldn't deny the anticipation she felt as she left her room and searched the walkways for some sign of him, or the need she felt to keep that anticipation in check when she knocked on the door to his room on the outside chance that he was a minute late, too, and they could walk to the truck together.

When all she heard on the other side of his door was silence, she gave up and hurried toward the parking lot.

Andy, the documentary audio tech had a doughnut in his mouth and his hands full with a coffee cup and doughnut box when she saw him walking toward the van.

"Hey," he mumbled, the greeting muffled by fried and frosted dough.

"Good morning to you, too," she replied, smiling, and noticed Ed walking toward the silver truck carrying a bag of his own. So much for talking to Matt now.

She made her easy smile stay right where it was. "I don't suppose you have a bagel in there, do you?"

"Nope," he replied, setting his breakfast on the hood. Keys jangled as he pulled them from the pocket of his tattered jeans. "But we can stop and get you one on the way. Matt said to make sure you're not skipping meals. I'm supposed to see that you take breaks more often, too. Don't want any repeats of yesterday."

Her smile died before she could stop it. "He's not here?"

"Just got back from taking him to the airport. He's got a problem on one of his other jobs."

"When will he be back?"

"Soon as he can be, I imagine. Depends on how long it takes him to get things straightened out."

Four days later, Matt still hadn't returned. But the roof was on, most of the doors and windows were in and the temperature had dropped. That was good news and bad because, while the first storm had stayed out at sea, a new one had developed and was teasing everyone with the promise of rain and blustery winds.

The possibility of bad weather was actually the last thing on Ashley's mind as she sat in her room late in the evening with her day planner, counting backward to the little witches' hat that indicated her last period a little over a month ago. It hadn't been much of one, far lighter than usual, and it had only lasted a couple of days. But she had been in the throes of beating herself up over her night with Matt and feeling the pressure and strain of catching up on a month's worth of work in three weeks, so she chalked up the deviation in her pattern to stress. All she'd cared about was that she'd had a period, which had relieved her enormously of the possibility of anything…unexpected. Even though she and Matt had used protection the first two times they'd made love that night at her brother's, they hadn't had anything to use the third.

She closed the leather-bound calendar, trying to dismiss the uneasy thought that she had been relieved too soon. She was only late by a few days. And her body was still under stress, only now from the weather. She'd even passed out from it.

That thought didn't help. Between being late and the

morning queasiness she'd blamed on everything from hurrying, to the heat, to not eating, she couldn't quite shake the thought that the reporter from the *Sun Daily News* might actually have the story he was looking for.

Chapter Ten

The day after Matt had left Gray Lake, another tropical storm started building off the coast of Florida. Last evening, he had heard that the National Weather Service had upgraded that tropical storm to a hurricane and issued a hurricane watch. By that morning, the watch had become a warning. That meant the storm would hit within twenty-four hours. Or less.

The Shelter project sat in the middle of its projected path.

Because Matt had been up to his hard hat in meetings and minor crises, he had asked the secretary in the construction trailer at the Newport mall site to keep an eye on The Weather Channel for him. He'd been on a steel girder, three stories in the air when she'd called him on his headset to pass the warning on.

Within an hour, he had been on the phone to Ed. His first thought had been that he needed to get back to help secure the project. His second was to get Ashley out of harm's way.

He had already decided that he wanted her gone, anyway. The storm had just made it easier to have her leave.

He had been away from her for less than a day when he'd realized just how much he didn't trust the pull he felt toward her. He had no trouble recognizing pure sexual attraction. Having had sex with her, he knew how she felt, how she made him feel and he'd have had to be dead not to want her again. And he did. He couldn't be within ten feet of her without craving her, especially the way he'd seen her lately, without the perfect makeup, the perfect clothes. She looked far more touchable. Softer. Sexier. He just wasn't sure if he wanted her in his bed because she was a beautiful, desirable woman or because he still felt some lingering need to prove something to himself. There had been a time when she had epitomized a class of women he couldn't have. As trusting of him as she had become, the last thing he wanted to do was use her just to prove that he now could.

He could think of a few other reasons to halt the direction of their relationship, too, a couple having to do with her brother and father, but those thoughts were canceled by the voice on the truck's radio. Dale had picked him up at the Gray Lake airport two hours ago. Now, six hours after first hearing of the impending storm and having stopped at three building-supply centers for materials, they had just pulled up to the nearly deserted Shelter site.

"*...moving much faster than expected. Hurricane Edwin is expected to make landfall by six o'clock this evening. Evacuation of coastal areas from Key West to Palm Harbor has been ordered. Storm surges are expected to reach...*"

"So much for taking our time," Matt said, as Dale cut the engine, killing the radio. "Looks like we have about an hour to get these boards up and get out of here."

Both men reached for their doors. Tidal surges wouldn't be a problem as far inland as they were, but damaging winds and torrential rain definitely would be.

Ed hurried for the truck, dust swirling past his feet in the breeze. "Did you get any more plastic?" he called. "I only had enough to cover the one pile of lumber."

Solid gray clouds blanketed the sky. The breeze that actually felt quite pleasant at the moment, carried the smell of impending rain.

"I think we got the last roll in town," Matt called back. "And the last dozen sheets of plywood. Everybody's sold out."

Dale was already at the back of the truck, lowering the gate.

Heading there himself to help pull sheets of plywood from the bed to cover windows and openings, Matt glanced toward the house.

The gray block structure rising from the construction debris on the dirt lot looked different with its roof on. It hadn't been shingled yet, but a solid deck of plywood covered the rafters. As long as the wind didn't get too greedy, whatever they put inside should stay dry.

It seemed strange not to see the place swarming with workers, or to hear the din of hammers and saws. It seemed stranger still for the street to be empty of gawkers with their coolers and lawn chairs out on the street. But with Ashley gone, even without the storm that would have kept them away, there was no longer a reason for them to be there.

Or so he was thinking when he caught sight of her through one of the newly installed front windows.

His eyebrows jammed together like lightning bolts. It was only then that he realized that the white van shouldn't have been there, either. He'd just become so used to seeing it parked across the street that its presence hadn't registered.

"Why is Ashley still here?" His glance landed on Ed. "I asked you to tell her to go home."

"I did. But she said she's not going anywhere. She said the last storm turned out to be nothing and this one probably will, too."

"If she believes that, she's the only person in the state who does. Hasn't she turned on a radio? A television?"

"Didn't ask."

Scowling at the back of Ed's head, Matt grabbed the end of a board so Dale could pull out another. He didn't want her there. Aside from the fact that it wasn't safe, he wanted her and all the potential grief she could cause him tucked neatly away from him and his very well-ordered life.

He glanced around, just now noticing what else was missing.

"If she's here, where are all the reporters?"

"I imagine they're all in Fort Myers or Sarasota getting ready to cover the storm. Haven't seen a single one today. Could be they're at the shelter they set up over at Gray Lake High School, too."

"She should have gone with them."

"Well, I'll tell you what," Ed said, grabbing the end of the cumbersome board so they could carry it to the new picture window by the new front door. "I'm glad she stayed. She's the one who got those documentary boys interested in working on the house and, if she'd gone, they would have left and we wouldn't have gotten near as much done as we did the past few days."

The documentary crew had taken to working more hours on than off, Ed told him. The older man also said he suspected they enjoyed the work far more than what they were being paid to do, since what they were being paid to do looked about as interesting to him as watching plumbers' putty dry.

"We sure wouldn't be getting things nailed down here like we are, either," Ed continued over the flap of the break awning in the warm breeze. "All of our volunteers are home securing their own houses and taking care of their own families. It's just been the four of us trying to get all the equipment and supplies inside. We just couldn't get the windows covered until you got here with the plywood."

"What happened to the plywood we'd stocked in case the last storm hit?"

"We used it on the roof."

Matt started to ask why he hadn't replaced it. But staying on top of supplies wasn't Ed's responsibility. It was his own. Just like it was his responsibility to get Ashley and her three shadows somewhere safe.

He and his two men could finish up here.

At least, that was his thought before Dale's colorful curse joined the slam of wood against metal. The stiffening breeze had caught the board he'd just pulled from the truck bed and ripped it from his hands.

Gusting wind wasn't a good sign.

"Hey, Matt," Ed called over that same gust. "You want these nailed as we go?"

"Hang on, Dale," Matt shouted behind him. "I'll help you. We might as well," he replied, turning back to Ed. "Otherwise we'll be chasing them down the street. I'll be right back."

He needed a hammer and nails. He also needed to help Dale carry the board he was wrestling. What frustrated him as he headed for the silver truck he'd left with Ed was that he couldn't be in both places at once.

The breadth of his frustrations widened as a distinctly feminine voice drifted from behind him. "We need to get those inside, too," he heard Ashley say. "And those rolls over there."

He turned at the efficient command to see her come out of the utility-room doorway and into the unfinished and open garage. Right behind her came her documentary crew.

The trio headed for the crated windows that hadn't been installed. Stacked beside them were dozens of rolls of ant-acid-pink insulation and boxes of roofing shingles. They had no way of covering the gaping hole for the garage door and everything in there now could be either broken, turned into missiles or blown away.

He watched the kid with the ponytail carry off two cardboard boxes of shingles. The director in his backward ball cap and his audio man in the red one picked up a crated window.

As if sensing his presence, or maybe just sensing that she was being watched, Ashley turned to look across chunks of cut lumber and swirling sawdust between the garage and the street. Her ponytail bounced with the movement. Beneath the bill of her cap, her mouth curved in a smile.

That smile was quick and welcoming. It also faltered in the space of seconds. He didn't know if he'd killed it himself because it seemed to take him a few moments to return it, or because she had noticed the palm frond flying by the truck and decided the storm wasn't going away, after all. Whichever it was, she turned without a word to grapple with a roll of insulation herself.

Gripping the bulky roll by its plastic wrapper, Ashley dragged it toward the doorway opening and ventured a cautious glance toward Matt. He had his back to her, his arms spread low and wide as he helped Dale fight the wind for possession of an eight-foot-wide board. They were saying something about having to cut the boards in half.

If Matt's faint and forced smile was any indication, Ed had just proved himself right. He had warned her that Matt wouldn't like it if she didn't do as he'd asked. And he definitely didn't seem all that pleased to see her there.

She couldn't believe how ambivalent she'd felt when Ed had told her that morning that Matt wanted her to go back to Virginia.

He said he didn't want you where you might get hurt, Ed had told her. *He wants you on the next plane out.*

If she'd had any doubt about Matt's protectiveness toward her, it had been pretty much erased when she'd then asked if he wanted the other volunteers to stay away from the site, too. Ed admitted that the only person Matt had seemed worried about when he'd called was her. The wizened old carpenter had looked a bit disconcerted when he'd said that, pausing as if he'd just realized how telling the admission had been. He'd then gone on to make it clear that he wasn't having any part of any argument over why she hadn't listened if Matt got upset about her ignoring his request.

The wind picked up, bending the tall palm trees in the vacant lot across the street and snapping at the blue canopy she needed to take down. She'd told Ed she thought this storm might go away like the others had, but she didn't believe that for a minute. She'd listened to the weather reports right along with the rest of them, and she hated the thought of the damage the storm could do. Yet the precarious weather now served to curb her concern about Matt's displeasure with her. As preoccupied as he had to be with getting the site secured, he probably wasn't worried about her being there at all.

After four days and still no witches' hat on her calendar, she didn't even want to consider what she was worried about herself.

Not that there was time for her to be concerned about much of anything other than the wind when she hurried out of the garage toward the canopy that was about to become airborne.

A gust caught inside the twelve-foot square of blue canvas, lifting enough to pull one of the aluminum legs from where it had been driven into dirt. She snatched at the pole across from it, thinking to collapse the whole thing before it turned into a kite.

"We've got it," Matt said from behind her. "Grab the loose one, Dale."

The burly carpenter snagged the silver pole before it could whip around and spear someone. As he did, she grabbed the flapping fabric.

"Hey, Andy! Steve!" Ed called from twenty yards away. "I need one of you to help me here!"

"Let them finish what they're doing," Matt called back to him. With a single jerk, he pulled another pole from the ground. "You and Ashley cover the windows in front. Dale and I will get the ones in back."

Ashley caught his unreadable glance. "Go ahead," he said, sounding intent only on doing what needed to be done. "We have to get that glass covered. We'll throw this in the back of the truck."

The need to hurry increased in direct proportion to the strength of the wind. The balmy breeze that had seemed so lovely to her earlier was now turning blustery and unpredictable. No sooner had she picked up one end of the wide board to help Ed cover the window than the wind caught the bill of her cap and sent it flying. With bits of vegetation from the overgrown lots around them also swirling past, she let the cap go and pressed her weight against the board to hold it in place so Ed could nail it to the window frame.

Within minutes the deep buzz of the saw filled the air as Matt and Dale went to work cutting plywood. The low, heavy clouds almost seemed to absorb the piercing sound, softening it as she hurried to help Ed cover the remaining pile of lumber with plastic. The wind grabbed and tugged at the protective sheeting, causing the ends of her hair to crackle from static when the plastic flew up at her face. The phenomenon seemed strange to her considering the humidity in the air, but even that dampness had a different feel to it now that the temperature had dropped. By the time they had secured the plastic with cement blocks so the wood wouldn't get soaked and warp, the odd feel to the air had her as edgy as Matt looked when she saw him come out of the garage and glance toward the threatening sky.

It took them the better part of an hour to get the remaining windows and door openings covered and for Ron and his crew to finish carrying everything inside that was small enough to get through a doorway. By then the size of the vegetation bouncing down the street had turned from fronds and leaves to small tree limbs.

"Okay, you guys, you're out of here!" Matt motioned Ron and his crew toward their van. "Ed said they've set up a shelter at the high school. You going there or to the motel?"

"The motel. We stocked up on food and stuff yesterday."

"Then, we'll see you there in a few minutes. Ed, you and Dale, too," he insisted. "We've done all we can here."

Ed started digging in his pocket. "You'll need your truck key."

"I've got a spare. Just get going."

"What about the sawhorses?" Dale called, spotting the two they'd used just outside the garage. On the ground between them lay the long orange extension cord they'd also forgotten when they'd rolled the saw back inside.

"I'll get them. You go."

"I've got them," Ashley said and turned on her heel.

Matt was behind her. "Get in the truck."

"You grab one. I'll get the other."

"Don't you ever listen?"

The wind tugged more strands of hair loose from her ponytail. The rest it whipped into a halo as she curled her hands around the battered wood supports and headed for the nearly empty garage. Behind them, the van started up with a roar. Truck doors opened and closed with sharp reports.

"I do when what I hear makes sense," she replied, but it was doubtful Matt heard her. The sounds of the vehicles, of the wind, of her words were all obliterated by a crash of thunder that almost had her dropping her load and covering her heart with her palm.

With one sawhorse already in hand, Matt grabbed the one she'd carried.

Her heart still jumping, she picked up the cord, hurriedly coiling it on her way into the garage and glanced behind her.

The white van had already pulled out and was leaving the dead-end street. The blue truck with Dale and Ed inside was right behind.

Wood met cement block with a clatter when Matt shoved his load up against the back wall. "Is there anything else?"

Her glance swept the ground. "Not that I can see. Do you think the house is secure enough?"

"It's as good as it's going to get." He took the cord from her, jammed it behind the sawhorses. "Let's go. That sky is going to open any minute. I want to get out of here while we can still see."

Hoping the house truly would be all right, she hurried beside him while he pulled keys from the khaki slacks he hadn't taken time to change. Wondering if the odd feel in the air was making him edgy, too, or if he was now as concerned as she was about what the wind might do to all their hard work, she glanced down the street once more.

The thought that the others were already out of sight had barely registered when she felt the hair on her arms stand on end.

Lightning flashed, a strange white-green glow against the slate-colored sky. Thunder cracked at that same instant, rattling the windows in the truck just ahead of them and jarring her teeth. But it was the boom and crackle beyond them that made her heart lurch an instant before she heard Matt swear.

A block away, a power line bowed and arched on the cracked pavement, sparks spraying like fireworks. As if in slow motion, the power pole beyond it tipped and landed with its crossbar on the opposite side of the street.

The street only had one outlet. Vegetation blocked one end. A live and snapping electrical line now blocked the other.

With her glance frozen on that whipping cable, Matt reached into the bed of the truck, came up with a hammer and locked his hand around hers.

"Into the house!"

The wind snatched his words, tore at their clothes, their hair as they turned and ran.

They'd barely darted under the garage roof when the rain hit with the force of a fire hose. The din of it beating overhead nearly drowned the howl of the wind. In the space of seconds the temperature seemed to drop another ten degrees.

Ashley backed up, seeking the dry space behind her as the deluge blew inside the threshold. The sheeting rain made it seem as if she was looking through cellophane. Wavering images of bending palms brightened with another flash of lightning. The stop sign that had been at the end of the street separated itself from its pole on its way by.

She turned to see Matt prying the plywood from the door opening that had been covered only minutes ago. He had the claw of a hammer wedged beneath the thin sheet and had just ripped it halfway off when she heard what sounded like another board flapping against the house.

Afraid it was one covering one of the new windows, she started to dart for the wide doorway—only to feel her arm nearly come out of its socket when Matt grabbed her and pulled her back.

"What do you think you're doing?" He spun her around, his expression as ominous as the storm raging around them. "You could get hit by something out there, if you don't get blown away first! And why in the hell didn't you leave like I asked you to?" he demanded, now that he had the chance.

"I'm trying to rescue a window," she shot back, defenses joining the pump of adrenaline as he hauled her toward the loosened plywood. The wind threw strands of hair across her face, flattened her white cotton shirt against her body. "And I didn't leave because I'm tired of having something go wrong with nearly everything I do. I wasn't going anywhere if there was anything I could do to help salvage this house."

"What are you talking about?" With the groan of metal reluctantly leaving wood, he pulled one side of the plywood back enough to expose the dim interior of upright studs and darkening patches of cement. "A hurricane is what went wrong here. You can't possibly blame yourself for that."

She slipped inside. "I can blame myself for anything I want," she insisted, watching him squeeze in right behind. "I'd blame myself for not staying to help," she informed him just as he snagged her arm.

With a jolt, he tugged her forward, moving her away from the pipes she nearly backed into. The motion also put her inches from his chest.

"If it's guilt you're after, then blame yourself for having to ride this out under a leaking roof. I didn't want you caught in this."

"And I didn't want to go." Her chin came up, partly in defiance. Partly because she had to tip back her head to see his face. If she had left, she was afraid she might never see him again, and that, over all her other reasons, was the very root of why she'd stayed. "I'm sorry we're stuck here, but I missed you."

The only light in the structure was what leaked in along with the rain between the gaps in the plywood overhead and where one large sheet lifted and slammed at the far end of the roof. She figured that was the board she'd heard, but she was far more interested in what the flickering gray light revealed in Matt's expression than in the cacophony surrounding them.

The quality of his tension seemed to undergo a subtle shift as he stood with his fingers coiled around her arms. His glance swept her face, his eyes glittering in the dim light.

She missed him. Of everything she might have said, Matt honestly hadn't expected to hear that. He hadn't expected the way the thought tugged at something long buried inside him, either. Or the sudden reluctance he felt to do what he strongly suspected he should do and ease away from her.

The rational part of his mind told him he should do just that, and go see what he could do about the board slamming at the other end of the house. He should let her go and find something to catch the drips and rivulets of water the pounding rain drove through the overhead cracks. The task would be futile, but it would give him something to think about other than how soft he knew her mouth felt, or the heavy ache he could already feel low in his gut when she looked at him so uncertainly and offered a faltering smile.

"If you stay mad, this is going to be a really long night."

He knew he didn't trust the pull he felt toward her. He just couldn't ever remember why that was when he was touching her. And now that he was touching her, now that she was trying to coax his smile, that was really all he cared about.

"I'm not mad." He smoothed her tangled hair from her face, catching the strands she hadn't already shoved away and brushing them from the corner of her mouth.

"You're sure?"

"Yeah," he murmured. "I just wish that you had listened."

She touched her hand to his chest. "How about I listen next time? Whatever you ask me to do, I will."

"Promise?"

"Within reason," she qualified, her hand splaying over his heart.

"Fair enough."

Thunder crashed as he lowered his head. He felt her jump, heard her quick intake of breath when his mouth brushed hers. He would have told her she didn't need to worry about the thunder as he framed her face with his hands, that it was the lightning preceding it that could cause the damage. But he brushed her lips again and she opened to him, welcoming the touch of his tongue with a sigh, and he forgot all about offering reassurances.

She tasted like warm honey, felt like pure heaven. She looped her arms around his neck, letting his hands drift down her body, letting him shape her, touch as he wanted to touch. Her breasts crushed against his chest, her slender thighs molded to his. Their breaths mingled. His heart began to pound. He could feel hers pounding, too, beating hard against him as that heady exploration slowly turned to more insistent demand.

He backed her up, edging her away from the board clattering against the door opening behind them and pressed her against a post six feet away. With her head resting against the column of wood, his mouth on hers, he tugged her shirt from her jeans and slid his hands up under it. The feel of her skin was like satin beneath his hands, but it was the feel of her breasts in his palms that shot lightning of a different sort through his entire body.

The need to feel her, all of her, grew more urgent by the second.

He found the clasp at the back of her bra, freed it to let her breasts spill into his hands. Greed tore through him as he lifted her shirt and lowered his head to capture one tantalizing bud in his mouth. He felt it bloom against his tongue, felt her tremble when he fastened his arm around the small of her back to pull her closer.

She seemed to urge him closer still. Threading her fingers through his hair, she splayed them over his skull as if to hold him right where he was.

Wind whistled through cracks. Something solid bumped the side of the house. He barely noticed as he drew her other nipple into his mouth and slowly rubbed away the moisture from the one he'd just tended. At his gentle ministering, he felt her sag a little, as if her knees were giving out and all that held her up was him and the post.

He rose up over her. Steadying her in his arms, he bent his head to her ear. He tugged at her lobe, kissed the smooth skin behind it.

"Ever make love in a hurricane?"

Ashley's breath trembled out. Ever make love on a sailboat? he'd once asked. Sliding her arms around his neck to keep from sliding right to the floor, she shook her head. As badly as he had her aching, she would make love with him anywhere. "Have you?"

His breath feathered her neck. "Never." With the tip of his tongue, he traced the shell of her ear. "So," he murmured, making her shiver, ''since we're both new at this, I guess we'll just have to improvise.''

His hands slipped to her waist.

There was nothing below them but concrete, much of it scattered with sawdust and a few growing puddles that they could see only when lightning illuminated the cracks overhead. But where they were, it was dry and as protected from the elements as they were going to get.

Not that Ashley much cared where they were or what surrounded them. They had the privacy of the walls, the cocoon of the storm. As Matt drew her down, then drew her over him, stretching her over the length of his body, all she cared about was him and the storm he was building inside her.

He captured her mouth with his as his hands skimmed down her back. He cupped her bottom, pulling her against him, arching a little himself, then caught his breath at the feel of her stomach against his erection. He kissed her deeply, ravenously, breaking only to pull her shirt over her head and drop her bra on top of it. She kissed him back, sliding her hands under his shirt, pushing it up so she could feel the washboard muscles of his stomach against her skin.

She had never before felt what Matt could make her feel. He pulled a need from deep within her, something that made her mindless and demanded only that she get as close to him as she could. Or maybe, that need had been there all along and what he'd done was simply unleash it. It was a primitive thing, something that felt basic and right and so essential that it struck to the very core of her being.

The smells of raw wood and rain mingled with the lingering scents of his soap and her shampoo. He had pulled the clip from her hair, freeing it to fall over her shoulders, veiling their faces as their tongues tangled.

His hand slid between their bodies. She could feel him

working at the snap of her jeans, tugging down the zipper. Made bold by his raw, unmasked hunger for her, she slipped down to help, groping for his buckle, unfastening his belt before he lifted his hips to tug his wallet from his pants and retrieve the little foil packet inside. Within a few frantic heartbeats, khaki and denim were shoved down and pushed away as they rolled to their sides, seeking each other with mouths, tongues and hands.

She mirrored his motions, touching him as he touched her, playing an erotic game of follow the leader that nearly drove him out of his mind. With the driving rain pounding all around them, the wind ripping at the boards, drafts of it swirling past them, Matt slipped the condom over himself and eased her back on top of him.

Need swept through him, sharp and pulsing as he closed his hands around her small waist. Drinking in the sweet taste of her mouth, he lifted her, raising her hips, then lowered her, slowly, slipping inside her feminine warmth. Sheathed within her, he swallowed her small moan and gritted his teeth against need so exquisite it bordered on pain.

He had wanted her beneath him. He had wanted her long, supple legs twined with his. But the ground was too hard, and his weight and the unforgiving concrete would leave her bruised if he drove into her the way he desperately wanted to now. He held himself in check as he eased her back to sit astride him, and traced the shape of her breasts with his hands. A flash of lightning shot pale beams through the overhead cracks, illuminating her, making her skin look like marble in that too brief instant. The feel of her tested every ounce of control he possessed. The sight of her with her head back, his hands on her body, his body in hers, nearly sent that control up in flames.

The hard muscles of his stomach clenched as he sat forward. Bracing his arm across her back, he held her against him, holding them both upright so she could lock her legs around his hips. Seeming as needy as he felt, she pulled off his shirt, her fingers biting into his skin. Her body trembled as she clung to his shoulders. Buried within her, he felt her move against him, heard her whimper his name.

He murmured hers, thrusting back, and claimed her mouth once more.

He had never craved a woman the way he craved her. The need burning inside him was like a living thing, clawing at his gut, coming precariously close to his heart. Something about that seemed terribly dangerous, like something he had meant to avoid, but then he felt the little tremors shuddering through her body, felt them building in his and he wasn't thinking at all. He could only feel. And what he felt had him wanting her all over again long after she fell asleep in his arms.

Chapter Eleven

The luminous dial of Matt's watch glowed two-eighteen in the morning. It had been an hour since the last clap of thunder had rattled the windows or lightning had illuminated the space where he sat with Ashley curved across his lap. Rain still beat with a vengeance and the wind still blew, but it no longer sent swirling drafts across the floor or threatened to tear the plywood from the roof.

With his back to the plastic-covered rolls of insulation, his legs outstretched, he felt Ashley stir. She curled against him, her legs drawn up, her head resting against his chest.

They had shaken out their clothes and pulled them back on hours ago, checking each other by feel to make sure labels were on the inside and not out. They had then proceeded to work most of them back off again after he'd pushed her hair aside to check the back of her shirt and started kissing her neck. Clinging to each other right where they'd stood, they had collapsed in each other's arms long minutes later, and they'd had to straighten themselves out all over again.

He couldn't believe how quickly his body responded to hers, or how badly he could want her so soon after finding release. He wasn't a man of extraordinary sexual appetite. He was just a normal, red-blooded male with normal, red-blooded desires, but with Ashley, he simply couldn't seem to get enough. It had been that way the first time with her, too. As he dipped his head to kiss the top of hers, he clearly remembered feeling the sharp need that had made it seem as if he'd barely taken the edge off his desire for her.

He felt that way now. Only now, with her sleeping in his arms, that need was getting all tangled up with concern and caring and something else that didn't feel terribly familiar. Enveloped by the darkness and the din of the rain, he told himself there would be plenty of time in the cold light of day to worry about why that felt so dangerous. Right now, he would just hold her.

Her hand edged to the middle of his chest. "You're awake," she murmured, the warmth of her breath stealing through his shirt.

The darkness was absolute. He could see nothing but the unrelenting blackness that provided his temporary reprieve. Yet, he had no trouble finding what he was looking for as he cupped her face and tipped it toward his.

With her head on his shoulder, he touched a kiss to her lips. "So are you."

Warm and drowsy, she snuggled closer and slipped her arm around his neck. "I've been awake for a while."

"Me, too."

He shifted a little.

"How uncomfortable are you?" she asked.

He would probably ache like the devil after spending the night on a slab of concrete. One leg had gone to sleep, then awakened with the sensation of needles prickling down his calf. A muscle in his back threatened to protest hours of being in one position. But he was only vaguely aware of those particular body parts. "I'm not."

She smiled against his mouth. "Liar. I heard you groan."

He smiled back as he slipped his hands under her shirt to stroke the velvety skin of her back. As he did, she shifted against him, one soft breast brushing the side of his chest. "That was hours ago. And that was only because of what you do to me."

Her breath trembled against his cheek. "Me, too."

"You, too, what?"

"What you do to me." Ashley's voice dropped to a tone of sleepy confession. "I've never felt the way I do when I'm with you."

Protectiveness merged with a sense of possession as he sought the sweetness of her mouth. Instinctively, he drew her closer, deepened the kiss. It would be so easy to turn her in his arms, to move her legs to straddle his hips and feast once more on her beautiful body. There was only one problem. They'd used the two condoms he'd had with him. Even though he ached for her, he wasn't about to play Russian roulette with their futures. They'd gotten away with it once. He wasn't going to push their luck again.

"If I don't stop now," he murmured, gentling his voice as he drew her arm from his neck, "I won't want to stop at all. And we have to." Weaving his fingers through hers, he clasped them near his heart. "We're out of protection.

"We got lucky on the boat. That last time," he quietly reminded her, drawing her head back to his shoulder. He pressed a kiss to the top of her head, soothed the faint tension in her body by slowly stroking her back. "I don't think it's a chance either one of us wants to take."

* * *

Ashley didn't know how long she lay in Matt's arms listening to the beat of the rain and the uneasy voice in her head that whispered they might already be too late. It seemed like hours that she lay there caught between feeling she should pull away because that was what he would do if he knew what she was worried about—and feeling that it was too soon to panic because she didn't know for certain that she had anything to panic about.

She didn't think she slept at all. At least, it didn't seem as if she had until she became aware of a thread of sunlight slanting across her face. The chirp of birds filtered into her consciousness. Beneath her ear, she could feel the strong, even beat of Matt's heart where her head lay against his chest.

Blinking at a deeply shadowed row of upright studs, she looked up to see tiny strips of light creeping between several sheets of the plywood overhead.

"We need to get up." Matt's deep voice rumbled in his chest, vibrating against her ear. His words sounded rusty, as if he, too, had finally fallen asleep. "The guys are coming."

The thought that they were about to be discovered curled up like the lovers they had become did what it usually took caffeine to accomplish. Suddenly fully conscious, Ashley felt him lift his arm as she raised her head.

"I didn't hear the trucks."

"I didn't, either." With a faint groan and the crack of his knees, he rose over her and held out his hand. "I can hear their voices."

Needing to hurry, she didn't stop to see if she could hear what had caught Matt's attention. Threading her fingers through her hair with one hand, she reached for his with the other.

In the shadows, his face looked craggy from the long, fairly sleepless night. A night's growth of beard shadowed his lean jaw. With her hair ruffled from the wind and his fingers, and his polo shirt hanging loose over his khakis and probably flecked with sawdust, she could only imagine how they must look.

"Matt! Ashley! You in there?"

"Yeah, Dale!" Unzipping his khakis, he started tucking. "We're here," he called back.

Though the carpenter's voice was filtered, it sounded close enough to tell Ashley it would only be moments before they had company. Spurred by the thought that held a hundred little insecurities at bay, she told herself she could worry later about what sort of future she had with Matt and tucked cotton into denim herself. As she did, Matt reached over and brushed at her shoulders.

In turn, she brushed his, then ridded him as best she could of the sawdust clinging to his back.

"You guys okay in there?"

"Hey, Ed," Matt replied, recognizing the older man's gravelly voice. "We're fine. How about you?"

"Spent the night playing poker," he called back. Something rustled, the sound like a limb being dragged away. "Never play with Bull. The man can't lose."

"You played with Bull?"

"He came down looking for Miss K. We were all getting worried about the two of you when you didn't show up. Started to get real concerned when we checked the shelter just now and didn't find you there."

"We couldn't get out. A power line blocked the road."

"Saw that." Ed's voice filtered through the thin plywood covering the doorways and window openings. "That's why we had to park the trucks a block away. Lost a few shingles over at the motel, and the power's out. Heard on the radio that Gray Lake just caught the edge of the storm. Most of the damage is a hundred miles north." His voice grew closer. "There really isn't much damage around here at all. Few tree limbs is all. How's it inside?"

Ashley watched Matt's glance move over her face. "Pretty much the way you left it," he called back, his focus on her as he smoothed something from beneath her eye. "The plywood on the roof has probably already started to warp, so we'll have to pull that off and replace it, but other than that, I think we came through it okay."

His hand slipped over to tuck her hair behind her ear.

"Is there water at the motel?" Matt called, intent on her even as he spoke to the man she could now hear in the garage. "Or is that out, too?"

"There's water. Just no power."

His voice dropped. "We'll go back and clean up after we've checked things out here." The sound of heavy footsteps had his hand falling away, robbing her of the reassurance of his touch. "Are you ready?"

Ashley didn't know if she was or not. Reality was on the other side of the walls that had sheltered them from the rest of the world, and reality was something she wasn't sure she wanted to face just yet.

The groan of metal and wood had him stepping away.

"Whenever you are," she replied and tried to pretend it didn't bother her when he so abruptly put that distance between them. She should feel grateful that he had, she told herself as the board he'd pried off halfway from the door opening last night came loose. Their relationship wasn't something she wanted out there for public consumption, and they didn't need anyone suspecting just how involved they had become. Matt was all too aware of how she tried to protect her privacy.

The thought didn't relieve the disquiet, though. He wouldn't want his own privacy invaded because of her, either.

The board moved aside with a clatter, allowing in the light that chased shadows from the corners. Ed walked in, checking out them and the suddenly more visible interior. Right behind him was Steve of the documentary crew, camera rolling.

Having brushed off and tucked as best they could, Ashley figured she and Matt were as presentable as they were going to get—considering that their hair still bore the effects of the wind from yesterday. But she needn't have concerned herself with appearances. As Matt moved with Ed through the maze of studs, hands on his hips, his attention completely absorbed by the work they now had to do, she realized there were no other reporters around. Even when she went outside to help the other men pull boards away from the windows and pile up the limbs scattered over the lot, she was spared the intrusion of another camera or microphone. In the aftermath of a hurricane, there were far more pertinent stories to report.

For the legitimate press anyway. The paparazzo whose presence she had noticed at the motel clearly had nothing better to do than cash in on her.

Ashley didn't know if the freelance photographer had checked in to the Cypress Motor Inn or if he was staying somewhere else and just came and went when he figured she'd be around. But she and Matt, who had spent most of the drive to the motel on his cell phone with someone at the Newport site, had no sooner approached her door than she caught a camera flash that had her groaning even as she turned away.

"That shot should get him a few thousand," she muttered.

Preoccupation melted to a scowl as Matt automatically blocked her from view. "What do you mean?"

"I hear the tabloids pay best for shots of people at their worst."

"Was that the same guy you were talking about the other night?"

She'd barely caught a glimpse of the man's dark head before she'd turned away. But that glimpse was enough. "I think so."

For the past hour, it had been apparent that Matt's thoughts were pretty much divided between his projects and the problems they were causing him. But that preoccupation faded as protectiveness slid neatly into place. "Go on inside. I think I'll have a little talk with him."

"No!" she called, not totally trusting Matt's deceptive calm as he started off. Her voice dropped. As much as she would love to have the man and his ilk out of her life, it wasn't worth the hassle and publicity it would bring if Matt got in the guy's face and the little toad decided to sue him for some sort of press rights violation. This particular nuisance was no worse than many others had been. She was more concerned about Matt, anyway. He didn't have time for this. "You have more important things to do," she insisted as the door next to hers flew wide open.

Her bodyguard must have heard her shout. Bull, wearing baggy Hawaiian-print shorts, a T-shirt and a scowl, was between her and Matt before she could blink.

"What's going on?" he demanded, his voice a low rumble. He clearly recognized Matt. It was just as clear that he wouldn't stand down until he heard from the woman he was being paid to protect while at the motel.

Ashley moved from where he had blocked her against her door with his tank-size body. "A paparazzo," she murmured, unable to imagine how a man his size could move so fast.

"I was just going to talk to him," Matt defended. "I wasn't going to do anything illegal."

"You talking about the short guy?" Bull asked him. "Kind of round? Dark hair?"

"You've seen him?"

"I've seen him around. Don't worry, Matt," the man who really did look more like a "Bull" than a "Jeffrey" assured, "he won't get close to her." Dark eyes sharp and intent, he looked to where Ashley stood with her room key in her hand. "Are you in now?"

"I'm just going to shower and change and go back to the site. Barring another hurricane," she said with a smile, "I'll be back at the usual time."

Matt's preoccupation returned as he glanced at his watch. "How long do you need?"

"May I have half an hour?"

He only gave her twenty-five minutes. She heard the knock on her door while she was tying her boots and listening to a news update. The electricity had come back on while they had been talking to her bodyguard, a little blessing that had made taking a shower so much easier than trying to clean up by Ed's flashlight.

After checking to make sure that it was Matt, she opened the door and stepped back so he could come in.

She didn't know if he'd nicked himself shaving because he'd been in a hurry or because his mind had been elsewhere. Whichever it was, he walked in with a tiny cut on the underside of his jaw, his hair still damp and wearing the same preoccupied expression he'd worn most of the morning.

"I still have five minutes," she pointed out, picking up her other boot as he closed the door. Sitting on the side of the bed, she pulled it on over her clean white sock. "But I only need two. Have you eaten?"

"I had some chips. I'll get something else later."

"That was nutritious." She hadn't done much better herself. All she'd had was a piece of plain bread. "You took a rain check on dinner the other night," she reminded him. "Do you want to cash it in on pasta here this evening?"

She watched his glance cut to the door adjoining her room and Bull's. Seeing it closed, he snagged the chair by the floor lamp and pulled it over to sit across from her.

An uneasy little knot formed in her stomach when he picked up her hands. His feet planted wide, elbows on his thighs, he clasped her fingers in his.

"I'm not going to be here tonight, Ashley. I have to go back to Newport. I'm leaving right after I drop you off at the site."

The knot loosened a little. For an awful moment, she thought he was going to say something she didn't want to hear. It was that sort of seriousness she sensed in him. But him going back to Newport wasn't so bad. It was his work, after all. And she knew how dedicated he was to it.

"How bad is the problem there?"

"Problems," he corrected. "As in, 'multiple.'"

"Are they anything that will stop construction?"

"Stop it?" Looking pensive, she glanced up from where his thumb brushed hers. "Nothing like that. They're just causing delays that cause more delays because I have subcontractors that can't come in and do their job until the sub before them gets theirs finished. By the time the contractor who caused the original delay finally gets his act together, the other subs are in the middle of other jobs they've contracted for and I've got this domino effect going that's nothing but a..."

"Mess," she concluded for him.

The sound he made was half snort, half sigh. "Yeah."

She tipped her head, smiled. "So why are you sitting here when you have so much work to do?"

His gray eyes skimmed her face. A faint smile tugged at his mouth. "Because I needed to say goodbye to you. And I didn't want to say something like that with all the others around."

Despite his expression, the knot seemed to tighten again. She didn't know if it was because of the way his smile faded just before he spoke. Or, because his phrasing made saying goodbye seem almost…final.

She blinked down at their hands, at the almost unconscious way he stroked her skin.

"You don't need to take me to the site," she told him, thinking of all he had on his mind, thinking that the last thing she wanted to do just then was add her insecurity to his stresses. He had been guarded with her around the others at the site, but she needed to believe that was only because he'd been doing his part to keep their relationship private. Not because he was questioning the direction it had taken. "It will save time if I drop you off at the airport and just drive myself over."

"I need Ed to take me. I have to talk to him about ordering more supplies."

"Would it help if I did that? Order the supplies, I mean. Just tell me what we need and I'll get on the phone."

He considered her for a moment. And, for a moment, she thought he might say that he would take her up on her offer. Or, at least, that he would have Ed tell her what materials they required and she could spare his lead carpenter the time on the phone.

Instead, he reached over and cupped her cheek in his palm.

''That still doesn't solve the problem of leaving you without doing this.''

Ashley couldn't count the times his kisses had altered her heart rate and her breathing and narrowed her awareness to where it included only the two of them. That was what he did now. Yet, there was something new in the feel of his mouth on hers. It wasn't the gentle discovery she had tasted so often. It wasn't hunger or heat or passion. It was a tenderness that she'd never felt in all those times before because this time that tenderness felt strangely bittersweet.

She pulled back, afraid to meet his eyes, afraid not to.

As she did, his fingers traced the shape of her jaw. His glance followed the path. The faint furrow of his forehead made it look as if he were memorizing the shape of her face and texture of her skin. Yet, when his eyes returned to hers, all she saw in the smoky depths was the hint of a smile.

''See my problem?'' He took her hand again. Rising, he pulled her to her feet. ''I couldn't do that out there,'' he said, nodding to indicate the outdoors. ''Especially if there was any press around.''

Relief allowed her own smile to return. Falling in love obviously created a whole host of new uncertainties. He didn't seem to be pulling away from her at all. If anything, he seemed to be thinking only of how discreet they needed to be. He wasn't saying goodbye as in ''forever.'' He was simply saying goodbye for now.

At least, that was what she wanted to believe when they left a few moments later to join the others at the site. It was what she needed to believe when he didn't say anything else to her before he and Ed took off for the airport less than an hour later. The belief that she would soon see him again was also the thought that kept her going during the first days he was gone.

* * *

By the afternoon after the storm, work on the house returned to the same pace as before the edges of the hurricane had swept through Gray Lake. Since damage to the entire area had been minimal, nearly all the volunteers were back, pacing themselves in the rising heat and the humidity while the sun slowly turned all that rain to steam. Within days, the wiring the professional electricians had started was completed and the plumbing and insulation installed. Within the week, the roof was on, shingles and all, and the interior maze of studs had been transformed into rooms as wallboard was nailed into place.

Ashley had been assigned to wallboard and trim detail and spent her days nailing baseboards and door casings into place while fantasizing about a long soak in a tub of cool, lavender-scented water, and wondering if Matt would call that evening. She spent her evenings on the phone with friends or her mom—always listening for whichever phone she wasn't using in case Matt had tried to call on the one phone and decided to try the other. Twice, she shared dinner with Jeffery who told her he spent his mornings sleeping, his afternoons playing pool at a local hangout and his nights watching old movies and listening for anyone who didn't belong outside her room.

As for the press, they weren't nearly so troublesome as they had been at first. Because someone at the high-school shelter had called the police to report that people were looking for her the morning after the storm, a mob of reporters had descended within hours trying to scoop the story—including Tony Schultz who had looked visibly disappointed when he'd found her working at the site. Appearing quite safe and well, she had totally ruined his shot at a story about a missing Kendrick. Other than that, the press pretty much left her alone to do what they'd seen her doing for well over a week. The gallery of onlookers was back, though. Its initial ranks had thinned a bit, but new faces eventually sprang up among the die-hards.

Since reporters no longer seemed to be following her everywhere, Ashley had asked Bull last evening to take her in his rental car to the little strip center by the grocery store. She'd needed to buy another cap to replace the one a volunteer had given her because the wind had taken hers. She also needed to run into a drug store.

She wasn't about to mention what she needed there. But any hope of discreetly purchasing a pregnancy test was lost within a minute of walking into the amazingly busy Wal-Mart. No sooner had she entered the feminine products aisle than she found herself faced with three smiling ladies who recognized her immediately. One said she was going to start volunteering to build houses because of her. The others chorused in that they would do the same, just as soon as they had the time.

She thanked them, earnestly told them she was certain their help would be more than welcome and kept going until she reached a display of sunscreen at the end of the aisle.

When she checked out with only a bottle of SPF 45 and a magazine, the cashier recognized her, too—something that gave Ashley pause only because it made her aware of how truly worried she had to be getting about the possibility of being pregnant to have not considered how recognizable she was in Gray Lake. Even if she hadn't had one of the more familiar faces in the country, the local newspaper had carried pictures of her for nearly two weeks. When she'd walked into the store, her only concern had been that paparazzi hadn't followed her in to take a photo of her buying a pregnancy test.

Now, on the phone with her mom twenty-four hours later, she felt even more concern about how late she was, but she felt even more grateful that she hadn't been caught making that particular purchase. Cord's penchant for bad publicity worried her mom enough.

"I don't think it's going to be the problem it could have been," her mother said, her voice as clear as if she'd been right there in the motel room with her. "Cord was able to prove to the attorney for the Securities and Exchange Commission that he didn't even meet the girl until long after the company ceased operations. There was no possibility of her passing him inside information about their stocks.

"Anyway," she continued while Ashley paced restlessly from the kitchenette to the front door, "I thought you'd want to know. I know you were worried about it when you told me that reporter had approached you. Knowing you, you've been worried about it ever since."

A quick tug of guilt made Ashley close her eyes and wrinkle her nose. She was a lousy sister. Preoccupied with her own problems, she had completely forgotten about her brother's involvement with the ex-Enron executive's daughter.

"This doesn't sound like it was Cord's fault at all, Mom."

"This one doesn't," her mom conceded. "But there was still that picture in the *Enquirer* of him and the girl on his sailboat. I understand she was topless."

That bit of news had undoubtedly gone over well at her parents' breakfast table, Ashley thought. She could picture it now. Her mother trying to be tactful as she casually mentioned that one of their staff had mentioned the photo to her, and her dad's rising blood pressure making the vein in his temple throb as he attacked his eggs Benedict and orange juice. "At least Dad doesn't have the hassle of having his holdings investigated," she pointed out, looking for the bright side. "I'm just glad for everyone's sake that it didn't turn into a bigger problem."

"So are we." The words were heartfelt. "It's been almost a year since Cord has been involved in anything disgraceful, so I suppose he was due. I always feel like I'm holding my breath with him, just waiting for the other shoe to drop."

From the weariness in her tone, it seemed that Katherine Kendrick always knew it was only a matter of time before her son managed to create some sort of scandal or embarrassment, or did something unthinking to reflect badly on the family. Until a couple of weeks ago, Ashley couldn't have imagined any member of her family more likely to do that, either. Yet it was now entirely possible that she was about to upstage her brother in the embarrassing publicity department.

Her pacing became more restive as she tried to shake off the nagging thought. She didn't even want to think about how disappointed her mother would be in her if she was pregnant. Or the gossip that would fly among their friends and staff.

"It would just be so nice if he would stop chasing women and settle down with one," she heard her mother muse. "I don't expect him to be a saint, but I hate that he's so careless and indiscreet." The admission came with a sigh. "At least your father and I don't have to worry about the rest of you doing anything irresponsible."

Ashley winced.

"Anyway," her mother quickly continued, clearly ready to move on from that distressing subject. "On a brighter note, has your sister called you yet?"

Grateful for the shift in subject herself, Ashley turned at the stove and paced back the other way. "Tess?"

"She's the only sister you have, dear. Of course, Tess."

"Not tonight. But I was on the phone with Elisa for about an hour going over a couple of new scholarship applications."

Something about her mom's flat, "Oh," held a hint of disappointment.

"Is everything all right with her?"

"She's fine. Wonderful, in fact."

"Then, what's going on?"

"She has news."

"Meaning you know, but you won't tell me?"

"Well, she didn't ask that I not say," her mom carefully qualified. Excitement entered her voice, her lovely, much-photographed smile filling her tone. "And I know she wants you to know. So, I guess I can tell you that your father and I are about to have our first grandchild."

Somewhere down the breezeway, a motel-room door slammed. Laughter rose, then receded. "She's pregnant?"

"About six weeks, she figures. She went to the doctor today."

"Are she and Bradley all right?" By Ashley's calculations, if she was pregnant herself, she was a week ahead of her sister. "I got the feeling when I had lunch with her last month that she was trying awfully hard to pretend everything was okay between the two of them."

"There's an adjustment period in any marriage. I'm sure they're fine," her mother insisted, sounding as if she were willing it to be. "She sounded very excited."

That was a good sign. Tess was an open book. She couldn't fake an emotion if she tried. "Good. If she is, then I am. Will she be going to Camelot soon?"

"She'll be here in two weeks. Bradley has meetings in San Francisco for a few days, so she'll spend that time here. Can you come?"

At the family home under her mother's too-keen eye was pretty much the last place she wanted to go. "Definitely," she replied, since she was accustomed to doing many things she would rather avoid. And she did want to see Tess. "I have one more week here, and I know I'll need at least a week to catch up at the office. The timing will be perfect. It will be good to see you both."

"You, too, dear. Now, call your sister. She's probably been trying to call you all evening."

Ashley told her mom that she would, quickly assured her that she was doing fine when her mom cut in to ask, and said good-night.

She'd barely closed the phone to cut the connection so she could punch out her sister's number when the phone played the first cheerful notes of a Strauss waltz to let her know she had another call.

Determined to sound cheerful herself for her sister's sake, she flipped the phone back open and answered with a bright, "Hi!"

There was a moment's pause before she heard a deep, "Hi, yourself."

Her heart bumped her breastbone.

"Matt," she said and sank to the edge of her bed.

He'd obviously heard the ease drop out of her voice. "You were expecting someone else."

"My sister. She's..." *pregnant,* she started to say, "...supposed to call," she concluded. "How are you?"

"Swamped. It's crazy here. That's why I'm calling." The connection hummed with his pause. "Ed says everything is pretty much on schedule there."

The lurch her heart had given at the sound of his voice settled into a quietly erratic beat. "I guess it is." He sounded tired, she thought. But it was just so good to hear his voice. "A crew came today and installed the kitchen and bathroom cabinets."

"That's what Ed said."

"You just talked to him?"

"A few minutes ago. I needed to let him know I'm sending a man down to fill in for him so he can take those days off for his anniversary. I'm sending the original site manager back, too. He'll take over for me."

"Take over for you?" She hesitated. "For how long?"

"Until the job is finished."

The awful feeling she'd had when he'd kissed her good-bye was back with a vengeance. Desperate to keep her tone even, she took a deep breath, slowly released it. "Does that mean you won't be coming back at all?"

The pause on the other end of the line seemed a little longer this time. "Not before you're scheduled to leave. I really am swamped here, Ashley."

"I see."

"It's been one thing after another," he hurried to add. "I'm hoping to get caught up in a couple of weeks. But it's just not going to happen before then. I'm not even sure when I could see you after that. Once I get this under control, I have—"

"Please," she cut in, wishing he hadn't called at all, wishing he had caught her more prepared. "You don't have to explain." She stood then, pacing to stave off the hurt waiting to be felt and making her voice as light and understanding as she could. "I know about the domino effect. You told me about it," she reminded him. "I don't know what stage your project is in, in Newport, but I imagine you need to get as much done as you can before we get one of our winters. At least the heat and humidity here don't have to be shoveled."

She honestly couldn't have cared less about the effect of weather on construction at that moment. When a man said he didn't know when he could see a woman again, it was a pretty fair bet that he was letting her go.

"There is that."

"Listen, Matt," she asked, determined to be brave if not gracious. "As busy as you are, I shouldn't keep you."

"Ashley—"

"You take care of yourself," she murmured, the hurt edging closer. "Okay?"

That hurt hit her square in the chest when she heard his slow intake of breath, and nothing else. There was no need for him to say anything else, anyway. He'd accomplished his purpose.

She wouldn't ask him why he didn't want to see her anymore. She already knew. She knew he didn't want commitment. She knew he didn't want anyone slowing him down, making demands, interfering with his plans. He liked his life just as it was. And she knew how much he disliked dealing with the press. If he kept seeing her, the time would inevitably come when they would be seen together and the speculation would begin. The media would barrage them with questions about where their relationship was headed— questions that would ultimately have pulled them apart anyway, because they would make him think about how very much he did not want the whole hearth-and-home routine, as he'd put it, and for her to continually fight how badly she wanted a home and family with him.

"Okay," she finally heard him say. His deep voice sounded quiet, and terribly subdued. "You, too, Ashley. You take care of yourself, too."

She told him she would, then said good-night because saying goodbye was just too hard.

Matt caught that betraying nuance. He'd heard the hurt, too, and the politeness she'd used to cover it.

He lowered his cell phone from his ear the moment she broke the connection, closed it and set it on the graphs spread between his elbows. His breath leaked out, the tension slowly leaving his shoulders.

He hated what he had just done, but he hadn't known what else to do. He couldn't be with her without wanting her and he couldn't let their relationship go any further than it had already. He'd told himself that exact same thing the last time he'd been away from her. And all he'd had to do was touch her and he'd kissed his common sense goodbye. He couldn't risk seeing her again.

Weary to his bones, he pushed himself away from the mahogany desk in his hotel suite and looked over the balcony to the lights glittering on the bay. Room service had delivered his dinner half an hour ago. It still sat cooling beneath the silver dome on the table the hotel employee had set.

He had put off calling her until the guilt wrecking his concentration and his appetite had finally forced him to pick up the phone. He'd known when he left Gray Lake that he wouldn't see her again. But it hadn't seemed right to tell her that only hours after the night they had just spent in each others' arms. It hadn't seemed right as the days away from her had passed to keep putting it off, either. He couldn't just let time and silence get his message across. Ashley didn't deserve to be left waiting, wondering. As well as he knew her now, he knew she never would have allowed herself to get so involved with him if she didn't care for him, and trust him completely.

He turned from the view, shoved his hands through his hair. He couldn't let himself think about how much that mattered to him. She was looking for Mr. Right and he wasn't about to lead her into thinking they had any sort of future together. It had taken him years to earn the freedom he had now. He finally had the financial means and the independence to do exactly what he wanted to do without being restricted by another's expectations of how and when he should be doing it. He knew that Ashley had never demanded anything of him that he hadn't willingly given, but her own life was constrained simply because of who she was. And who she was, was even more important.

She was his friend's sister, and his friendship with Cord was one he didn't want to louse up. He especially didn't want to louse up the business relationship he now had with Cord's father. He had worked far too hard to establish it, and he could only imagine how unwelcome he would once again be if he truly hurt the man's daughter.

Ending things now was definitely the wisest choice. He just didn't know which he felt more as he turned back to face his empty room, a profound sense of relief over having finally made the call, or the strange and unfamiliar sense of loss that left him feeling oddly hollow inside.

He was not a man to dwell on a decision once it had been made. Refusing to do it now, he told himself to stop thinking about it, to eat his dinner and get back to work so he wouldn't be up until 1:00 a.m. again tonight. If he was feeling anything at all, it was just fatigue, and the hollow sensation was simply a need for food.

As rationales went, he considered his logical enough. Yet the void inside him wouldn't go away. Work didn't fill it. A day climbing rocks with Cord and a couple of other buddies took his mind off it as long as he was dangling against the face of a cliff, mostly because his life depended on paying attention to what he was doing at that moment, but the disquieting sensation came back within minutes of his feet touching solid ground.

It didn't help matters that he saw her picture nearly every day at the magazine stand by his hotel. Two women's magazines had her on the cover. One had a shot of her looking as regal as the society princess she was in a stunning ball gown, another bore a photo of her at the Shelter site, amazingly radiant in a white ball cap and pearl earrings. A tabloid displayed a grainy shot of her outside her motel-room door in Gray Lake, her hair wild and an uncharacteristic frown on her face. Since the photo took up half the page, he could only assume that she had been right. The tabloids paid well for catching people at less than their best.

Two weeks passed. Then, three. Still trying to ignore that sense of loss nearly a month later, he gave up and tried to call her. But by then, Ashley was nowhere to be found.

Chapter Twelve

It took Matt the better part of a week to learn where Ashley had gone. He'd been fairly subtle about trying to contact her at first. He'd called her office, only to be told that she would be out for the next couple of weeks. He'd then tried her cell phone. All he got there was her voice mail. All six times.

He checked the newspapers, but he'd seen nothing to indicate her whereabouts or what she was involved in.

Knowing no other way to reach her, short of calling her mother, he called Cord, who immediately wanted to know if he had time to go with him to catch the big waves on Oahu's north shore. Matt had the time. He could have made the time, anyway. He just didn't have the inclination. So he'd declined, then told Cord that he needed to talk to his sister. He just couldn't find her. And asked if he knew where she was.

Because Cord tended to do his own thing, he rarely had

any idea of what was going on in his siblings' lives, so he didn't have a clue where she was, either. He also wasn't interested in calling any member of his family to ask. But he did call Ashley's assistant—the same one who wouldn't give Matt any information other than that Ashley was gone—and learned that she had gone to their grandmother's.

"She's in Luzandria," Cord had told him. "At Grandma's place."

"Can you give me directions?"

"To Luzandria, or Grandma's?"

"I know where Luzandria is." It was less than an hour's flight out of Paris. The gambling Mecca on the Mediterranean was as famous as Monaco. "Your grandmother's."

"You have a thing for Ashley?"

The surprise in Cord's voice wasn't unexpected. "You might say that." It was a "thing" all right. Something that had kept him awake nights. Something that made him so restless that he found no pleasure in much of anything anymore. He missed her smile. He missed the way she cared about everyone, the way she cared about him. Mostly, he missed talking to her, sharing with her. "So, are you going to give me directions or not?"

Matt swore he heard a smile in his friend's voice. "Sure, man. Just grab a cab from whatever hotel you're staying in. I recommend the King Alphonse. Grandma's is the big house at the top of the hill. You can't miss it."

Matt hadn't realized what a gift Cord had for understatement. He also now understood part of the reason for the grin he'd heard in his buddy's voice. The "house" was indeed hard to miss. From its perch on the cliff above the curved harbor of yachts and sailboats, five-star hotels and world-class restaurants, Le Palais du Luzandria overlooked just about everything.

Grandma's house indeed, he thought as the driver of the cab pulled up to a massive iron gate topped with gold scroll-work and trumpeting cherubs. Beyond the gate a wide drive lined with tall conical cypress trees curved through a sweep of velvety green lawn.

Guardhouses flanked the gate. Guards in serious blue-and-gold uniforms and hats with curved gold feathers flanked the guardhouses.

One of those guards executed a smart turn and approached the shiny black cab as it slowed.

The official language of Luzandria was French. Since the only French Matt understood had to do with food, he had no idea what the cabbie said to the guard before the guard stepped to the back window and tapped on the glass. The old cabby's English had seemed limited so to make sure he got where he needed to go, Matt had simply pointed to the top of the hill and asked him to take him there.

The guard was as tall and thin as a spear, his gaze sharp and penetrating. His English was also flawless. "Your business at the palace, sir?"

As Matt looked up at the man's humorless face, it suddenly occurred to him that after four hours of sitting in airports, numerous security checks, nine hours of flying and a quick shower and change in his hotel room after a much-apologized-for hour delay checking in because the computer had lost his reservation, that he might not get any further. Ashley didn't have to allow him in. "I understand that Ashley Kendrick is here. The queen's granddaughter," Matt expanded. It occurred to him, too, that he'd never thought of her in exactly that way before. "I'd like to see her."

"Your name, sir?"

"Matt Callaway."

"One moment."

One moment led to two. Two stretched to three.

As the cab's meter ticked away, Matt began to wonder if he would have to go back to the hotel and try calling her, if he could even get a phone number that would do him any good. If that didn't work he could come back and try scaling the wall, he thought, only to then wonder if he might get himself shot in the attempt. An uneasy frown had just formed at the possibility when the guard returned to speak to the driver. Moments later the wide gates swung open.

Within thirty seconds, the enormous palace with its towers and turrets, marble statues and formal gardens came into view. A minute after that, the cab stopped beneath a small portico to the side of what Matt assumed was the main entrance and a footman in black tails opened his door.

"Bonjour, monsieur," the gray-haired gentleman greeted, his accent heavy. His glance made a surreptitious sweep over the dark beige jacket and slacks Matt wore with a collarless black shirt. Looking faintly approving of the classic Italian styling, he gave him a nod. "You will accompany me, if you please?"

He held open one of the double doors for him, then solemnly led him through a gleaming marble foyer filled with more flowers than a funeral parlor. Had Matt not been so absorbed with what he needed to do, he would have been sorely tempted to check out the architecture. But his only thoughts were of the relief he felt that Ashley hadn't had him sent away.

His escort stopped beside a set of open double doors outside an opulently appointed sitting room and waited for him to enter.

"Her majesty, she will be with you in a moment," the gentleman informed him, then closed him inside.

Her majesty?

With nothing to do but cool his heels, Matt glanced around the opulent room. The enormous paintings on the wall depicted stalwart men draped in capes and medals on horseback, women in jewels and flowing gowns. The fireplaces were marble. Red velvet draped the high, arched windows. The furniture gleamed with gilt. Huge gilded mirrors reflected a gold chandelier dripping with crystals.

Matt had always thought the mansion on the Kendrick estate impressive. It had been the model for what he someday wanted for himself. Even now, though he rarely spent more than a night or two a month in his well-appointed condo overlooking Boston's back bay, his own life lacked for nothing. But he hadn't been prepared for the grandeur Ashley's mother had left when she'd given up her title and married Ashley's dad.

With a refined whisper of the rarified air, the doors swung open. Turning from his examination of the ornate plasterwork on one of the walls, he saw the footman who had escorted him through the grand foyer stand to one side. ''Her Majesty, Queen Sophia.''

Matt halfway expected the woman who entered the room to be wearing a crown and a ball gown. He also expected her to be taller, but it was possible that, at one time, she had been. The petite, white-haired lady in the sedate powder-blue suit and heavy sapphire jewelry had to be eighty if she was a day. Despite her visible age, the blue eyes behind her silver-rimmed glasses were as sharp as glass. Remaining by the doors that had just been closed behind her, she held out one wrinkled hand.

''Mr. Callaway,'' she said.

He didn't know if he was supposed to shake her hand or kiss her ring. Totally unprepared for an audience with royalty, he fell back on the only manners he knew.

''Ma'am,'' he replied, and went for the handshake. He clasped her soft hand in his, carefully so as not to bruise her. She looked as if a breeze could blow her away. "It's a pleasure to meet you."

"Yes," she murmured, obviously preferring to reserve her own opinion about the meeting. She motioned toward two gold silk-covered chairs facing each other across a marble coffee table. "I must say I'm quite surprised to see you here."

Matt didn't know if the woman was naturally about as warm as an ice cube, or if the coolness in her tone had to do with him personally. He had no idea what, if anything, Ashley might have said about him. He also wasn't quite sure what he was supposed to do when the queen sat and arched her eyebrow at him.

Her glance cut to the chair directly across from hers.

Moving to it, he tugged at the knees of his slacks and lowered his rather large frame between the elaborately carved arms.

"Did my granddaughter know you were coming?"

"Ah...no, ma'am. Ashley and I haven't spoken for a while."

"How long a while?"

It had been four weeks and three days, not that he had been counting. "A month or so." He glanced toward the door. "Is she here?"

Looking as regal as the monarch she was, Queen Sophia Regina Amelia Renaldi sat with her back as straight as she could make it, her beringed hands clasped on her lap. Her shrewd eyes weighed and measured. Her keen mind judged and assessed.

Matt sat perfectly still himself, his powerful body radiating a sort of tension that had nothing to do with being subjected to the royal eagle eye. It would take more than this woman's silent examination to unsettle him. He'd always had a bit of a problem with authority anyway, though he had to admit he'd long ago outgrown any significant need to prove it. All he wanted was to talk to the woman's granddaughter, not to subject himself to some sort of pregame interview. There were things he needed to say to Ashley before he lost his nerve—and before he let himself start worrying too much more that she might not be interested at all in seeing him again.

"She is," her highness finally allowed. "Though I haven't told her that you are. Why do you wish to see her?"

"That's between her and me."

The royal grandmother didn't seem accustomed to being refused an answer to a question. The eyebrow that had arched before, rose even higher.

"No disrespect intended," Matt quickly qualified, wondering if palaces still had dungeons. More importantly, if they still used them. "But I really don't think it would be fair to Ashley to discuss her with you."

"I am her grandmother."

"I know that. And I know you're a queen and that you could probably have me hauled off and…"

"Beheaded?" she suggested blandly.

He hadn't even considered that one. "I was thinking more along the lines of 'banned,'" he explained, thinking she'd certainly given him pause. "I was under the impression that they stopped doing the other in the Middle Ages."

"Only in some countries," she replied, suddenly looking as if she was enjoying herself. "Fortunately for you, Luzandria is one of them. In earlier times, you would have been quite headless by now, and all your land holdings confiscated and turned over to the Crown. It was only last century that saw an end to the use of the guillotine in the civilized world."

Civilized? he thought, still back at the part where he would have been without his upper extremity. She made it sound as if he were guilty of some unpardonable transgression. He just wasn't quite sure of the nature of his crime—unless hurting someone related to the ruler had once been a punishable offense.

Guilt coiled like a fist in his gut. He knew he was guilty of having done that. It seemed her royal grandmotherness did, too.

"I can only assume that you have come to do right by our Ashley," she continued, her amusement fading. "At least that is my hope. The women in this family do not give their hearts lightly, young man. And it speaks well of you that you are here. I will not coerce, but do keep in mind that my confessor is on call at all times and that the royal chapel is quite available."

At the mention of her confessor and the chapel, Matt's forehead pinched in confusion. He was missing something. He was sure of it. He just didn't have time to figure out what that something was.

A small gold bell sat among the tasteful arrangement of flowers and art books on the table. Picking it up, the queen rang it lightly. She had no sooner set it down than the doors swung wide.

"Your majesty," the silver-haired gentleman said with a slight bow.

"Is Lady Ashley still on the south terrace?"

"I believe she is, your grace."

"Escort Mr. Callaway to her," she commanded, and held her hand out to Matt so he could help her rise.

Ashley loved this time of year in Luzandria. The late-September air still held hints of the balmy summer and the rains of October had yet to arrive and shroud the bay in gray. That bay sparkled below her, as blue as the sky above and stretching out to the endless sea. Beyond the low terra-

cotta railings and the stair-stepped terraces, the homes of
the little kingdom's fifty thousand residents dotted the lush
and verdant hills.

She'd always found it peaceful here, but peace wasn't on
her mind at the moment. Taking another rose from the bas-
ket of those she'd just clipped, her thoughts were torn between sending Matt a letter, calling him, or flying back to
tell him in person that he was going to be a father.

He had the right to know. He also had the right to know
before the rest of her family learned she was pregnant and
he heard the news through Cord.

Only her grandmother knew her little secret. Neither her
mom nor her sister had suspected a thing the weekend she
had spent at the family estate. But then, they'd had no reason to. As far as they were aware, she wasn't even dating
anyone in particular, though she did notice that her mom
was quite interested to know how she had gotten along with
Matt on the Shelter project. She had even commented again
on how much he seemed to have changed—an opinion she
might well reconsider after she learned he was the father of
her unwed daughter's unborn child.

She already knew how her grandmother felt about him.
But then, her grandmother was terribly old-fashioned. She
was also quite astute. Ashley had arrived at the palace ten
days ago. Within twenty-four hours, Nana Sophia had informed her that she could tell she was hiding again, though
not from the public this time. This time she had the feeling
from the absence of her smile that she was hiding from a
man.

They had sat down then with cups of herbal tea served
from a porcelain pot on a tea cart and Ashley had confessed
that she wasn't hiding. The man didn't want her, so there
was no one to hide from. She had sought the solitude of the

palace because she needed time to figure out how to tell him she was going to have his child.

She had expected to see profound disappointment. She had expected to hear her grandmother say that she would never have imagined that she would compromise herself in such a way.

The disappointment had been clear in those sharp, blue eyes, but she had also seen sympathy. Her grandmother had asked if she loved the man. She had then told her to take as long as she needed to make her decision, but to keep in mind that no female with Renaldi blood in her veins ever pined for any man who was stupid enough to not realize how fortunate he would have been to have her for his wife.

She wasn't pining, she insisted to herself as she broke off thorns so she could add the rose to the vase on the mosaic-covered table. She was preparing herself. She'd heard that recovery from a broken heart should never take any longer than the relationship had lasted. The only problem there was that their relationship never would totally end. She didn't know how involved Matt would want to be with their child, but the man she had come to know would never walk away from such a responsibility.

She should call, she decided. No, she should go see him. Or, maybe, she thought, spearing the rose into the vase and picking up another, she should call and then tell him she needed to see him. She loved their baby more by the minute. The life growing inside her was the most precious gift she had ever received. She needed to tell him that, too.

Over the distant peal of church bells ringing the hour came the sound of a terrace door opening. Wondering if her grandmother was sending for her, certain that the stoic-yet-sensitive woman responsible for a small kingdom would never be so indecisive, she glanced up.

The rose in her hand landed silently on the flagstone at her feet.

Matt watched the flower fall.

He had seen her through the tall windows, watched her as she thoughtfully arranged the flowers. With her shining hair swept back and swinging loose against her shoulders and wearing a knee-skimming silk shift as blue as the sea, she was once again the cool, poised beauty he had once thought so untouchable.

She stood frozen as he crossed the terrace to where she stood, her lovely face betraying little beyond shock and maybe a hint of disbelief. As he bent to pick up the rose, his only hope was that he hadn't totally destroyed whatever chance he'd had with her.

Disbelief vied with a healthy dose of caution as Ashley watched Matt's fingers close around what she'd dropped. Her glance skimmed his sun-bleached hair, his broad shoulders, then met the same caution she felt in the carved lines of his face when he straightened. He looked big, powerful and commanding—and maybe just a little uncertain when he held the rose out to her.

Blinking at the blood-red bud, she took it, then looked back up to where he stood carefully watching her.

"Why are you here?" she asked, trying hard to comprehend that he was actually standing in front of her.

Matt drew a mental breath. He was there to talk her back into his life, to fill the void that had opened when she left. He was there to see if she could ever feel about him the way he'd come to feel about her. "I wanted to see if you were interested in going out to dinner."

"Dinner?"

"You know. A little food. A little conversation."

His gray eyes carefully searched hers, his expression totally guarded. The tension she'd been too stunned to notice before slowly edged toward her.

"I figured if you agreed to dinner, that meant you were at least still talking to me. Then, I could tell you how much I miss you. And how I wish we'd never had that last conversation."

He missed her. The knowledge caused a flutter of hope in her chest. Knowing what she had to tell him, that hope faltered. "You want to pick up where we left off," she said, her voice quiet with conclusion.

"That's what I'm hoping we can do." He ducked his head to catch her glance when she looked away. "Or, am I too late?"

Ashley set the rose in the vase, the gentle breeze lifting the flower's sweet fragrance toward her. She had never in her life felt as torn as she did at that moment. Or, so uncertain about how to explain that she very much wanted what he wanted, but that it wasn't quite possible. "It's not that easy."

"Okay," he said, pushing his hands into his slacks pockets. "I suppose I deserve that. I shouldn't have just—"

"It's not that," she cut in, wanting to make sense, afraid she wouldn't. "It's that we can't go back to where we left off because things have changed since then. I mean, they're the same," she qualified, because technically they were. She'd been expecting then. She was expecting now. "But I just didn't know for certain at the time and I didn't want to say anything until I was."

Confusion narrowed his eyes. "What are you talking about?"

"That night on the sailboat," she began, only to decide there was no point in putting off the inevitable by explaining the obvious. "I'm pregnant."

Matt could only recall one other time in his entire life

that he had been rendered speechless. That had been the evening she'd told him she had once been afraid of him. As he stood watching her watch him so uneasily, he figured he felt just about as stunned now as he had been then.

Only then, he hadn't been able to think of a thing to say. Now, the questions piled up like dead leaves in the fall. He just didn't know which to voice first in the moments before he saw her cross her arms protectively and turn away to hide her hurt at his silence.

Caution gripped him as he walked up behind her and settled his hands on her shoulders. He thought he felt her stiffen at his touch. All he cared about was that she didn't pull away.

The first thoughts to push their way to the surface were of how hard she had worked at the Shelter site. How she had pushed herself in the heat. How she had passed out...

"Are you and the baby all right?"

Sunlight shimmered in her hair as she nodded. "The doctor said everything is fine."

"How far along—"

"Three months."

He hesitated. "When were you going to tell me?"

"As soon as I worked up the courage." Ashley took a deep breath, blew it out. The way Matt's face had drained of expression and his silence as he'd simply stared at her had made her heart feel as if it had stopped and fallen straight to her toes. The supportive feel of his hands on her shoulders at least had her heart beating again.

"That's why we can't go back to the way things were," she said, her tone subdued. "I know you like your life the way it is, Matt. And I know you don't want anyone else putting demands on you. I don't want to ask anything of you..."

"Stop."

"…that you don't want to…"

"I said stop," he repeated, turning her around even as she spoke.

"I know what I said about liking my life as it is." He remembered that conversation quite well. He also remembered that, at the time, he'd meant every word. "Once I was finally able to be on my own, I never wanted to account to anyone but myself again. But that was because I'd never met anyone who made me want to know where *she* was going, or what she was doing, or wanting to hear about it at the end of the day. My life was good enough before," he admitted, slipping his hand to the sides of her face, "but since I last saw you, nothing has been the same.

"I love you," he said simply. "I came up with every excuse I could think of to let you go. I've just never been in love before so I didn't realize that you can't just let someone that important…go."

The admission wasn't as eloquent as he might have liked. And it certainly wasn't poetic. But it came far more easily than he would have thought. He'd never said such things to a woman before. He'd never allowed himself to be so vulnerable. But he'd been vulnerable to her in one way or the other since the day he'd met her. He couldn't begin to explain what it did to his heart to know that she'd always been vulnerable to him, too.

The blue of her eyes looked luminous as she searched his face. Looking as if she couldn't believe what she had just heard or, maybe, as if she was afraid to, she slowly raised her hand to his cheek.

"What?" he murmured.

She shook her head, still searching. "What did you say?"

"You heard me." He traced the line of her jaw with his thumb. "I love you."

Her smile came slowly, softly, curving her lush mouth, filling her eyes as her fingers drifted to his chest.

Ashley flattened her hand over his heart, wondered at how quickly it was beating. "I love you, too."

Desperately, she might have told him, but he cupped her face in his hands and his head descended, blocking her view of the cloudless sky, the turrets and the hot-pink bougainvillea climbing the side of the palace walls. Something fierce swept his expression in the moments before his mouth settled over hers, warm, full and faintly hungry.

Having ached for him, she sagged toward him, kissing him back. She wanted badly for him to deepen the kiss that held so much from her now, and promised so much later. But he seemed as aware as she was of where they were—in full view of the town below, and servants who were undoubtedly peeking out windows at that very moment.

She lowered her head even as Matt lifted his.

"So…" he murmured, easing her closer so her forehead rested against his chest. Over the low terra-cotta railing ahead of him, he could see the sweeping view of the ocean and the town below. Touching his lips to the top of her head, he considered that normally he would never have given any thought to the fact that someone below could see them with binoculars. Or a telephoto lens. But "normal" had gone out the window along about the time he'd began to realize how he felt about the woman in his arms. He'd known he was in love with her when he realized he really didn't care.

"So…" she murmured back, her voice muffled against his shirt. "Do you still want to go to dinner?"

He chuckled. "Sure. But I think we're beyond what I'd originally planned. I was thinking we'd take this slow," he admitted, more relieved than he could believe to be touching her again. "I'd thought we'd go out for a while, then do the engagement thing, then get married when we wanted to have a family.'' He was going to be a father. The reality of that hadn't sunk in. He was sure of that. But he was also certain that having a baby with Ashley felt very…right. ''Since the beginning of our family is on the way, I think we need to accelerate that schedule.''

Ashley lifted her head, looked up at the strong, certain lines of his face. Knowing that he loved her already had her heart feeling unbearably full. Knowing that he'd wanted to marry her even before he'd known about the baby, made her heart feel as if it would burst.

''I want you,'' he said. His hand slipped to her stomach, his touch amazingly gentle in the moments before his eyes met hers once more. ''And I want our child. But right now, I want to protect you from the speculation that will start once the world realizes you're pregnant. They're going to talk anyway, but if we're already married that should at least help with your family.''

''Oh, Matt,'' she murmured, falling in love all over again.

''Oh, man,'' he muttered back, looking at her as if he'd just been struck with a bolt from the blue. ''The chapel. Now I get it.''

Utterly bewildered, Ashley blinked up at him. ''What?''

''Your grandmother,'' he explained, thinking it no wonder the woman had greeted him like a pariah. She knew Ashley's condition. She knew he was her baby's father. ''She said her confessor and the chapel were available. I thought she was planning my funeral. But I think she was thinking more along the lines of a wedding.''

Ashley gave a small laugh, the sound as bright and welcome as spring sun. ''I'm sure she was,'' she replied, seeming to need no explanation for the funeral remark.

He touched her cheek, lost himself in her smiling eyes. ''So, how about it?''

"Now?"

"Now works. Or, sometime in the next few days if you want time for your family to get here."

Her smile nearly stole his breath when she curled her hands around his lapels. "A small wedding in the palace chapel would make my mom and my grandmother very happy."

"Good." He locked his hands at the small of her back. Since she didn't seem concerned about who might see them, neither was he. "I wouldn't want your family upset with us. Especially Grandma."

A flash of consternation shadowed her expression. "There's just one thing you should know," she murmured, that unease entering her voice. "Grandmother thinks we've been in a relationship for longer than a few months. She would never understand if she realized I got pregnant the first night we—"

He silenced her with the brush of his lips over hers. "There's nothing for her to understand, honey. We've known each other for over fifteen years." He bent his head toward hers once more. "What happened between us during any of that time isn't anyone's business but ours."

National Week-in-Review Magazine, October 15.
People and Entertainment

One of the best-kept secret romances in the nation was revealed this week when William Randall and Katherine Kendrick announced the marriage of their daughter Ashley to longtime family acquaintance Matthew Callaway. The intimate wedding took place two weeks ago at the royal palace in Luzandria, home of Ashley's maternal grandmother. Katherine Kendrick relinquished her place in succession to the throne there in 1965 when she married William. The bride wore an off-the-shoulder raw-silk gown by Versace. The couple plans to build a home on a two-hundred-acre parcel recently purchased by Callaway in northern Virginia.

* * * * *

Don't miss the culmination of
THE KENDRICKS OF CAMELOT *miniseries*
in HER PRODIGAL PRINCE CHARMING.
Available July 2004, only from
Silhouette Special Edition!

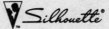

If you enjoyed what you just read,
then we've got an offer you can't resist!

Take 2 bestselling
love stories FREE!
Plus get a FREE surprise gift!

Clip this page and mail it to Silhouette Reader Service™

IN U.S.A.	**IN CANADA**
3010 Walden Ave.	P.O. Box 609
P.O. Box 1867	Fort Erie, Ontario
Buffalo, N.Y. 14240-1867	L2A 5X3

YES! Please send me 2 free Silhouette Special Edition® novels and my free surprise gift. After receiving them, if I don't wish to receive anymore, I can return the shipping statement marked cancel. If I don't cancel, I will receive 6 brand-new novels every month, before they're available in stores! In the U.S.A., bill me at the bargain price of $3.99 plus 25¢ shipping and handling per book and applicable sales tax, if any*. In Canada, bill me at the bargain price of $4.74 plus 25¢ shipping and handling per book and applicable taxes**. That's the complete price and a savings of at least 10% off the cover prices—what a great deal! I understand that accepting the 2 free books and gift places me under no obligation ever to buy any books. I can always return a shipment and cancel at any time. Even if I never buy another book from Silhouette, the 2 free books and gift are mine to keep forever.

235 SDN DNUR
335 SDN DNUS

Name	(PLEASE PRINT)	
Address	Apt.#	
City	State/Prov.	Zip/Postal Code

 * Terms and prices subject to change without notice. Sales tax applicable in N.Y.
** Canadian residents will be charged applicable provincial taxes and GST.
  All orders subject to approval. Offer limited to one per household and not valid to
  current Silhouette Special Edition® subscribers.
  ® are registered trademarks of Harlequin Books S.A., used under license.

SPED02   ©1998 Harlequin Enterprises Limited

™ *Silhouette*®

SPECIAL EDITION™

One family's search for justice begins in

ROMANCING
THE ENEMY

(Silhouette Special Edition #1621)

by award-winning author
Laurie Paige

When beautiful Sara Carlton returns to her
hometown of San Francisco to avenge
her mother's death, she doesn't count on
falling in love with the handsome single father
next door—who just happens to be the son of
the enemy. Does she dare tell him the truth
about her return, or risk losing the love of
her life when he unravels the mystery?

The first book in the new continuity

The Parks Empire

Dark secrets.
Old lies.
New loves.

Available July 2004
at your favorite retail outlet.

Silhouette®

COMING NEXT MONTH

SPECIAL EDITION

#1621 ROMANCING THE ENEMY—Laurie Paige
The Parks Empire
Nursery school teacher Sara Carlton wanted to uncover the truth surrounding her father's mysterious death years ago, but when she met Cade Parks, the sexy son of the suspected murderer, she couldn't help but expose her heart. Could she shed the shadow of the past and give her love to the enemy?

#1622 HER TEXAS RANGER—Stella Bagwell
Men of the West
When summoned to solve a murder in his hometown, ruggedly handsome Ranger Seth Ketchum stumbled upon high school crush Corrina Dawson. She'd always secretly had her eye on him, too. Then all signs pointed to her father's guilt and suddenly she had to choose one man in her life over the other....

#1623 BABIES IN THE BARGAIN—Victoria Pade
Northbridge Nuptials
After Kira Wentworth's sister was killed, she insisted on taking care of the twin girls left behind. But when she and her sister's husband, Cutty Grant, felt an instant attraction, Kira found herself bargaining for more than just the babies!

#1624 PRODIGAL PRINCE CHARMING—Christine Flynn
The Kendricks of Camelot
Could fairy tales really come true? After wealthy playboy Cord Kendrick destroyed Madison O'Malley's catering truck, he knew he'd have to offer more than money if he wanted to charm his way toward a happy ending. But could he win the heart of his Cinderella without bringing scandal to her door?

#1625 A FOREVER FAMILY—Mary J. Forbes
Suddenly thrust into taking care of his orphaned niece and the family farm, Dr. Michael Rowan needed a helping hand. Luckily his only applicant was kind and loving Shanna McCoy. Close quarters bred a close connection, but only the unexpected could turn these three into a family.

#1626 THE OTHER BROTHER—Janis Reams Hudson
Men of the Cherokee Rose
While growing up, Melanie Pruitt had always been in love with Sloan Chisholm. But when she attended his wedding years later, it was his sexy younger brother Caleb who caught her attention. Both unleashed their passion, then quickly curbed it for the sake of friendship—until Melanie realized that she didn't need another friend, but something more....

SSECNM0604